WILL HAUNT YOU

BRIAN KIRK

This is a **FLAME TREE PRESS** book

FLAME TREE PRESS
6 Melbray Mews, London, SW6 3NS, UK
flametreepress.com

Distribution and warehouse:
Marston Book Services Ltd
160 Eastern Avenue, Milton Park, Abingdon, Oxon, OX14 4SB
www.marston.co.uk

Thanks to the Flame Tree Press team, including:
Taylor Bentley, Frances Bodiam, Federica Ciaravella, Don D'Auria,
Chris Herbert, Matteo Middlemiss, Josie Mitchell, Mike Spender,
Cat Taylor, Maria Tissot, Nick Wells, Gillian Whitaker.

Front cover design by Todd Keisling.
The font families in this book are Avenir and Bembo.

Flame Tree Press is an imprint of Flame Tree Publishing Ltd
flametreepublishing.com

A copy of the CIP data for this book is available from the British Library.

HB ISBN: 978-1-78758-138-8
PB ISBN: 978-1-78758-137-1
ebook ISBN: 978-1-78758-139-5
Also available in FLAME TREE AUDIO

Printed in the UK at Clays, Suffolk

WILL
HAUNT
YOU

BRIAN KIRK

FLAME TREE PRESS
London & New York

I read a book much like the one you're holding now. And this is what happened to me. Don't make the same mistake. Please, put it down. Or better yet, throw it away. This is your last warning. Turn the page, and you're on your own. Actually, that's not true. Turn the page and he'll be there, watching you.

The book was the last thing on my mind when I got to the gig that night. Though something should have triggered my memory when I saw Solomon. The burn mark creeping up through the collar on his neck. That goddamn glint in his eye.

"Jesse, my man!" he hollered when he saw me enter the hazy room. Solomon's a dour asshole, not the jolly chum welcoming me like some hero returning from war. "How you been?"

We clasped hands, exchanged an awkward hug. He was hot. That could have been another clue. His chest and back were radiating like he was running a high-grade fever, but I blamed it on the summer heat. Nervous excitement before the show.

Caspian was already at the bar, downing what appeared to be his third shot of Jameson. Two dead soldiers were sprawled on the bar in front of him and I knew what that meant, the kind of night it prophesied. Caspian with a bottle of whiskey was more ominous than a clown in a dark alley. And the flashbacks it produced almost made me turn and walk back out the door.

Not that leaving would have mattered. I was screwed no matter what I did next.

The little reunion was brief. We hadn't played together in a decade but we'd all kept in touch. Caspian still tooled around – had a sycophant fan base that followed him wherever he went. Solomon had gone in with a merchandise company, selling concert shirts and bumper stickers and other crap tchotchkes. Kevin's been working as a sound engineer at a reputable studio, making decent money from what I understand.

I've been…well, I'll get to that, I guess.

I'd arrived just before the show was supposed to start in order

2 • BRIAN KIRK

to avoid the pre-game festivities. The temptation was still too strong. I know my limits and avoidance is the best way for me to stay clean. Not that the Full Moon Saloon has a backstage green room where the heavy stuff goes down. But, still. One slip-up and I could kiss the last seven years goodbye. Why take the chance?

The bar manager signalled it was time and we made our way to the stage and got our instruments set up. Solomon took a seat and thumped the bass drum, pattered the snare. Kevin positioned himself on the right-hand side of the stage, me on the left. The guitar strap felt snug on my shoulder, my Jim Root Telecaster thrummed in my hands. And it all came flooding back through me in that moment. That otherworldly energy that comes when the amp is turned on and the audience is tuned in – even in half-empty dives like this.

Caspian, standing centre stage, stomped his foot to the beat of the bass drum. Then, right on cue, threw his fist in the air and for the first time in ten years summoned the dead to rise. A chorus of drunken howls came from the meagre crowd, the faithful few who had come to watch their favourite cult band from an era they hardly remembered.

I turned to Caspian and grinned at the absurdity of what I saw. The greying hairs sprouting from his armpit were fluttering like the tentacles of some diseased sea anemone. Ten years ago he would have been shirtless, oil glistening off his rock-star abs. But tonight he was wearing a tank top to conceal his sagging gut and fleshy breasts. At least the pentagram printed on the front of his shirt reinforced the rage that still existed in his ageless heart. And the ink on his arm sleeves remained as bright as fresh blood.

Solomon was now pounding the foot pedal, a ritualistic war beat that counted down to showtime. Three, two, one....

I strummed the guitar as hard as I could; a single downstroke that turned time back ten years, blasting a chord of distortion so loud it caused one of our old roadies, Sam Holt, to stumble back and drop his beer. Sam had been fired from three jobs, ditched by two wives, and lost the bus keys more times than I could count. But this was the first time I'd ever seen beer slip though his veteran hands.

We opened the set with 'Coffin Dust', a power ballad about unrequited love that Caspian had written after being dumped his sophomore year in high school. It was a lewd metaphor for what his ex-girlfriend was like in bed. Lance Caspian, always the class act. Next came 'Within a Cage of Hate'. There are no lyrics to this one, only screams and guttural howls. The guitar riff is basically me raking my pick across the E string as fast as I can while Kevin drops bombs with his bass.

I spread my legs and hunkered down, assuming the pose I had always imagined striking in front of an arena filled with screaming fans. That had never come to fruition. This would have to do.

Still, it felt damn good.

The crowd had loosened up by the third song, the sixty-or-so people who were scattered around the stage. Old metal-heads from the Eighties. Still wearing their black concert shirts tucked into too-tight jeans. Heads banging on rigid necks. Clinging to whatever hair they had left. Arms raised riotously in the air, fingers forked in devil horns.

Fuck yeah, I thought. *The dead rise again.*

Time grew elastic around the sixth song, and a calmness descended upon me like the eye of a deadly storm. Peace inside fury. My happy place. I stood in this pocket of tranquillity watching sweat fly from our old fans, their faces contorted into angry sneers of post-hormonal rage.

The burn in my arm had faded several songs ago. I could play all night if needed. In fact, given how the past ten years had gone, that was exactly what I needed. Needed it more than I had known. And, for the briefest moment, I didn't even miss the booze, or mind being at a bar. Even a shit shack like this.

We were nearing our ninth, and final, song when I first saw the chick three rows back, watching me, trying to catch my eye, swaying her hips so hypnotically it could have put a venomous snake to sleep. She smiled when she saw me looking and began to raise her shirt, a faded halter top with our old logo on the front. A foetid zombie crawling up from the earth. RISING DEAD etched across the leaning tombstone behind. Solomon sells these now for $14.99.

She raised her shirt in slow, incremental spurts, teasing me, incorporating the movement into the gyrating way that she danced. She was much younger than everyone else, still in her twenties. Which may have put her around seventeen or so when we'd split up. I wondered which of us she'd slept with. Wasn't me, I would have remembered. That was part of what had brought the whole thing crashing down, anyway. Some one-night stands last a lifetime, I've learned.

Her stomach was flat and tight, with a vertical crease down the middle. Tan. She had a steel stud pierced through her navel and, as I saw when she licked her lips, another through her tongue. She swayed her hips, childbearing hips, the old man in me mumbled, and raised the shirt further to reveal the swollen underside of her breasts. Just a couple of inches more and the baby feeders would be shown.

That's the worst part about having a kid. Tits take on new context.

Her eyelids closed as she yanked the shirt up and over her chest, the fabric snagging for a second on her nipples. I flubbed my next chord but didn't care. We were just producing one big soundgasm at that point anyway. A cacophony of discordant noise designed to invoke chaos. To shatter the walls of what had become our structured lives.

Caspian's voice was fading and starting to crackle, which was just as well. We were building towards the final climax. No encore tonight. We had decided to leave it all on stage. Blow it out in one ecstatic set that would leave everyone dazed and trembling on the floor.

We all pounded our instruments as hard as we possibly could and then quit at the exact same time, letting the combined sound crash against the walls. My eyes were shut, imagining a sea of people. When I opened them, reality hit. Half the crowd had left, the few remaining howled as the last notes faded and feedback screeched from the amps. An anti-climactic conclusion to a show ten years in the making. That's another thing I've learned: we never fully live the dream.

Sure, it may not have been everything I imagined, but it was still mighty fine. And as I looked out on the die-hards who had stuck around, seeing the girl who had flashed me still swaying and batting her eyes, the only regret I had was that we couldn't do it again. This was the final chapter, the last act.

The stage manager cut the show lights and brightened the ones over the bar. The spattering applause petered out and those left turned to stake claims on empty stools.

Caspian stepped beside me. "Tore their fucking arses open," he said, speaking with the affected British accent he had adopted years ago to sound more like Lemmy.

My ears were muffled and ringing. We'd likely given tinnitus to half the crowd. "Fuck yeah, man. Buried 'em in their graves."

I turned to see Solomon smiling while slowly twirling a drumstick with a faintly dazed look, like he'd just been lobotomised. On the far right, Kevin had set the bass guitar down and was bent over talking to a frizzy-haired blonde with cleavage deeper than the Grand Canyon. She could have been anywhere from thirty-five to fifty, which was fine for Kevin. His type was anything with a hole.

"You still off the sauce?" Caspian asked.

I set my guitar in its stand, taking a moment to collect myself. It was a stupid question. Then again, Caspian was a stupid man.

"Yeah man. Seven years now."

"Shame," Caspian said, shaking his head. His pale scalp shone through the threads of his long, slicked-back hair. "But, on the other hand, we still get one more round on the house. I'll take yours."

"Knock yourself out."

I stayed on stage as Caspian led the others down and started cleaving a path towards the bar. People patted their backs as they walked by, bleated at them with loose smiles and bleary eyes. This had been our lives once. Crammed into a filthy bus, crawling from town to town, blasting the eardrums off rowdy drunks in dirty, half-filled bars. And I had loved every minute of it. But that time was over now.

Except for tonight.

In this rank hall of misfits, the dead had risen again.

I took one last look from atop the stage and then stepped down. Mortal, once more.

The bar smelled like pickled eggs and stale piss, which produced a stinging nostalgia. These were my favourite haunts. Places where you could be your most derelict self and no one gave a shit. I closed my eyes and let the babble of conversation reverberate inside my ears, catching snippets within the general drone. It was a soothing sound, mindless. It conjured memories from the countless hours spent in rooms just like this one, hunched over a cold, sweaty mug of pale yellow beer. Watching sports highlights on blurry screens while the mind melds into the babble of talk so much like a gurgling river. Flowing with whiskey.

The crack of gunfire startled me, and I looked up to see a line of people slamming empty shot glasses down against the bar.

"Keep 'em coming!" Caspian shouted, throwing his arm around the woman on his right. A roar of approval followed, and the bartender turned a bottle of Fireball upside down.

Tastes like heaven, burns like hell.

Takes you to hell, too.

Solomon peeled away from the bar, his eyes watering, and shouldered his way towards me.

"This must suck for you," he said, eyeing my soda water with mild disgust.

"Eh, what are you going to do?"

"Is it hard?"

I took a sip. It tasted like corroded metal. "Man, everything's hard."

"For sure." Solomon's once-white concert shirt had yellowed around the collar and under the arms and was now a half-size too small. "Booze makes it easier, though."

I still hear the screams from that night years before. Hers, mine. I swear they get louder and clearer every time they enter my mind. "Not for me. For me, it makes everything much harder."

"Yeah...." Solomon drifted off, his eyes losing focus as he watched his thoughts. There's nothing more terrifying to a drunk than someone going dry.

Caspian walked up holding two beers; the cling-on he'd left watched wistfully from the bar. He handed one to Solomon.

"Cheers, mates," he said, and we all clinked glasses; me admittedly feeling like a lame third wheel. Caspian took down nearly half his Miller Lite in three gulps.

"Anyone seen Kevin?" Solomon asked.

Caspian's laugh expelled halitosis. "Saw him take some hood rat outside for a good rutting. Ain't nothing changed with that one."

He looked at me with a scowl of disappointment. "What about you?" he said. "What's it like imprisoned behind a white picket fence?"

I felt the heat rise to my face. "Shit, my life's good, man. Living the American Dream."

Caspian slapped Solomon on his back just as he was taking a sip, creating another stain on his filthy shirt. "More like a fucking nightmare. Cutting jingles for commercials, right? How's that for rock 'n roll."

"Yeah, at least it pays."

"Sure it does. That's why they call it selling out."

Crushing ice cubes between my teeth helped calm me some, but not enough. Strangulation may have done the trick.

"Hey!" Caspian backhanded me in the stomach, and it hurt. "I'm just fucking with you, mate! I don't care if you turn into Mickey fucking Mouse. If it works for you, if you're truly happy, then that's great. You weren't getting anywhere as a lush, that's for sure."

Caspian and his backhanded compliments. I would have preferred warm spit to the fizzy water in my glass, but I took another sip. Anything to fill my mouth with something other than the words that wanted to spill out.

In retrospect, it hadn't been the partying and Cassie's pregnancy that broke up the band. It had been Caspian.

Solomon's eyes were glazed and unfocused. He must have taken something as soon as the show ended, if not before. Then I remembered the book. "Hey man, I read that book you told me about."

Solomon didn't seem to hear me. He was slowly nodding his head as though envisioning some drum solo he never got to play. His black hair plastered to his face with sweat. An oily sheen that smelled vaguely musty and made his face look like warm cheese.

"Dude." I elbowed his arm. "You in orbit?"

A doughy man in a Slayer shirt walked up and tried to enter the conversation, but Caspian boxed him out. We were standing in a loose triangle, and we each took a step forward to close it in. Amidst the drunken mayhem, it had a ceremonial feel. The tightening of a knot.

"Dude!" I yelled right into Solomon's face. "Wake the fuck up."

He blinked from surprise. "What? What's up?"

Caspian was surveying the room in search of better prospects, but I could tell he was listening.

"That book." I enunciated each word slowly and carefully as though speaking to my brain-damaged son. "The one you told me about. I read it."

"Oh." Solomon's face slickened with a fresh coat of oily sweat. "What'd you think?"

I shrugged. "Felt bad for that girl. Pretty grim little read."

"Yours had a girl?"

My phone began vibrating against my leg. I could faintly hear the harmonic opening to 'Welcome Home Sanitarium' through the fabric of my jeans. I checked, it was Cassie calling. Normally this would have annoyed me, but I actually felt relieved.

I plugged my outside ear and listened. "Yo, babe. What's up?"

"Hey! How was it?"

Caspian was still listening. That big, droopy, perforated ear angled towards me like a satellite dish. I cupped my mouth for privacy.

"Uh.... Good, babe." In my mind I saw the woman lifting

her shirt, her pert nipples vibrating like doorstop springs. "A little rusty. But a good time, nonetheless. Crowd had fun."

"Of course they did." I could hear Cassie's smile. Could see her perfect, ivory teeth, which were impervious to stain. I wondered if her cravings were still as bad as mine. If so, she hid them well. Seemed to get high off motherhood instead. Her fix coming from morning cuddles, nightly baths, and innocent 'I love yous'.

For me, fatherhood had felt more like a constant come down.

"I'm so happy you were able to do that," Cassie said. "You needed it."

The fog of cigarette smoke was thick, but not enough to account for the stinging wetness in my eyes. "Yeah, well...."

"So, how much later will you be out? I mean, how are you holding up?"

I peered through the dregs of soda water to the bottom of my glass. The burgundy floor was a dime-shaped blur. A hungry black hole with a gravity field that would never stop pulling until it sucked me back in, leaving only a burp behind.

I uncupped my mouth and spoke louder than necessary so that Caspian could hear me. "Yeah, I can shut it down. I'll be—"

His hand shot out like an angry mongoose and snatched the phone. "Is this the lovely Cassie Wheeler? How are you, my dear?"

The prick's smile looked menacing. Abusive, if such a thing could be said of a smile. He had tried to fuck Cassie twice that I knew about. The first time I decked him in the mouth, starting a fight that lasted twenty furious seconds and left us both lumpy and smeared with blood. We went out boozing the following night and ended it with our arms around each other. The second time Caspian had just shrugged as if to say, 'What do you expect?' We skipped the brawl that time and went straight for the reconciliatory booze – on Caspian's tab. It was his backwards way of saying he was sorry. He'd probably tried more times than that, and Cassie just hadn't said anything. With men like Lance Caspian, there wasn't much point. He did it less out of lust than spite.

Caspian's eyes glazed over while listening to whatever Cassie had to say. "Look here, love. The dead don't rest. This is a once-every-decade deal we're working on right now, and I got to break the ball from the chain. Your boy's doing lovely, you have nothing to worry about. We'll send him home safe and sound and you two can get back to the exciting, spontaneous life of raising toddlers. Okay? Ciao."

He disconnected the phone and stuffed it down his back pocket.

"Dude," I said.

Caspian held out his hand and shook his head. "Nope. Mate, I'm saving you from yourself."

The girl who had flashed me walked up then. And, with a sixth sense acquired at birth, Caspian moved aside and let her through.

|

Her name was Mandy, or Marie. I couldn't tell. Her Southern twang was accentuated by her drunken slur. She kept trying to interlace arms, but I wouldn't let her, so it became a kind of wrestling match that must have looked like a mating dance between two amorous snakes.

Caspian and Solomon ditched as soon as she walked over and started slamming drinks at the bar. I counted four in the thirty minutes since Mandy-Marie had stumbled over. That was in addition to the six before the show, and several during. They were both on their way to being smashed. And Caspian would want a ride home. That's why he had shut Cassie down and commandeered my phone. Fucking mooch.

Tired of wrestling with my arm, Mandy-Marie grew bolder, pretending to stumble into me while mashing her boobs against my chest. A timer starts when tits touch a married man's chest, and I let it go on long after the buzzer should have rung. Look, I couldn't help it. The effect of feeling twenty-year-old tits is the same as mainlining amphetamine, and I should know. Finally, I mustered the resolve to push her away and heard her moan like a petulant child.

"Oh my God. I'm so sorry. I'm such a klutz, I swear. You must think I'm a mess." She stuck out her lower lip in a pout.

"No, you're fine." I held her at arm's length, trying to get the guys' attention. It was time to go.

"Aw, you're sweet. I swear I—"

"Wait here." I swerved around her and weaved my way to the bar. I was definitely the only sober one there, and was starting to get a contact high. The room was swaying. Manic laughter echoed off the walls. A diffused corona blurred the white Christmas bulbs that encircled the bar's overhang year round, and the smell of unfiltered cigarettes had grown enticing.

I grabbed Caspian by the shoulder. "Hey, man. I need my phone back. Time for me to roll."

His eyes were half-lidded, the pupils bobbing in a sea of red. "Why don't you stop being such a pussy and get yourself a drink? It won't kill you."

There was a spot on Caspian's face, just below the eye, that was begging to be punched. Or the chin. Put him to sleep and drag him out by his fleshy, old-man arms. "No, I'm good. Night's over. Time to head home."

His eyes seemed to steady for just a moment. "No, mate. Night's just begun."

"Huh-uh, not for me." I reached behind him and ripped the phone from his back pocket. "It was fun, though. Let's do it again next decade."

"Man, why you got to be such a buzzkill?" Sweat had washed the hairspray from Caspian's hair so that it fell lank to each side, revealing the yellow skin of his scalp. It was speckled with liver spots. The man enjoyed his toxins, and a liver could only do so much. He pushed away from the bar, swaying. "Fine, fuck it. I need a ride."

"You leaving?" Solomon said. He had a hangdog look, like his feelings had been hurt.

I grinned, put my arm around Solomon and gave him a side-armed hug. "That was fun tonight. Good show. Let's do it again soon."

Solomon squeezed, holding me in place. "Be careful, okay?"

The hug went on longer than it should. "Thanks, I'll be fine."

"I'm serious." Solomon was struggling to hold his eyes steady, making some gurgling sound as though he'd suffered a stroke. "It's still out there."

That was when I noticed the pink, striated strip of flesh running underneath Solomon's chin down the side of his neck. It was partly concealed by some kind of skin-colour goo that sweat had turned to paste.

"Oh, right." I figured Solomon was trying to spook me. "Yeah, I'll watch my back."

I cupped Caspian's elbow and guided him through the stragglers who were still at the bar, too wasted now to even notice the band was breaking up. Again. By tomorrow, most of them would have forgotten the show.

"You're a fucking quitter, mate," Caspian was saying, stumbling on unsteady legs, head bobbing. "Quit the band, quit booze. Got married. Bet you quit pussy too."

"Yep, sure did."

Caspian freed his arm and pushed through the door out into the parking lot. The air was cool and crisp and smelled like fresh asphalt. Gravel crunched underneath our feet, and as tempting as it was to let Caspian slip and fall, I helped guide my old front man to my car.

I took a quick survey of the lot but didn't see Kevin anywhere. He must have taken his love connection home. Then, as I like to do at night, I looked up into space and scowled at the low-hanging curtain of black, the stars drowned out by the light pollution from Atlanta. We traded our view of the cosmos for the ability to work late into the night and gazers like me got the shaft.

A car whooshed by on the backwoods highway as I eased Caspian into the bucket seat of my Toyota Camry and closed the door. The marquee sign for the Full Moon Saloon was still lit up. RISING DEAD REUNION. Show starts at 8pm. $2 pints.

Yeah, of piss.

But now, in the great history book of the world, we will have forever rocked the Full Moon Saloon on this sleepy Saturday night. And that made me smile.

The Camry turned over on the first try, a near miracle. It had travelled over 180,000 miles and I was waiting for the inevitable breakdown, which would mean a new car. Or an old car, actually. But a new payment. Which would require more commercial work. At forty-six, I'm no longer at the top of the call sheet. But we'd find a way to make it work. Cassie and me. We always had. Some one-night stands are meant to last.

I used to obsess over the life I'd given up for her. The freedom, the years on the road. But looking back, I know who really got the better end of that deal.

Caspian was already starting to nod off in his seat, wheezing like a geriatric with emphysema. That could easily have been me.

He got a second wind as we turned onto the highway, however, and sat up, switched on the stereo and cranked the volume loud. "Radio out here's for shit," he said.

It was 'Beds are Burning' by Midnight Oil. I liked that song. "So turn it down."

He did. Barely. I reached out and turned it down more.

"Fucking princess," Caspian slurred.

Yep, this is exactly where I would have been had I not gotten Cassie pregnant. Drooling in a drunken stupor. Looking ten, fifteen years older than I am. But where would she be? Cassie had been working as an art designer for a music label when we met. Making shit money, but loving what she did. Doing good work too. She had talent. Still does. Just applies it towards decorative covers for our photo albums now. A little freelance work when she can get it. Mostly wedding invitations and stuff. She quit the label when The Accident happened.

I still call it that, 'The Accident'. My mind does, anyway. My protective ego. But it's with a capital T and capital A. The Accident.

Okay, here goes. I had gone out for drinks after working a double shift at Best Buy. I hated that fucking job, but needed money to help support our baby – our Big Surprise (capital B, capital S, believe me). I gave guitar lessons on the side and used that for bar money. Being a regular helped; they'd give me breaks on my tab. Plus I'd play happy hour every so often. 'Sweet Child of Mine' and shit like that.

Razz, the bar manager at this place called The Mule Kick, was testing a new drink special. Two-for-one Long Island Iced Teas. Fresh pours, not the mix. Liquor all the way to the brim. A couple of those and the bar lived up to its name. A couple more and the night got dark and murky. I have no idea how many I had that night. My tab was never over ten bucks.

Cassie and I took turns caring for our son, Rox, at night, with her leading the charge. Shoving me out of bed whenever it was my turn. She was still using then, but not nearly as much as me. That night, though, she must have had more than usual, because she was passed out deep. I crashed in the bed beside her, still clothed, and woke up hours later to the most dreadful silence I'd ever heard. That place was never quiet, man. Rox had a set of pipes that could put Caspian to shame.

Cassie and I woke at about the same time. Checked the clock and saw the blurred digits showing 4-something. Way past my nightly shift. She rose from the bed and I stayed put, partly due to the hangover already setting in, but also from some premonitory fear. I knew something was wrong. Could sense it like a silent alarm.

Then I heard her scream. Like something I'd conjured. A shriek that zapped my brain with an electric shock. I leapt out of bed and rushed into the living room where we kept Rox's crib tucked in a corner. The only space for it in our four-hundred-square-foot studio. I looked and saw that the crib was empty and my first thought was that someone had kidnapped my son. An overzealous fan or jilted lover. We'd have to call the police, send out an Amber Alert. Then I saw the way Cassie was hunched over and staring at something on the ground. Rox wasn't stolen. He'd crawled out of his crib at some point in the night and landed on the hardwood floor. I won't describe the scene any more than that. I can't, really. I've done everything I can to block it out.

He survived, but his future was destroyed. So were my tenuous rock aspirations, which is fair penance for my negligent behaviour. Actually, none of what happened is fair.

Cassie quit her job to stay at home. Good thing she's a great mom. Rox requires a lot of care. In many ways he's still an infant. Where-oh-where would she be without me?

The singer from Midnight Oil was singing about paying the rent, about paying our share, while, beside me, Caspian had begun to snore.

↑

I remember looking down at the front console right as the clock struck midnight and being happy that I'd made it through another day. Feeling a mixture of pride and shame over having put myself in this position in the first place. Wondering where the scale tipped in terms of trade-offs. What the biggest mistake had been. The lifestyle, or bringing others into the mix. Would things have gotten so bad if I'd never met Cassie? If we'd never had Rox?

Here I am thinking back on the past seven years, how much I've changed in such a small amount of time. Wishing I could bring the two versions of myself together, work out a reconciliation, find a way to forgive myself and move on. The night had been a blast. Being back on stage, back with my old bandmates, back in a seedy bar with loose rules and looser women. But how long would it take for the old patterns to reemerge? I couldn't afford to find out. I had just recently gotten to a place where I could even look at Rox without cringing. Where I could look in the mirror without averting my eyes. Nothing was worth giving that up now. Certainly not a night of blurry memories followed by a crushing hangover. No matter how much fun it might have been at the time. I felt like I'd passed some kind of test, and it felt good.

I glanced back down at the clock and it was still 12:00, making this the longest minute of my life. I thought maybe the clock had stopped, so I counted to sixty in my head and looked again. The glowing red digits remained at 12:00.

Fine, whatever. I started watching the yellow line bifurcating the road, the pulsing stripes ticking by like seconds. 'Personal Jesus' by Depeche Mode was just coming to an end on the radio. Caspian would have hated that one too, but I didn't mind it. Better than 'Coffin Dust', that's for sure.

The late-shift DJ spoke over the fading track, his voice soft and gravelly, like they'd just woken him up and stuck a mike under his nose.

"Welcome to The Midnight Hour. We've got a long night ahead of us, and it's just getting started. It's dark out tonight. Quiet. Half the world lost in the delirium of sleep while the other half toils away their sad, meaningless lives, counting down the days towards their inevitable death."

I snorted laughter. Sounded like someone had gone off his Zoloft.

"And out there right now, a lone rider drives down an empty highway, listening. An old acquaintance sleeps beside him, snoring like little baby Jesus in His cradle made of hay."

That was a little strange. I stiffened, and cocked my head. Looked down to see the clock still stuck at 12:00. The yellow hash marks flashed by.

The DJ chuckled, a deep, rattling grumble laced with lung plaque.

"That's right, The Midnight Hour. Let's get things started with our first guest of the evening. Get up close to that mike, there, and tell us your name."

That chuckle again. Like a death rattle.

"Kevin," the guest said. He sounded hesitant, scared.

"All right, yeah. So, Kevin, welcome to The Midnight Hour. Do you have any requests for us tonight?"

The guest said something that sounded like, *Want to me?* but had moved away from the mike so it was hard to hear. Then he grunted in pain and brought his mouth to the mike again.

"Okay, okay, okay," he said, his voice wavering, breathing hard. *"He's listening?"*

"Yes, I assure you, we have his complete and undivided attention right now. Go ahead."

I must have gotten a bigger contact buzz than I realised. I was feeling the paranoia you get when the trip goes sideways.

"Hey," I said to Caspian, trying to wake him up, but my voice sounded frail and pathetic and vanished as soon as it escaped my mouth. His answer was a riotous snore.

A loud, despondent exhale reverberated through the car speakers.

"*Okay then. Hey, Jesse.*" A pause, followed by another loud exhale. "*Man, I don't know what you've gotten into, but there's some dudes here looking for you. Rough bunch, man. I guess you're driving home right now? And this is coming through your car radio? They lifted me from the lot. Been watching, I guess. Fucked me up good.*"

It was Kevin, no doubt about it. He had never come back from banging that chick out in the lot. If that had even happened. Had that been a ruse? Was this some twisted stunt? If so, it was fantastically authentic. Kevin spoke like he was chewing cotton balls. Or else his jaw was broken.

"Hey." I grabbed Caspian by the shoulder and shook. "Dude, wake the fuck up."

Caspian gurgled and a string of drool wetted his chin. I needed a second set of ears on this so I gripped his jaw and pressed his face against the headrest, hard, looking helplessly at the white crescents of his vacant eyes. His head bobbed forward as soon as I let go.

"*So, man, listen,*" Kevin continued in that thick, swollen voice. "*I'm not even sure what I'm supposed to say. But I wouldn't fuck with these guys if I were you. Okay, man? Whatever this is over, just do what they want you to do. These guys, man. Wearing masks and shit. Fucking Halloween shit here.*" More breathing. The road hissed under the tires. "*Look, I don't know what y'all want me to say.*"

"*You're doing fine, Kevin. Just fine. This is The Midnight Hour, longest hour of the night. In fact, tonight it may never end. But you'll want it to, Jesse. You'll beg for it to be over. Do things you never thought you were capable of to make it stop. Are you ready for that?*"

Right then the interior lights cut off, the headlights sputtered and faded. The car engine seemed to choke. Then the engine died completely and we were coasting, the steering wheel stubborn in my hands.

The deep, gravelly laugh was louder without the ambient noise. Intimate.

"Look out, listeners. It's a hazardous night out there. Not a good night to be out on the road. You may want to look for a place to pull over and park. Some of you may not have a choice."

The car drifted and I eased it over to the emergency lane, which seemed like the wrong thing to call it. More like the *Figure Shit Out For Yourself* lane.

The tyres crossed over the rumble strip, and the car rattled. The interior lights flickered on and off like a strobe. That prick DJ's menacing laugh came in and out in a discontinuous staccato. I mashed the accelerator against the floorboard, but it was useless. The engine had shut off. There was nothing else for me to do but bring the rolling Camry to a stop. Chalky dust swirled in the soft glare of dim headlights.

"So, Kevin. You never told us. What is your request?"

I listened to Kevin's cynical laugh, suggesting a hint of defiance. Maybe that was good. *"Let me go?"*

"Hmmm." It came out like a purr, or the beginning of a growl. *"No, that's not on the set list tonight, I'm afraid. Let me rephrase my question. Do you have any last requests?"*

Kevin's next laugh was less defiant. And higher pitched. *"Come on, man."*

The speakers fell silent. Then I heard some talking in the distance, too far from the mike to make out. More humourless laughter. Then Kevin: *"Dude, seriously. What the fuck!?"*

The screech of a chair, something banging sharply against a wood table. Kevin grunting in pain.

"Your final words, Kevin? Anything for our audience?"

It sounded like the mike was moved back to Kevin's mouth. He was breathing hard and fast. *"Fuck you, man."*

"Well, okay. Good thing the FCC isn't monitoring this station, otherwise I don't think that would have gotten through."

Deep, sickening laughter. A man-size frog.

Kevin's sudden scream rattled the car speakers. Even Caspian flinched in his sleep.

"No, no, no no no—" Kevin stopped talking and started

groaning, an expression of pain that was almost like a plea. Then came a wet, gurgling sound. Like he was gargling something thick and viscous. I could hear a strange hissing noise, a leaking tire, then water splashed against a table.

No, not water.

A tearing sound, a knife through a chicken joint. Someone grunting off-mike, but getting closer. Breathing hard.

All the while the DJ chuckled. A portly man warming by a fire while petting a purring cat.

Something hard rattled as it rolled unevenly across wood.

"Ah, yes. We're off to a good start here at The Midnight Hour. And we're just getting warmed up. For our listeners out there on this special night, buckle up. Things are about to get bumpy. But don't worry. Help is on the way."

The lights cut off, casting the car in silent darkness.

P

My lungs were burning and it took me a minute to realise I wasn't breathing. If I had to bet on what I'd just listened to, I'd say it was the sound of Kevin's head being cut off. At least that's what it was supposed to sound like. That carving sound, the hissing of air, the waterworks, the rolling of the head.

It had to be a prank. There was no better explanation. No way had it been real. Yet, if that were true – and it must be, it must – then it meant my friends were master organisers, and Kevin had missed his calling as a Hollywood star. I had never before heard such terror in a man's voice. Such genuine, primal fear.

I have heard it since, however. My own.

There were no streetlights on this backwoods highway. Utter darkness pressed against the windows. I pulled out my phone and almost crushed it in my hand as the battery icon flashed once, twice, and then went blank. It had been fully charged at the bar. I'm sure of it.

At least it had been before Caspian confiscated it. He must have drained it somehow, the mischievous prick. He was probably faking sleep right now.

"Hey, asshole." I was not in the mood to be fucked with anymore. I grabbed his shoulder and started shaking him. His body rocked lifelessly. I shook him harder, rocking him against the side door. Harder, banging his head against the window. "Caspian. Wake the fuck up!"

He mumbled, blew air through rubbery lips. Paused, inhaled a snore.

Tiny pinpricks of light flashed in the rearview mirror. Headlights on the horizon, coming our way.

I slumped back against my seat, suddenly relieved. This whole setup must have something to do with that stupid goddamn book

Solomon had gotten me to read. Right, okay. That's what this was all about. He had even offered some cheese-dick warning when I was leaving the bar; I had just been too distracted to pay attention. He had been tipping his hand.

Christ, how long had they been putting this together? Was that the point of the whole reunion, just to fuck with me? Why?

Because I was the domesticated one, that's why. The one in most need of a little thrill.

"This is good, Caspian," I said, still unsure whether or not he was pretending to be asleep. "I don't know whether to be pissed or impressed. I think both."

I could now hear the hum of the engine from the approaching car. The headlights were growing brighter.

"So, what now? We just sit here?"

Caspian continued to quietly snore. These bozos must have gone to Martin Scorsese's acting school.

"Dude!" I backhanded him hard in the chest, paying him back for the gut shot earlier. Caspian groaned, shifted, but didn't wake up. "Hey." I grabbed his long, thinning hair, and twisted it. This was getting irritating; prank or not, I needed to get home. Cassie would begin to worry if I was out too late without my phone. I jerked his head harder and harder until I could hear strands of his hair ripping out by the roots.

Finally, he chuffed and raised his hand up defensively. "The fuck," he said in a sleep-addled slur. Still gripping his hair, I turned his head to face me.

"Rise and shine."

Caspian's face seemed to register something for a second, then fell slack. His lids stayed open, but his eyes glazed over. There was nobody home. Either Caspian could no longer hold his liquor or he had been drugged. This was a performance that could not be faked.

I heard the rumbling of tyres and watched as the approaching vehicle pulled over into the emergency lane behind us. Its headlights reflected off the rearview mirror, blinding me until I flipped the deflector. The engine was a loud, angry-sounding diesel. Judging by the general height of the hood and shape of the headlights it looked like a tow truck. It came to a stop several feet behind my rear bumper, brakes squealing, and then it released a frightening gasp of pressurised air. It was impossible to see past the blinding lights into the windshield.

"Don't worry," that smug DJ had said. *"Help is on the way."*

"Goddamnit, Caspian. I don't have time for this shit. Wake up, you asshole."

I didn't expect him to respond. I just wanted to hear my own voice. See how steady it sounded. Try and enforce some dominion over the present situation, which was feeling less and less under my control.

The truck rumbled, its glaring headlights casting a spotlight into my car, making me feel exposed and vulnerable. I turned and faced the truck head on, giving my best Fuck You face. Wanting to exhibit a little confidence. Show that I wasn't about to cower or be pushed around.

The engine cut off, but the lights remained on. Both doors opened and two men exited the cabin at the exact same time, their movements synchronised. Backwoods mechanics, by the looks of them. A matching pair wearing denim overalls, striped shirts with rolled-up sleeves, and cotton engineer caps. Older men. Late fifties, early sixties. Thick, wide-rim glasses obscured their eyes. Dark blotches stained their forearms. My eyes flitted back and forth. They looked identical. What the fuck were the odds of identical twins arriving the instant my car broke down to tow it away?

I pressed the seatbelt release, and felt a rush of panic as the button caught. Please don't let me be trapped in here. Don't let them have rigged the clasp. But then the buckle popped free.

They shut their doors at the same time, the noise echoing in the silent night, and started walking my way.

"No, no," I muttered. "Fuck all of this."

I opened the door and got out, never once seeing the little button on the steering wheel containing a camera. Just like the one now watching you.

The road felt barren, the night sky loomed in its endless expanse. I learned from my days of partying that nothing good ever happens after midnight. Statistically, you're more likely to die in the wee hours. More likely to disappear.

The two men stopped when I stepped out. Yes, they were definitely identical. At least they appeared so from this distance. Hick brothers who had only been separated when the embryo split.

"Ran into a little trouble, there?" they said together, their thick Southern accents reverberating as one. No way this was random coincidence. It was too theatrical. Too strange.

I figured I could take one of them in a fight, if it came to that. I wasn't sure I could handle both. "I'm fine," I said. "I've already called Triple-A. Thanks for stopping, though."

"Triple-A?" the one on my side said, standing motionless, hands hanging down.

"They don't service these parts," the other one said, working together to complete a sentence.

"Ain't nobody out here but us," they both said as one.

They were about twenty feet away. I was happy for the distance, but wanted to show that I was willing to stand my ground. I figured this would be over soon, and I didn't want to arm my friends – if I could still call them that – with ammunition to use against me later. Some hidden camera shit of me running from these oafs or pleading for them to stop.

I raised my arms to each side and shrugged. "So, what's the plan? Any way we can cut to the chase and get this over with? I've got a wife and sick kid at home. I don't want to keep them waiting."

"Just trying to help," the man closest to me said. He reached behind his back and retrieved something from a loop on his belt. Pulled around a large steel wrench, almost comical in size. More weapon than tool.

The man on the far side snickered – a dopey, wet sound as though it loosened his dentures. "It's a long walk to get anywhere from here, and ain't much traffic this time of night. Let us give you a hand." He pulled a tire iron from the back of his belt loop. Tweedledum and Tweedledee, carrying their instruments of death.

"Okay, so we've got to act this out I guess?" I decided to get theatrical myself. There wasn't much else I could do but play along. "Well, gee. Yes, guys. My car here's broken down, and, as you mentioned, there's not much traffic out tonight. To make matters worse, my phone's out of juice. But I can't tell you how glad I am to see you two with your handy tools. I mean, what a relief."

They began walking towards me, raising their tools. Their heavy work boots crunched over grit and broken glass.

"Seriously, I don't have time for this. Not tonight. I've got to get home. Let's do this some other time." They kept coming, closing the distance by half. Twiddledee on the far side snickered again. Shadows obscured their faces as they stepped in front of the beaming headlights.

"Dude, give me a break. I don't feel like running around out here half the night," I said. And I was going to run, I knew it. I wasn't convinced they would seriously hurt me, but they weren't about to throw down their tools and tell me they were kidding. Not according to that book. And I figured that's what this was about.

"That's okay," the one on the left said.

"There ain't nowhere to run," said the one nearest me.

They were taking slow, deliberate steps. Brandishing their tools. Old men with their old-man strength. Large, mechanics' hands. I checked the side of the road for a rock, or some piece of debris to use as a weapon. I saw a shredded flap from a blown tyre and bent to pick it up, but one of the steel wires sticking out pricked my hand.

They quickened their pace, loose gravel skittering under their feet. I backpedalled away from my car to maintain distance. Getting in would just trap me there.

"Where you going?" the near one said, coming faster now.

The other one was coming around the far side of the car. "We're only here to help," he said, and snickered. The one with the sense of humour, I guess.

They'd reached the back end of my car, and the guy with the wrench stopped for a moment, pretending to inspect the tires.

"Well, ain't that a shame," he said. Tire Iron was still coming around towards me with that dumb chuckle. "I'm afraid this car here is totaled."

He set his feet and raised the wrench in the air with both hands, then swung it down with ferocious strength, smashing in the back window. "Sure hope you have insurance," he said, and now they were both laughing. The bark of two hyenas – a family tree with a single branch.

I looked through the windshield and saw Caspian still passed out in the passenger seat. The shattering glass hadn't stirred him. I had locked the car when I got out, but clearly these guys weren't against breaking windows. Something told me Caspian was in on this, though, and would be okay. It was me they were after.

Tire Iron had reached the front of the car and was coming around, now less than ten feet away. Decision time had arrived: fight or flee. I'm not one to run from trouble, but that's exactly what I chose to do. And it was the first of many mistakes I made.

The road was four lanes of tar that disappeared into darkness. I've never been much of a runner, nor am I in very good shape, but I figured all I had to do was stay ahead of these lumbering idiots until I could flag down a car. One was destined to drive by sooner or later. It was strange one hadn't already, although I'm no longer surprised.

I peeked over my shoulder after going twenty feet or so. Wrench was walking slowly, but Tire Iron had picked up his pace. That was okay, I could cut over to the other side of the highway if I had to. I was high on adrenaline and knew it would give me the energy I needed to elude these old men until they gave up, or their ageing hearts did. No way they wanted to run around all night either.

A shadowy figure emerged from the side of the road up ahead. He was hunched over and holding something beside him. I couldn't see it clearly, but it had a long shaft that came to a sharp point. If I had to bet, I'd say it was a machete. Or something similar. I slowed just a bit, and heard the crunch of Tire Iron's feet quicken behind me.

"Here I come, big boy," Tire Iron said with his dopey snicker. "I got you now!"

I jolted forward and felt a twinge in my upper hamstring, just below my ass. It was the fastest I'd moved since high school, which was thirty years ago, and even then I'd never played any sports. But I didn't let the pain slow me down. I cut across to the far side of the highway and used my hands to hurdle over the guardrail. I landed on a decline and my feet slipped as I waved my arms for balance. Then my feet slid out from underneath me and I landed hard on my side and kept sliding, scraping my palms as I placed them down to brake. It was a forty-five-degree descent, maybe twelve feet or so to the strip of grass bordering the pine wood hill opposite the highway. I wouldn't get far in there, the trees were too densely packed. The hill too steep. At least it was dark down here at the bottom. It would be hard for them to see me from the road.

I stooped low to the ground – the back of my leg was now burning – and turned back the way I had come, figuring I could loop around and come up behind them. Up ahead I saw something that gave me a better idea. The opening to a circular culvert that tunnelled under the highway. That would put me clear across to the opposite lanes where I could run – limp, more likely – towards the nearest off-ramp and a gas station. I lurched towards it and scrambled inside.

Something had died in here. The smell caught in the back of my throat, the cloying stench of flesh rotting in stagnant water. It felt like a bad omen – this place knew death – but I was running low on options. The back of my leg was throbbing and growing tight. I had obviously pulled something, and wasn't sure how far or fast I could run before it gave out.

I ventured farther into the tunnel. Light only penetrated five feet or so. Beyond that, total darkness. There was no way to see the other side, but it had to open out on both ends. It had to.

The rounded ceiling was low, forcing me to hunch over. I felt a strain in my lower back much like the one in my leg. Fuck, if nothing else this escapade had revealed what kind of shape I was in. The ungainly shape of a squash.

Water stewed in the centre of the tunnel. I straddled the stagnant river to avoid splashing. It forced me to waddle but I kept moving forward, towards the smell. It was growing thick. I was entering its atmosphere, a cloud of noxious fumes. Of putrid decomposition. I hoped this wasn't something's lair. The death den of some scavenger that poached roadkill from the highway and feasted on it here. Or on people from broken-down cars.

I heard a splash from the far side of the tunnel. I stopped, and listened, breathing as quietly as I could, fighting to keep from gagging on the blooming stench that was now coming from right underneath me.

Another splash, but it didn't sound like a footstep. More like a fish, or the swish of a tail. It was coming towards me faster than anyone could walk. It sounded like something swimming.

"Hello?" This was Tire Iron, calling from the opening I'd entered from, blocking that entrance. I knew I was too far inside for him to see me. "Anybody in here?"

"I'm in here!" This voice came from the opposite end, from the direction I was heading.

"Me too! We're having a party." A third voice, a girl's. High-pitched and manic with glee. "I've invited all my friends."

More splashing, coming closer. Whatever it was must have arrived at the dead thing because it stopped momentarily. And then it started thrashing, splashing me with water as it attacked the decomposing meat.

I felt something bump my foot, then whip against my leg. It hissed.

I kicked my foot out reflexively and felt a hot poke in my calf, just below the knee. Searing pain set my leg on fire. I reached down and caught hold of something clinging to my leg. Something long and slippery with a rubbery feel, writhing in my hands. I pulled and it coiled around my forearm. I couldn't stay quiet any longer. I screamed as I flung it away.

That was a snake. There were snakes in here.

Joyous laughter came from the girl. "Oh, goodie! My friends have found someone to play with!"

Then, from Tire Iron, "No fair, wait for me."

I was surrounded, and I'd just given up my location. And that goddamn snake had bitten me. This was not a game.

Cold fire burned the spot where the snake had bitten me, my calf was cramping. There was no telling what type of snake it was or the brand of venom now coursing through my veins. Whatever it was, it was fast acting. And I doubted these maniacs had any antivenin on hand.

I heard the hiss of another snake and felt it slither over my foot, curling briefly around my ankle before letting go. It must have been at least three-and-a-half-feet long. Another one swam down the channel between my legs. How many were in here?

What was the thing lying dead beneath me? The odds of it being human were increasing.

I had to get out of here, now. "I've got a gun!" I screamed. Or tried to. It came out in a strangled croak that echoed down the concrete tunnel and couldn't have convinced a child.

"Now would be a good time to use it then, sweetie. We've come to kill you, you know."

I felt myself deflate. My head drooped until my chin rested against my chest. How could my friends think I would enjoy this? Even if this ordeal ended in a Swedish message with a happy ending, I'd never talk to them again. This was too far over the line. Hell, I was prepared to press charges. Put these assholes behind bars.

"You guys are so fucked," I said. The tunnel's acoustics accentuated the squeamish quality to my voice. It would have been interesting to record vocals in here. If, that is, we hadn't just given our final performance. And assuming I ever got out.

Fuck that. Of course I would.

The tunnel had turned quiet, except for the occasional splashing of snakes. I couldn't tell if my pursuers were approaching or staying put. Strange colours began to bleed into blind darkness. Burnt-orange window blinds. A flash of teal tracing the arc of a blade, or the wing of a bird. A swirling maroon that gave me momentary vertigo, making me lean forward for balance.

The darkness, the venom. Toxic hallucinations.

A deep, guttural vibration filled the tunnel. Someone humming, or Tire Iron's dim-witted guffaw. It was impossible to locate its source as it built towards a pulsating OMMMM.

Then someone whispered right beside me. "Jesse. Mate, it's me." Pain streaked down my left arm, and I nearly prayed for a heart attack to put me out of my misery. I was too stunned to speak.

"Mate, don't worry. It's all just a gag."

I heard the clink of metal, the scrape of flint. A small spark flashed and faded out. The flip-top lighter flashed again, this time producing flame.

It felt like I was being electrocuted. A mixture of fear and absolute relief. Like jumping to your death from a tall bridge, changing your mind midflight, and surviving the fall.

Caspian was standing next to me. The small, orange flame illuminated his face in a corona glow. His eyes were still half-lidded. His mouth was drooping in a drunken sneer. He hardly looked conscious, and I wondered how he had managed to navigate the channel in total darkness.

Who cared? Just moments ago I was ready to file charges, now I just wanted to give him a hug.

"Dude, Caspian!" I stepped towards him. His expression didn't change.

Then my eyes adjusted to the flare of light and I saw the tendrils of sinew and spinal cord dangling from Caspian's serrated neck. Another face came up next to his out of the gloom. Dark shadow in deep sockets. An old man's weathered face. Orange light flickered off his thick lenses, obscuring his eyes.

Then the light went out. Something stepped in the water behind me.

"Told you we'd get you, boy," Tire Iron said behind me. The last thing I heard was his inbred snicker.

I crumpled into a ball of light that wasn't really there.

ᚠ

More light. It blinds me. A headlight shining right into my eye, bright as the sun. My left eyelid shuts and the other one opens. It's forced open and exposed to another beam of blinding light, examining me. Looking straight into my brain. My right eyelid shuts and I hear the flick of a button.

A hand on my shoulder, a gentle nudge. A man's soothing voice. "Mr. Wheeler, are you awake?"

I am at the bottom of a well, the back end of a long tunnel. The man's voice is close, but I – the conscious me – am far away. Deep down inside myself.

"Take your time," the man says.

Slowly, I drift to the surface, towards the light of shallow water. Water, putrid water. Running along the bottom of a culvert drain. The memory jolts me awake, but I'm unable to move. My body's paralysed. My eyes flash open and the brightness stings.

I'm lying in a bed in what appears to be an operating room. The windowless walls are covered in white subway tile. An adjustable lamp is hanging directly overhead. Sharp surgical tools are arranged atop a steel tray beside me, several of them stained red. The lone man is dressed in a blue smock, his head covered in a scrub cap, his face hidden behind a white surgical mask. His brown eyes gaze into mine as he removes yellow latex gloves. I notice that they are speckled with blood. I presume mine.

My first thought is that I'm alive, and it brings tremendous relief. I made it out of that tunnel. Maybe they left me for dead, I don't know, but they didn't kill me. And now I'm somewhere safe.

I open my mouth to speak but all I can do is croak.

"Let me get you some water." The man fills a small paper cup from a bedside spout. It's cool and refreshing, although it burns a little as it wets my throat. He refills it and I drink again, easier this time. I gasp it feels so good.

I feel ready to speak. "What am I?" I say, mixing "What happened?" with "Where am I?"

The doctor's eyes crinkle, the mask hides his smile. "You've been in an accident. It was quite serious, but you're going to be okay. Just relax."

The last memory I have is of that twin mechanic doubled over in the narrow culvert holding Caspian's severed head. The tunnel was dark, though. And I was scared witless. It could easily have been a prop. It must have been.

I'm not sure what knocked me out. Could have been a needle to the neck or a knock to the head. That snickering hick with the tire iron had snuck up behind me – *"Told you, boy."* – just before the world had gone black.

My mind is whirling. "Where?" is all I manage to say.

"Someone reported the accident from the scene of the wreck. Your body was thrown from the car and had rolled down into a ditch by the side of the road. You're lucky they found you when they did. You must have landed near a snake's nest. You've suffered a copperhead bite, but we've administered antivenin and treated the wound. The more serious injury was to your head, where we've had to alleviate internal swelling to mitigate intracranial pressure. Your condition is stable now."

"The wreck?" I say. I try and lift my arms, my legs, but I'm immobile. I can't even turn my head.

The doctor nods. "It may take some time for your memory to return. Assuming it does. With a concussion as serious as yours, you may never recall the accident."

He removes the scrub cap to reveal a high forehead framed by a shock of dark grey curls. "We tested the alcohol content of your blood, and you came out clear. The police were here earlier, and will be back. They're still looking for the passenger who was in the car with you. Do you have any idea where he might have gone?"

Caspian? Do I tell him about the culvert? What I heard on the radio? Where do I begin?

I try to shake my head but can't.

"You can't remember," the doctor says. "That's okay. Don't strain. It'll either return or it won't, you can't force it."

He pulls the mask down from his face. Deep grooves line the side of his mouth. Dark whiskers are visible just below the surface of skin that sags from stress. He yawns from exhaustion and I'm either looking at a set of the world's most masochistic dentures or an orthodontist's wet dream. He doesn't have teeth, he has walrus tusks. Clumps of food – little sticks that look like grasshopper legs – are caught in between them. These yellowing tusks are growing in every direction and overlapping like warped fence posts. They crowd his mouth so obscenely it's surprising he can talk, a miracle he can eat. His mouth continues to open so wide I'm waiting for his jaw to unhinge, for the skin at the corners of his mouth to split.

Could be a trauma-induced hallucination. Or caused by the swelling of my brain. Or just a man with God-awful teeth and a coincidence of timing. Although the stuff stuck in his teeth is definitely from insects. I see the iridescence of a wing.

"You will no doubt notice that your motor skills have been compromised. That's from the anaesthesia, which will soon wear off and you'll regain complete mobility. All things considered, your injuries are minor and you can expect a full and expedient recovery. I'll have a nurse check on you soon. Best wishes."

He pats my chest and stands, placing the penlight on the instrument tray. He swings the overhead lamp away from the bed, giving me a clear view of the mirrored ceiling, where my reflection is marred in darkness, and exits through the door. A second goes by, then a ring of lights rimming the ceiling begins to grow brighter, bringing my reflection into view. My head is fixed in place so that I can only look up, and I'm mesmerised as my features take form in the mirror above me. The blue sheet covering my body. My pale face with its salt-and-pepper goatee. There's a red cap covering my scalp, which must be some kind of protective bandage. Although I can't feel the wrapping, and the closer I look the more I realise that it's not something covering my head. Rather, something is missing from it. The top half of my cranium has been removed and the red cap I see covering my scalp is my exposed brain. A dollop of blood oozes from my severed scalp line and I feel it drip down towards the corner of my eye.

I'm starting to breathe uncontrollably – I'm about to hyperventilate. But the rush of oxygen awakens my paralysed limbs, causing pinpricks of pain as the blood returns. My arms and legs are heavy and clumsy, but at least I can move them around. Blood begins to seep from my scalp from my exertions, stinging my eyes. I rock forward, once, twice, then sit up. I probably shouldn't be doing this. Fuck, there's no way I should be lying here alone with my brain out in the open. I'm going into shock. Finally I get to where I can control my arms and, without thinking, reach up and touch my head.

I feel hair. Wet hair, but hair. Not the slippery folds of my gelatinous brain. It doesn't hurt to touch, I can feel that my scalp and cranium are still in place. It's not even tender as I would have expected from getting clubbed over the head. According to the mirror, however, I'm caressing my most delicate organ – the source of all my dreams and grave addictions.

There's a small hand mirror on the instrument tray beside me. I grasp it with wet, red-stained hands. Hold it up and see my matted hair soaked in red liquid. Fake blood apparently. I look up, see my brain. Look to the mirror in my hand, see my blessed scalp and blood-soaked hair.

It's a fake mirror. The one above. Some kind of carnival trick like they have at fancy theme parks. Just an elaborate illusion. Which means, I'm still engaged in this sadistic hoax.

This realisation drained me of energy. All I wanted to do was lie back down in the hospital bed and go to sleep. Who knew what other tricks awaited me right outside the door the fangled-toothed doctor had just walked through. I had no other choice but to find out.

I swung my legs off the chair, pushed myself to my feet and tested the strength of my legs. They trembled and the world began to wobble so I lay back down. Then, before I could try to rise again, the door opened from the other side and the young woman who had flashed me at the bar walked through.

It looked like my nurse had arrived.

人

Mandy-Marie had exchanged her concert shirt for a costume nurse outfit with a short, hip-hugging skirt. The open top showcased the pert tits she had flashed during the show. I assumed that had just been a few hours earlier, but she had been wasted at the club and appeared sober now. Blue eyeliner rimmed her bright, alert eyes; glittering mascara caused her eyelashes to sparkle. Those eyes were all I could look at as she strutted towards the bed where I lay in an atrophied puddle. That doctor had said he'd administered antivenin for the snakebite, but I wondered if I wasn't succumbing to the poison now and dying, drawing my final breaths.

She stopped when she reached the bed and stared down at me with a look of mild indifference, as though examining a pet turtle. "You won't last the night." She clicked her tongue. "I should just kill you now." She picked through the utensils on the instrument tray and selected a scalpel, brought it towards my neck and ran the tip along my jawline. "Is that what you want? Trust me, it's the best offer you're going to get, the easiest way out. Continue on and you'll be told many lies; this isn't one of them."

I wanted to reach up and grab her wrist, but I was still woozy and it wouldn't take much for her to stab the scalpel into my neck. I could feel the sharp tip pricking my skin, right on the brink of breaking through. Still, I couldn't buy into this whole thing being anything more than a well-orchestrated charade. The fake mirror alone seemed to prove this point. I was on one of those stupid prank shows and in just a little while my prick friends would come in howling with laughter at how frightened I had become during their ridiculous stunt.

"You're the trustworthy one, huh?" I said. "Right."

"I didn't say that. But I am the only one you can trust."

I sighed. I was tired, still drugged. It blunted the fear that was soon to follow. "Look. I'm sure there are people who get off on this. I'm just not one of them. And this is all a bit much to waste on someone who really is not going to appreciate it. Let's cut our losses and call it a night, okay?"

Mandy-Marie frowned, removed the scalpel from my face and returned it to the tray. "I'm sorry you feel that way. This must be a big mix-up, then. I'll just take you to your car and we can forget this ever happened, all right?"

I chuckled, a pebble rattling in a rusty can. "Yeah?"

"Sure, silly mistake." Her hair was midnight blue with straight bangs. Bright, glossy red lips. Her tan had faded since I'd last seen her. "Whoops! Happens, you know."

The way she said 'Whoops!' produced a flash memory. From the tunnel. The party girl with her fork-tongued entourage.

"No worries," I said, trying to sound more casual than wary. Tiptoe past the sleeping bear. I started to sit up and had almost righted myself when she put her hands on my chest and slammed me back down against the operating table, then pivoted and swung a leg over to straddle me, pinning me in place.

Here came the howling laughter I had expected. Not from my maniac friends from behind the hidden cameras, but from this psychotic chick straddling me. "You dumb fuck!" Her breath smelled like corroded battery; I could see her uvula quivering. She grabbed my fake-blood-soaked hair and slammed my head into the padded table. "You clueless waste! Think you can ask your way out of this? Think you can plead? Did that help me, huh? It doesn't end, dummy. You're never getting out."

This was hysterical anger, this was real pain. Padding or not, she was slamming my head hard as fuck and it hurt. Clawing my scalp with sharp nails and tearing my hair.

"This is no joke. And you're the one who made a mistake, not us. You're the one who asked for this. Now you have it. Now it's here. The only question is how the story ends for you. Because it's only just begun."

She stopped slamming my head and screaming into my face.

She straightened and shifted her hips, settling down on my lap in a way that would typically trigger arousal. But I had never felt less aroused. Given the chance, I would gladly break this girl's nose. Would strangle her unconscious as soon as I regained my strength. This had stopped being a game, and I was no longer playing around.

"Okay," I said. "I get it. Help me, then. Please, tell me what's going on."

Nose to nose, mouth to mouth, we shared one breath. Naked, this would be the most intimate position two people could share. She pushed herself upright and looked down at me, her pet turtle. "Why did you do it?" she asked.

My mind had never been so empty. "Do? Do, what?" I was surprised to muster a single syllable, much less two.

"Stop acting like you're surprised by all this. You had fair warning. I should know."

Solomon's book, had to be. She was right, it was time to stop playing coy. "This didn't happen in the book I read. Forgive me if I'm caught a little off guard. So, Solomon's behind all this?"

She seemed puzzled. "I don't know a Solomon."

I leaned back and looked at my brains in the mirror above. "This is crazy." I was stating the obvious, which was just as well. I could see no way of talking my way out of my predicament. "Can't you just…please, just help me?"

"Absolutely." She smiled and it was patently adorable. Plump cheeks, cleft chin, dimples. I couldn't wait to rearrange her features with my fist. "That's what I'm here for."

My exposed brain was pulsating in the carnival mirror, oozing blood. "You're the fucking cavalry? Fuck."

"I'm your only chance of getting out of here."

"Which is where?"

She giggled remorsefully. "A place I call Fucksville."

Mandy-Marie pressed down on my chest and gave a silent look that meant, 'Be nice, don't move.' I nodded, and she swung her leg off of me to stand beside the table again. I noticed the nametag for the first time: Malia. I had yet to see her blink.

"You're in the manifestation of a maniac's imagination. One

who has been stalking you for months. Exploring your history, studying your psychology. Learning your fears and discovering your regrets. But you know this already. You know what's in store. Fun, huh?"

I didn't cry the night Rox fell from his crib, I didn't know how. I felt like crying now. "This can't be real. What's the point of putting me through this? Please, cut the bullshit."

She slapped my face with a stinging hand that turned my cheek to ice. "I'm the one truth in a house of lies."

There was nothing fake about the sharp pain her slap left behind. "I'm going to fucking kill you guys."

She nodded. "I wish you would. How else will it end?"

I came to the realisation we were being watched, listened to. That my threats were not confined to this isolated room that had begun to offer a false sense of safety. I forced myself to reflect back on the book Solomon had given me, one very much like the book you're reading now. I'm your future, don't you understand? There you are, lying in your bed, riding on the bus, squatting on the can. Safe, comfortable. Enjoy it while it lasts. You're already past the point of no return. His eyes are on you right now, I guarantee it. My voice travelling through time to this present moment – a fire alarm ringing from a mound of smouldering cinders. Were I to switch places with you, I'd start planning my escape now. I mean today, tonight. Maybe there's a way out if you leave early. Leave everything behind and never stop running. Maybe...but I doubt it. Might as well learn as much as you can about what comes next. Not that it helps much. This I learned thinking through the scenarios I read about, knowing the nightmares waiting beyond this one room. This recovery room. Here with Mandy-Marie-Malia, my nurse. My curse.

I sat up. My head felt clearer, my mobility had returned. "Where do we go from here?"

She pointed towards the door. Light brown, plywood. Maybe birch. A veil of ignorance I didn't want to lift. Didn't want to see beyond.

I sighed. "The only way out is through."

She smiled smugly and offered her hand. Mine was wet, hers dry. She tugged and I stayed in place, peering down at the sharp objects on the instrument tray.

"Kill me and you die." I still hadn't seen her blink. "Means nothing to me. I gave up long ago."

A puzzle piece clicked into place. I had read about her. Or at least, I was supposed to believe I had. "No, I'd rather be friends. Show me the way out of here."

"This way." She led me to a grey box on the wall beside the door that looked like a circuit breaker. That's what I expected to see when she opened it up. Instead, I saw a joke. A glass box with the words BREAK IN CASE OF EMERGENCY tucked inside the outer box like a Russian doll. A straight razor hung from a chain inside the glass enclosure.

"This is the quickest exit. The only chance you'll have. I'd take it if I were you."

Given a second chance, I would. But the same blind arrogance that led me to read the book delivered false optimism at this critical moment. Know this: it is the last opportunity you'll have.

"I'd rather take my chances," I said, and she blinked for the first time that I saw.

The door opened onto a dark hallway. I tried to step forward, but couldn't. Glued to the ground. Turned to stone. I may have stood there until I crumbled to dust had Malia not shoved me through.

ᛈ

Darkness is inherently scary, and it shouldn't be. So are confined spaces. Rather than remind us of the womb, the safest and most hospitable place in our primal memory banks, it awakens our imagination to monsters hiding in the shadows, waiting to pounce. Which means the memory must come from a time before birth, from a shared experience of such terror it was encoded into our DNA.

Sorry, you think in abstract terms when death feels close. The mundane becomes profound. *All of this for me*, I remember thinking as I stumbled out into this dimly lit hallway.

All of this for me.

The hallway reminded me of the mansion from the board game Clue. I wanted to be Colonel Mustard, but felt more like Professor Plum. Either way, I was sure to be the murder victim, but it wouldn't come by candlestick or lead pipe. No, no. Nothing as pedestrian as that.

A wall sconce flickered muted candle flame a dozen steps farther down, offering just enough dim light to see the paisley wallpaper, the warped shoe moulding. I fluttered towards it like a moth.

As I entered the halo of light, I got a clearer look at the wallpaper pattern. It looked like potted ferns. Or heads of cabbage framed by African shields. But as the images became clearer, I realised the head of cabbage was actually a human head. Peering closer, I saw that the face on the head was mine, silkscreened in faded yellow print on maroon paper. My face, watching with bland curiosity; my head planted in a pot, wispy fern leaves sprouting to each side like windblown hair.

You know how you can animate a series of drawings by flipping the pages? That was how my face was printed on the wall. As I walked I saw my open eyes begin to droop, closing the farther I went. My silkscreened mouth sagged open as though preparing to speak, or scream in agony. A red slash cut sideways across my throat. Red paint spilled out, drooling down the wall. Real liquid, seeping through miniscule slits in the paper that I could reach out and smear with my finger, taste with my tongue.

All of this for me, I thought again, scanning the opposite wall to see the same tableau. Feeling delusional as I watched myself die on a wall that was watching me walk towards my death.

"Cute," I said to my guide behind me, motioning towards my decapitated head. "Nice touch."

Mandy-Marie-Malia, her skirt ending one millimetre below her womanhood, reached out and swiped a dollop of my lifeblood, unfurled her long, pink tongue and ran a red track down its centre. "Mmmm, Type O," she said.

I am Type O. I can donate blood to anyone, but only receive transfusions from my own kind.

"Good guess," I said, knowing it wasn't. There was a square, head-level recess in the wall up ahead on my left, like an unfinished window. I've been to haunted houses; this is where the zombies reach out to grab you. If only that's what this place was.

I approached with caution, peered in to find two elliptical holes on the far side of the opening. Eye sockets with soft light streaming through. Back to Clue Mansion, I thought, realising this was the observation end of a fake portrait that allowed one to spy into the room on the other side. All around this head-size cutout were images of my decapitated head planted in a pot. Nothing ominous about that.

Curiosity is a son-of-a-bitch. It caused me to do two things. First, to swipe a dollop of the liquid dripping from the wall and taste it, proving it was indeed blood, or at least a convincing facsimile. I was not familiar enough with the taste of my own blood up to that point to know whether or not it was mine. Second, to push my face through the window in the wall to peer through the eyeholes into the far room.

The smell inside was the same as the taste in my mouth. A biting copper reek, familiar as rot. And the air in here was dank.

The recess, contoured in the shape of a face, was damp with wet splotches seeping through the paper lining, shining dark in the diffused light streaming through the eyeholes. It was like an inverted papier-maché skull, just large enough for me to fit my face inside. A stupid move.

A panel in the wall slid down around my neck, trapping my head inside the snug enclosure. My face flush against the contours, nose crammed into an impression that smelled like fresh blood. Dampness bled through the thin liner, wetting my cheeks, my hair. I planted my hands against the wall and pushed, but the panel was clamped securely against my neck. I was stuck. My head buried in the wall, waiting for the blade.

My breath quickened, turning loud in the cramped space. My heart hammered. I felt panic rise as a tightness in my chest threatened to crush my lungs.

The eyeholes looked out onto a game room, a hunter's trophy room with two plush leather chairs facing the wall from which I looked. A circular mahogany table was in the middle of the room with a cigar box on top, a chandelier with green lampshades hanging above. Rich oriental rug. Hunter-green walls with wood-panelled wainscoting. Animal busts mounted to the walls. A boar with tusks like the doctor who had been in the room when I awakened, but cleaner. An oryx with some decomposing rodent impaled on one of its antlers. Several deer that had not been taxidermied so they were dangling by limp necks, pulp oozing through eye sockets, plasma or some other sap-like substance seeping down like a shroud. My throat closed when I saw the head mounted on the wall opposite mine and my heart stopped beating. There, mounted on the opposite side, was Kevin's severed head staring back at me, hung like a trophy kill. His long hair combed shiny and flowing down either side of his waxen face. The waxen face you see staring up from a coffin during a funeral viewing – rouge on the cheeks, lips and eyes glued shut. Inanimate as a goddamned doll. That was Kevin's decapitated head, not a prop.

Which made me think about the head that I now inhabited. The ripe stench of blood.

A door on the far side of the room swung open. The thing walking through was crippled with yellow, wrinkly skin, like larvae. Thin and hunched over with a tragically disfigured spine. One arm longer than the other. Stark collar bones and vertebrae. Lank, colourless hair. It looked up at me with a misshapen face, swollen and flushed red with spider veins. Staring into my eyes, it grunted and drooled and hastened its lopsided shuffle.

The back of my head pressed against the solid panel as I tried to pull away. This was no spyhole; that maggot thing knew where I was positioned. It stared right into my eyes after every few ambling steps – its lips stretched in a permanent sneer – until he, I think it was a he, rounded one of the two plush chairs and bent down out of view to manipulate something on the wall underneath me. Seconds passed, then I heard the click-click-click of a starter fuse. Followed by the whoosh of a gas flame.

I was the mantel trophy over a fucking fireplace, stuck inside what I felt sure was Caspian's scooped out head, still wet from its recent cleaning.

The lady in the book I read never went through shit like this. What then is waiting for you?

The figure's hunched back returned to view as he or she hobbled over to one of the plush chairs and eased itself down, grunting and then sighing with relief as the worn leather contoured to its frame. I could feel heat rising from underneath my neck, and wondered if this person was going to sit there and watch me burn alive. Sit there and listen to my screams, my pleading. Watch as my eyes liquefied and melted down the front of Caspian's taxidermy face.

A voice began speaking directly into my ears from tiny speakers. A woman's voice – polite, yet stern, with the slightest affectation of a British accent. A stewardess for a fancy airline.

Foregoing preamble, she began to relate a story. The hunched figure watched with indeterminate interest from the leather chair, moaning periodically from the pain that sitting caused to its contorted back.

My trapped head grew ever warmer from the fire below.

*   *   *

The Story None of Us Should Know

*as related by an anonymous female narrator
to me while being cooked alive*

This is how you make a homunculus. Extract semen from a fertile male, preferably one in the peak of virility. Allow the sample to age in an environment that imitates the conditions of a vaginal canal. Once the sample has begun its mutation – usually occurring after forty days of gestation – extract the sample and inject it into the unfertilised egg of a hen. The hen must have lived in its natural habitat for proper insemination to occur. It must not have been treated with hormones or antibiotics of any kind.

Once the egg has been inseminated, it should be kept in an incubator for a minimum of twelve weeks. A horse womb can serve as an incubator. So can the womb of swine. When the shell has blackened and begins to moult, you may then carefully peel open the shell and extract the specimen, presuming the insemination was successful.

A proper homunculus will be anatomically identical to a full-scale human despite its miniature size. It will be able to move its appendages and swivel its head. Given time, and while being sufficiently fed the Arcanum of human blood, it may grow to the size of an avocado and sprout wiry hair. But it will never establish a personality or demonstrate even the most rudimentary form of human cognition.

Hostility, however, is a common trait amongst homunculi, suggesting an instinct for self-preservation. The last homunculus created at the end of Phase One was observed hissing and ejecting a toxic liquid from its mouth that contained acidic properties strong enough to burn human skin. Its ability to aim this discharge suggests spatial awareness, despite lacking observable faculties for sensory perception. Its skin was translucent yellow. Its undeveloped eyes were black.

This homunculus was terminated and homunculi were deemed incompatible for Doctor O's experiments despite further specimens that grew to the size of a dwarf human and could follow rudimentary instructions. Doctor O is also referred to as Mister O and Professor O, depending on his occupational capacity pursuant to current project scope.

In the spring of 1963, a group of villagers found a six-year-old boy devouring the slaughtered remains of a goat with a pack of wolves in the deep forest of Musafirkhana, about twenty land miles from Sultanpur. The boy was dark-skinned with sharpened teeth and long, hooked nails. His hands and knees had developed thick, calloused pads from travelling on all fours. A thin pelt of fur covered his naked body, and he slept among the pack alongside the younger pups.

After days of observation, the boy was eventually separated from the wolf pack and brought to town, where villagers attempted to indoctrinate him into the community. Dr. Soledad Rujmitari, a prominent anthropologist stationed in New Dehli, was alerted to the discovery of this feral child and brought in to document his condition and catalogue the process of his enculturation. Despite intensive efforts, the boy never learned to speak, nor even to understand the simplest commands issued by his caretakers. He remained a quadruped, and refused to eat anything other than raw or cooked meat. His eyes roamed wild, fearful, without the faintest spark of human understanding. After several months, with no significant indication of progress, he was terminated following an attack on a human infant he had been observed stalking in a predatory manner consistent with the hunting practices of his wolf pack.

In April 1965, another feral child was found living among a pack of Vervet monkeys in the jungles of Uganda. This time a young girl, around the age of seven, who was later named Little Niki. She, too, had calloused limbs and hooked fingers. A fine pelt of fur on her face and body. She was a proficient climber, capable of leaping between trees, and could mimic the vocalisations of other Vervets. Dr. Cyrus Parsifal's book, *A Return to the Jungle*, chronicled the attempts to enculturate Little

Niki by his team of renowned anthropologists – a three-year ordeal that ended with the return of Little Niki to her family pack while being kept under close observation. Having injected a homing device under her skin, Dr. Parsifal and his team were able to monitor Niki and her pack for the next eighteen months, before she died of injuries sustained from a fall. During that time, she was observed caring for toddler monkeys, grooming and feeding them insects and nuts. Even attempting to feed infants from her undeveloped breasts.

These cases, and others, formed the construct for Phase Two.

Phase Two began with specimens of various ages – age being the most predictable determinate of outcome – followed by length of exposure to feral conditions. Specimens entering the experiment after the age of two had a higher likelihood of adopting a modicum of social acuity, although were never able to meet the same standards of a child habituated from birth. Speech was limited to a few basic commands. Toilet use was widely rejected. Genuine affection for other humans was never fully attained, although some specimens learned to display affectionate behaviour in order to obtain certain rewards. Specimens' eyes remained distant and incapable of expressing emotion beyond anger and fear, except for an unsettling sadness that was reported among children removed from society at an older age, as though longing for something faintly remembered. The longer specimens were removed from society, the less favourable were even these most modest of outcomes.

Specimens entering the experiment before the age of two were almost universally incapable of adopting any human acuity if left exposed for a year or longer. Some physiological adaptations were noted in the specimen depending on age, length of exposure, and animal habituation. Specimens often displayed darker, thicker skin, coarser hair, sharper teeth, and hooked claws. Vocal adaptations occurred, allowing for vocalisations mimicking the species of animal to which the specimens were exposed. Gut fauna evolved to accommodate diets endemic to their familial species, and inoculate the specimen against harmful micro-organisms ingested while consuming raw meat, insects, untreated water, faecal matter, and soil. Visual and olfactory capacities were often supremely enhanced.

Specimens deprived of human interaction during formative years adopted the primal characteristics of their familial herd, and were incapable of later integrating with human society. Yet, unlike the homunculus, these specimens were impressionable and established a habitual construct based on the nature of stimuli to which they were exposed. Explained plainly, feral children disproved the argument for innate human instincts, while displaying the unique capacity to take on the operating system of the species to which they were exposed during the developmental window following infancy.

Recruitment tactics for Phase Two are classified. The funding of Phase Two is classified. All field data from Phase Two is classified. The status of specimens following the conclusion of Phase Two experimentation is classified.

The nature of personality has long eluded scientific inquiry. A soul has never been measured or observed. Genetically identical twins present a compelling case for an individualised personality separate from genetic sequencing and environmental influence, presenting polarities as early as seven months even within the same controlled environment. Based on this evidence, Professor O formed the hypothesis that the origination of personality – or soul, to use a more esoteric term – must not be predicated on biological imperatives.

In an airlock lab, stationed 2,000 metres underground, Doctor O prepares the petri dish as part of Phase Three. You may picture a man in his late fifties with a white goatee and a full head of fine silver hair styled away from his forehead, if it will aid your visualisation, though his true description is classified. While the embryonic DNA extraction technique is classified, I can disclose that patient zero for Phase Three was a Caucasian male with brown hair and eyes, and Type-O blood, as were all his genetic replicates.

Within the quiet, underground lab, you will see specimens in various stages of development – all cut off from any potential human interaction, separated from one another by metres of reinforced steel that block all sound, natural light, and electromagnetic waves. The foetus develops within an artificial womb, intravenously fed synthetic nutrients that have been engineered within a sterile laboratory setting.

At forty weeks, the infant is extracted from the artificial womb and placed in a sealed incubator that prevents any visual or auditory stimulus from entering the enclosure. Everything within its enclosure is sterilised, including oxygen, so that the specimen never encounters external biological agents. The enclosure is equipped with a sanitation system designed to clean the specimen with water purified through reverse osmosis.

The laboratory is silent. The specimens never once make a sound – not a mewl nor whimper, much less the boisterous cries of a newborn infant. Specimens within the first wave developed an umbilical cord that sought attachment to a placenta wall. Lacking one, it withered and detached and the specimen died of starvation. The biological imperative to feed through an umbilical cord was redirected by the fourth wave – the first to accept nutrients fed intravenously. Current specimens lack navels.

The fourth wave was the first to survive the incubation phase. Specimens were removed from incubators during sleep – EEG monitors revealed no change in brain activity during sleep, suggesting the absence of dreams – and placed on a rubber floor, free to move at will within the confines of their isolated cell. Here they would lie supine on the floor, silent and motionless. Cataracts formed over their brown eyes from each specimen's inability, or refusal, to blink.

The fifth wave received a radio tuned to classical music, opera, and NPR. Then, later, to the chanting of various spiritual traditions, religious hymnals, and *a cappella* youth choirs. These additional stimuli elicited no change.

The sixth wave received a television monitor showing maternity films, nature shows, cartoon musicals, and live video feeds whereby Professor O attempted to establish direct interaction. This additional stimulus elicited no change.

Specimens in the seventh wave were subjected to a mirror secured overhead. This was the first stimulus to elicit change, disrupting the specimens from their catatonic stupor, prompting preliminary signs of physical mobility. First, blinking. Followed by the subtle articulation of head and limbs. After gradually attaining muscular dexterity, specimens eventually tried to reach out and touch their reflected image. Specimens were unable to sleep underneath the mirror, and the mirror had to be removed under the cloak of darkness in order to facilitate rest. Finally, at this seventh stage, the EEG monitor presented a disturbance in brain waves, indicating visualisation during sleep. The mirror combined with a radio prompted the first attempts at vocalisation, although these vocalisations never evolved into cogent verbal articulations, so the radio was removed.

All documentation for wave eight was destroyed.

The stimulus for wave nine is classified. Specimens from wave nine were introduced to the classified stimulus during the incubation phase, in an enclosure lined with mirrors on all sides. Upon completion of the procedure, specimens would immediately animate and began vocalisation, typically screaming or howling, but sometimes laughing and giggling, sometimes grunting, sometimes growling. Several specimens were recorded babbling in a structured dialect that contained all the markers of a codified language for which we lack translation.

Specimens from wave nine showed an appetite for solid food soon following the incubation period, and actively roamed the interior of their cells, some crawling, others walking upright as early as sixteen weeks. Specimens appeared inquisitive and displayed critical thinking while exploring their habitat. While previous specimens were impervious to habituation of any kind, specimens from wave nine quickly adapted to their habitat and proved capable of assimilating new information at a rate associated with supreme cognition. Once communication was established – Latin being the first known language specimen from wave nine universally acquired – nearly all specimens began to describe imagery and recount events occurring outside their enclosure, displaying knowledge of information beyond the extent of their educational programming. While classified, these memories are considered fabricated, and professed knowledge to be falsified through an advanced form of emotive imitation.

The first attempt at societal assimilation was through a private orphanage owned and operated by colleagues of Mister O for purposes of research. Here, among other areas of inquiry, researchers studied the effects of myriad traumas on youths of varying ages. Fields of study included methods of personal rehabilitation and causes for behavioural degeneration. The elasticity of a moral codex. Means of cognitive conditioning and the disruption of fixed beliefs. The reaches of radical delusion; i.e., belief in gross falsehoods lacking affirming evidence.

John B was biologically seven when he entered the orphanage. Brown hair, brown eyes, Type-O blood, the same as his genetic donor. While specimens from early phases were inherently anti-social and intellectually stunted, children from wave nine matured rapidly and were drawn to social interaction – despite expressing initial inhibitions strategically utilised to disarm defence mechanisms among traumatised individuals or to subvert the hierarchical nature of social networks.

John B was placed in a dorm among five other boys his age. As part of a control group, these boys had experienced minimal trauma in the way of physical or sexual predation, and had been orphaned from stable, respectable families lost through non-violent and/or natural means. By the end of the first week, John B had indoctrinated himself into the group, earning an elevated sense of trust and empathy above standard expectations.

Days in the orphanage were very regimented. Early rise, exercise, personal hygiene, breakfast, group education, lunch, group education, group therapy, exercise, quiet study, meditation, supper, personal hygiene, sleep. By the end of the third week, John B had convinced another orphan to exchange cots with him, moving from the outer edge to the centre of the room. Unlike the other boys, John B required little sleep and could function after staying up for several consecutive nights. Hidden cameras observed him walking silently between the rows of cots at night, stopping beside each one and studying the sleeping child for periods of an hour or more. He was observed whispering into the ears of his bunkmates without ever waking one, and exhaling into their open mouths. Conversely, he was observed inhaling their exhalations. He would place his hands on their head, mouth, throat, chest, stomach, pelvis, and reach underneath to cup their scrotum.

John B's hair grew more rapidly than his peers. His resting heart rate was 140 and core body temperature was 104 degrees Fahrenheit. His IQ score fluctuated randomly from 6 to 162, with various measures in between. On one test, he provided answers in non-sequential numbers and letters that were later found to mathematically describe the rate at which the universe expanded and propose a date for a sudden reversal and period of rapid contraction. On another test he created a coded language that, once deciphered, read, MY MOMMA SPANKS ME BOTTOM RED RED RED SO NOW ME BLUE BLUE BLUE.

By the end of the sixth week, John B's roommates had stopped eating. When asked why, they would universally answer, "Why eat when I am full." None of the boys lost an ounce of weight during their time of fasting. Their resting heart rate decreased from between 70 and 120 beats per minute to less than 40 beats, and their core temperature dropped to 97.1 degrees Fahrenheit. When John B came around to their beds at night, they began to open their eyes and weep as he whispered in their ears. Hidden microphones recorded the contents of John B's whisperings, which more closely resembled the echolocations of odontoceti and Microchiropteran bats than any human language, and were indecipherable to expert linguists and pattern recognition programs. None of the boys expressed any recollection of these nightly encounters, but under hypnosis would begin to transmit the same echolocations as heard in the recordings.

All the linguists stopped eating for a period of nine days after studying the recordings, as did the psychologist who interviewed the boys under hypnosis. None of those afflicted have any recollections during this period of time despite engaging in regular activities. Their memories were erased.

By the end of the ninth week, John B's roommates had either lost the capacity to store memories entirely or had entered into an agreed-upon group deception to fabricate a shared condition. They began to act as a single unit, assuming identical bodily postures and facial expressions, displayed stigmergic traits common among animal swarms such as walking at the same pace, sitting and standing at the same time, taking simultaneous bites of food, chewing and swallowing as one. Distance did not disrupt this shared behaviour. Placed in separate rooms, the boys would cross their legs, scratch their chins, or run a hand through their hair at the exact same time, as though obeying a common impulse. Their voices took on the same tone and inflections to the point where unique vocal signatures collapsed into one shared profile. Interests regressed solely to activities required for physical survival: eating, sleeping, and waste removal. If asked how they were feeling, they would say, "Hungry", "Full", "Awake", or "Tired". If asked to reflect on past events, they would remain mute. If asked to ruminate on future desires, they may say, "I must find food when hungry. I must rest when tired."

The boys lay down for bed during the fifteenth week following John B's arrival, the one hundred fifth day to be precise, and fell into a collective coma. John B lay in his cot in the centre of the room in a similar catatonic state, although EEG machines were unable to detect brain activity for him during this period. Medically, he was brain-dead.

All attempts to pull the boys from their coma failed.

Microphones stopped recording during this period. Cameras malfunctioned. Those who entered the room fell into a fugue state and experienced short-term memory loss upon exiting. The temperature in the room dropped from 70 degrees Fahrenheit to 51 degrees before the digital thermometer short-circuited.

The boys awoke three days later. Lacking surveillance equipment, it is unknown if they awoke simultaneously or in turns. The guard stationed outside the door reported sudden, hysterical laughter occurring approximately at the time cameras turned back on. Every boy was sitting up in bed except for John B, who was lying down. Unlike before, their laughter was no longer synchronous or identical in tone. Sound analysis presented incongruities between the vocal profiles for each individual pre- and post-coma – these new vocal signatures being unique and heretofore un-catalogued. The deep, husky vocalisations of three mature adult males and two adult females, not those of the seven-year-old boys who had entered the orphanage.

The laughter soon devolved into violent retching and gurgling coughs as the internal organs of each boy swelled past capacity and ruptured. Blood ejected from gaping mouths and spewed from bulging eyes. Their facial expressions during their dying moments have been analysed and described as joyous, despite the agony they must have experienced as their organs liquefied and evacuated their bodies. In just under four minutes, the five orphans fell back in bed like deflated bags, while John B opened his eyes and sat up, surveying the carnage around him.

He turned and faced the hidden camera assigned to his cot, this brown-haired boy replica of the man he was cloned from. "More friends, please," he said. "These didn't last."

John B was removed from the orphanage and his status is classified. The status of Doctor O's/Professor O's laboratory work is classified. You are a point of classified data. You are a new wave of specimen, classified. You are in your son's head.

Imagine hearing this story while stuck inside the world's most claustrophobic sauna. I was sweating so much it was pooling in my ear canals and causing the woman's voice to warble. That calm, unrelenting voice telling me about abominations. The inside of the wall cavity had to be nearly two hundred degrees as the fire burned underneath me, ripening the copper stench of blood seeping through the interior lining. Meanwhile, the hunched figure lounging in the plush leather chair appeared to be enjoying an afternoon snooze.

The story had ended, but the airline stewardess wasn't done with me quite yet.

"You are inside your son's head."

My beautiful son, Rox. I am his damaged brain.

A static rasp hissed through the speakers, scratchy and painful. "Signals are scrambled. Thoughts come packed in locked boxes. Memories are shadows on a sunny day."

I know I'm not in my son's actual head, the space is too large. In fact, it's too large to be whose head I thought it was, unless they expanded it somehow, which is a possibility I suppose. That, or it's a sculpture. Same, I hope, as Kevin's head mounted across from me, but I have no way of knowing. I smell blood. I smell the talcum scent of bone.

"Loud noises are ice picks to his ears. Silence is empty confusion."

We can't take Rox to the grocery store for that very reason. You can see it in his eyes; it's Armageddon. Can't watch a movie because he loses track of the storyline and begins to cry. I took him fishing once and he started screaming when I hooked the worm. You'd have thought I'd murdered Mother Teresa when I caught a brim.

To think of all the nights we leave him in his room alone while watching reality shows. Left in isolation while I eat ice cream as a reward for another night of not getting trashed.

My skin is contracting from the heat. So this is how I'm going to die, baked alive in the skull of my friend while having the specifics of my son's handicap shoved in my face like truth manure? And it dawns on me why decapitated heads have played such a prominent role in the theatrics so far. Great, I get it.

"Hormone function is disrupted, dopamine and serotonin receptors go dormant."

But he responds to hugs, from Cassie at least. Probably because she gives them wholeheartedly. Mine are always timid, like I'm going to break the little guy. Like too hard a squeeze will give him a concussion. I realise I don't know how to love my own son. I treat him more like a hospice patient than a growing boy intent on living a full life. All I've ever known about being a father I learned from movies, and I like to watch horror flicks.

The static distortion intensifies; the searing heat scalds the underside of my chin and I can smell hair burning. Panic fills my chest and I'm ready to either break free or die.

"Hey!" I scream, trying to wake the pale mutant in front of me. "Fucking wake up! Please, I need help!"

"Patterns are elusive. Faces, too. Sometimes he lives with strangers."

I've seen him look at me with fear in his eyes. "Please!" I scream. Attempts to pull my head free just cut off my air. "Help!"

The figure in front of me stirs, lifts its head. Looks at me with those beige patches in place of eyes. That yellow parchment skin. Oh, shit. It's one of those experiments from Phase One. That half-human hummus thing born in a horse womb. It spills off the chair and waddles towards me, maybe three feet tall. Drool dangles from its sneering mouth and I wonder if it's toxic.

"No, no!" I shout, the static buzz assaulting my ears. "Don't, no!" I'd rather burn to death than have that thing spit acid in my eyes.

It lifts its head, opens its mouth to reveal four square teeth, two on the top, two on the bottom, spaced out about an inch apart. Its throat begins to convulse like it's choking or trying to clear a hairball. There's no soul in that thing; the woman told me. It's pure hostility without any saving grace.

"You are his father!" says the woman, shouting in my ears. It sounds like she's reporting through a Category 5 hurricane. "His protector!" I don't know how to raise my boy. I ask the doctors for advice without realising they don't know either – they're just regurgitating bullshit they learned from textbooks twenty-seven years ago. My face is on fire, my mind about to melt. Yes, I am in my son's head. This frightening, tumultuous lair from which neither of us can escape.

I try and work my fingers underneath the panel trapping my neck, but can't find a seam. Where is Malia, and why isn't she helping me?

The homunculus thing whips its head forward and spits at me like a viper. Misses. A ribbon of smoke rises up past the eyeholes as the figure's convulsing throat chambers another round.

"Please let me out of here!" I'm not sure to whom I'm pleading. I don't expect sympathy from the abomination before me. Malia, then? The stewardess berating me about my son's damaged brain?

"He is a wound that will not heal. He is exposed skin dipped in saltwater. The world is too much."

"Okay!" *This* is too much. And I've only been experiencing it for about fifteen minutes. Rox has had seven full years. "I'm sorry! I get it, and I'm sorry!"

"There are no accidents. You were chosen as his father." Underneath her voice and the static maelstrom I can now hear sonic chirping that I associate with bats in a cave.

"Please! I can do better! Please, give me another chance."

The static screech falls silent, so do the sonic chirps. Seconds pass where all I can hear is the crackle of flames from the fireplace and the perverse snorting from the figure as it extracts poison from whatever glands secrete it.

"Request granted," the woman states plainly in my ears, and I feel the panel rise behind me, releasing my head. Cool air hits my face like ice water as I stumble away from the wall and fall to the floor. The panel descends to cover the hole and it's as though it never existed. There's my potted face staring down at me in condemnation. My planted head.

Ever bake a tomato? That was my face, red and soft and runny. Steam rose from it like a matchstick. Gasping, I looked around for Malia and found her lurking in the shadows with her back turned and her hands cupped over her ears, her body trembling. I could hear fearful mewls coming as she willfully ignored my cries.

I shuddered from relief and the chill of cooling down, and my first manic thought was to go back, break the emergency glass and use the straight razor. I was done; finished. She had me pegged at first glance. There was no way I could last through the night.

Shit, but I had to. The pleas I had just made had been a promise to my son. If nothing else, I had to get back home to make sure my family was okay.

It took a couple of minutes for my head to cool down enough to think clearly. Malia had peeked over her shoulder and swooned with relief when she saw me. Strange, as I figured her concern for my safety was pretty low after she slammed my head into the hospital bed. Mascara ran in streaks down her face as she approached me, sniffling. I had placed her in her mid-twenties when I first saw her, but she looked much older now. A middle-age mom stumbling home from a Halloween party after the keg had run dry.

I shook my head, trying to fill it with something to say.

Malia knelt next to me, felt my forehead with the back of her hand and winced. She leaned forward and blew cool air on my face and my whole body broke out in gooseflesh. My nurse. Right, I'd forgotten. My guardian.

"Are you okay?" she said, actually looking sincere.

Nothing about this was funny, but for some reason I laughed. My throat was sore from breathing hot fumes and straining against the wall panelling. "I'm done," I croaked, shaking my head.

She combed her fingers through my hair. "He won't let you quit."

"He? Who's he? Mr. O or whatever the fuck?"

With mascara streaking down her face, she looked like the Cheshire cat.

"I didn't say I was quitting," I said. "I said I'm done."

Her cool breath was like a glacial breeze. "Just rest," she said. "You've made it this far. That's farther than most."

I remembered how Solomon had looked back at the club. Zoned out, with that gnarly scar running down his throat. Had he had his head stuck in there? No, probably not. This was all for me. His had been for him.

I rested my head against the wall. "What's next?" I gulped air. "All my ex-girlfriends come and castrate me?"

"Oh." She stifled a laugh with her hand. "I sure hope not. But, then again, I'm not in charge of programming."

All around the world, there are places where people explore the reaches of depravity. Suburban houses hosting bondage parties. Blood rituals in church basements. I heard there are underground clubs in Thailand where powerful businessmen pay to kill runaways. Some people have wicked ways to get off, and we let them.

I play music. That's my plug into the power source. And I hardly even do that anymore. I didn't sign up for this, and I don't need it. Most likely, neither do you.

"Okay, cut the bullshit. Who the fuck are you?"

I could have sworn her eyes were grey, but now they were emerald green. "That's complicated," she said.

"Really," I said, letting out such a long sigh it felt like venting steam. Who knows how long it had been since I strummed my last chord at the Full Moon Saloon. Several hours, at least. And I was beginning to feel the draining effects of shock. "How so?"

"Because our lives are fluid, not fixed. Tell me, are you the same person you were, say, five years ago? Ten?"

She had me there.

"Are you the same person when you're mad as when you're happy? At work and on vacation? When falling in and out of love?"

"If you think I'm in the mood for philosophy, you're wrong." What I was in the mood for was a cheese pizza and my comfortable bed. "Please," I said, sitting up straight to avoid getting drowsy. "No riddles. I'm confused enough as is. Just start with your name. Is it really Malia?"

She scrunched her nose by way of apology. "No. The letters are true, but the name is a lie. Some names are too powerful to say."

"Fine. What's on your birth certificate, then?"

"Good question." She licked her thumb and began wiping the mascara from her face. "Never seen it."

I grabbed her wrist more firmly than intended, digging into the bone. Despite my earlier talk about rearranging her face, I'm not too keen on hurting women. Intentionally, at least. "You're going to stop playing dumb right now, understand?" I could feel her blood pumping against my hand, her pulse steadier than my own. "I want to know what you're doing here. And I want to know how I can get out."

"Hurting me isn't going to help you. It will only make things worse."

I released my grip. Could see grooves in her wrists from my fingers.

"Let's walk and talk," she said, standing. "You don't want to get too relaxed."

"You think I'm relaxed?" Standing seemed like an Olympic sport, but I managed to climb the wall to my feet. "I'm about to have a goddamn heart attack."

Malia laced her arm with mine like an escort. This time I didn't fight her off. "It's a bad night, I know," she said, walking me towards the shadowed end of the hallway. I slowed and she urged me forward. "I think you deserve a break."

"No, I deserve answers. I deserve the truth."

Darkness blanketed the wallpaper, concealing my severed heads. Several blind steps brought us to a door.

"That's what everyone says," she said, swinging it open. "Until they get it."

It indeed looked like a break room, but even this was another lie.

ᚠ

The room we entered looked just like the break room at the recording studio where I cut jingles. A rectangular table in the middle surrounded by six mesh ergonomic chairs. A small side table held a coffee urn and a sealed carton of Krispy Kreme donuts. The far wall featured a large mirror stretched horizontally. I waited to see what false image this mirror would show me, but my flushed face and manic eyes looked authentic enough.

"Coffee?" Malia said. "Donut?"

"Sure." I expected sewage to pour from the urn and snakes to pop from the carton. "Why not."

I was wrong. The coffee was steaming hot with a rich, nutty flavour. The glaze still wet on the warm donuts. The first bite dissolved on my tongue. "Good Lord, almighty," I said, the words tumbling from my mouth.

We sat facing the mirror, staring at our reflections. I flinched when something clicked on overhead, then relaxed when I felt the cool breeze of centralised air blowing through the vent above.

It dawned on me, then. A two-way mirror. We were being watched.

"Truth is," Malia said, breathing in the fragrant steam rising from her cup. "I don't know much. Probably not much more than you."

I would have called bullshit but my throat was clogged with sugar-glazed dough.

"I'm still stuck in this thing. I don't even know for how long now. Forever, it feels like."

Another donut, another drink of coffee, sugar and caffeine rushing straight to my brain. I cleared my throat. "Bullshit." There, I said it.

A sorrowful smile, a budding tear. "I'm serious. It's like a recurring nightmare I have to go through every day. A game everyone's in on but me. Sometimes I get out. Or I think I do. Once for several weeks, even went to the police and got this big investigation started. Was taken to a safe house and put under constant surveillance. But it was all a sham, just part of the same elaborate scheme. And it's got to where I don't even know when it all started. Maybe this is my whole life."

I wondered if Mister, Professor, or Doctor O was on the far side of the mirror, looking in. "It's the book, isn't it? Where it starts?"

Her face corkscrewed. "Right, the book." Words rancid as bile. "You think you found that book by chance?"

Solomon had told me about the book, and there is no way he would have intentionally subjected me to this. Not without a dire reason, and I couldn't imagine what that would be. "Yeah," I said. "What's the alternative, the book found me?"

"If there's one thing I've learned, it's that there's nothing coincidental about any of this." She misinterpreted my sugar high for cynicism. "Don't believe me?" she said.

"You told me not to believe you."

She faced me, forcing my gaze from the mirror. How old was she? Twenty-four or thirty-four, I couldn't tell. "Okay, I'll prove it."

Mentalists and magicians propose the impossible with equal bravado. "By all means."

Her questions came in rapid-fire sequence.

"Are you an orphan?" No.

"Adopted?" No.

"Any near-death experiences?" Clinically, no.

"Been hypnotised?" No.

"Religious upbringing?" Uh.... Sure, along with over a billion others. Try again.

"Methodist?" Ye-ah?

"Youth ministries?" Yeah, but it was more like a social thing. Had a band that played metal tunes and hit on chicks.

"Retreats?" Your point?

"Love Week." Wait, say that again?

She paused, dipped her pinky in the coffee and sucked it clean. Flecks of teal polish clung to the nail. "Let me guess, campsite near Waycross. Close to the Okefenokee. A week of spiritual reflection and purification."

My mom had forced me to go to that geek retreat in the eighth and ninth grades. It was her meek version of boot camp. A plea for divine intervention to corral my wayward soul. Hoping the group counsellor could fill in for my absent dad. Tame my rebellious spirit with scripture. Soften my heart with fireside songs. Like singing 'Kumbaya' would get me to quit smoking weed. Come on, that song was written by a stoner. And s'mores afterwards? Please.

"Good guess," I said. "I'd love to see the file you guys have on me. Must put the one my doctor has to shame."

"Oh, God." Malia leaned back in her chair and covered her face, spoke through splayed fingers. "We couldn't have gone at the same time, obviously. But, Love Week. That's our connection."

"What, same church? Same retreat? Bare your soul for a week in Waycross and you wind up here?"

She lowered her hands, placed one on my knee and dug in with her nails. Those green eyes speared mine like skewers. "You're acting awful damn cocky for someone who was just pleading for his life."

Another bite of donut and this was the highest I'd been since I quit the band. "And you're acting awful friendly for someone who was threatening to kill me."

She relaxed her grip, but left her hand resting on my leg. "Fair enough," she said, her eyes softened. "Although, that wasn't actually me."

"What, then? Multiple personality disorder, or bitch stunt double?"

That smile again, chock-full of charm. Dimples that could make you weak in the knees. Truth was, I was happy to let her talk. Considering what I'd been through, I wanted to stay in this break room with its little luxuries for the rest of the night, or day, or whatever side of the sun we were on. It beat the hell out of the drainage culvert or the inside of my son's head.

"Go ahead," I said. "I'm listening."

Malia pulled her skirt down an inch and closed her top in her first show of modesty. "Actually, I didn't go to the same camp you went to. The church camp, I mean."

Great, another lie. I pressed my lips together to prevent anything sarcastic from slipping through. My mind was fizzing.

"Mine was with a rehab centre for women – or girls, actually. We were all under eighteen. Spring Rivers Rehab Center, though we called it The Dam. As in a place that cuts you off from everything you know. Backs you up. Sucks your energy. Then releases you like a raging flood."

Holy shit, I had forgotten about the Spring River chicks. A group of crooked girls shipped out to the wilderness to get straightened out. It had seemed so ridiculous, even then, to schedule their stay at the same time as ours – with a bunch of hormone-fueled boys being force-fed religion. Half the girls were there for acts of promiscuity, and, church retreat or not, all my fourteen-year-old bunkmates and I thought about was getting laid. It was our perfect temptation, and the ultimate form of corruption for girls who got off on breaking rules.

Painful nostalgia squeezed my heart. Those beautiful, don't-give-a-shit chicks. Our same age, but more sophisticated and experienced by aeons. Half our time at camp was spent concocting dimwitted ways to hook up with them. Trying to figure out who would pair with whom. How far we'd go when we got our chance. Then they'd approach us out on the trails when the counsellors weren't around, or swim out to our diving platform on the lake with their bikinis, and we'd clam up or get our lips caught in our braces or start stammering some nerd bullshit until they rolled their eyes and swam away. Exotic life forms we'd never understand.

This memory unearthed a fearsome craving. My life for a whiskey.

"I remember," I said.

She put a charge in her gaze. "I bet you do."

I noticed for the first time she hadn't sipped her coffee or taken a bite of a donut. And here I'd had two cups and half the carton. Surely this was a mistake. Oh well, at least my death would be delicious.

"So...." she said. "How to make a long story not so long?" Her hair shifted when she scratched her scalp and I realised she was wearing a wig. That porcelain skin was painted on, maybe even latex. "Okay, well. I was orphaned, after being adopted. Double fucking whammy, right?"

"Wait. You were adopted, and then orphaned by your adopted parents?"

She nodded. "Shot during a home invasion. Two men in ski masks, classic dickwads. Left me tied up in my room. Probably meant to kill me too, but the cops came and they ran away."

"Fucking A." Got to give it to her, she didn't mess with cute little fibs.

"My adoptive dad survived the shooting and dragged himself to my room to check on me, leaving a trail of blood all the way from his bed." She traced her first two fingers across the white underside of her arm as a reenactment. "I'll never forget his ghost-white face when he finally opened the door." Much like hers was now. "Lifting himself up to reach the knob must have exhausted the last reserves of whatever energy he had left. He looked in on me. Got this pained look on his face seeing me hogtied like that, then collapsed. Landed smack on his side with his face turned towards me. And as much as I wanted to, I couldn't look away. I watched as his eyes turned to glass, his lips whispering words I couldn't hear."

No, her lies could win blue ribbons at the county fair. "Christ, Malia. How old were you?"

"Seven." Said without hesitation. She had this thing rehearsed.

Still.... "Christ," I said. Rox was seven now. Another connective thread?

She nodded, squeezed my knee as though I was the one in need of comforting. "I know. Went to a foster home in Columbus, Georgia. Strict Protestant family with more rules than they've got in North Korea. The father was an accountant for a few of the fast-food places in town. Had a bald head that gleamed like he polished it or something. The wife was a court clerk. Or maybe she worked for the DMV, I can't remember. I just remember she had these really big jelly arms that jiggled when she waved her hands. These girly charm bracelets that jingled all the time."

Malia's eyes zoned out as she gazed into the past. "I used to get in trouble for my night terrors. For screaming in panic from the sound of a cabinet closing at night, certain some maniac was breaking in.

"There were five of us total. Me, the youngest. So the other kids used me as a scapegoat for all the shit they weren't supposed to do. A spill on the carpet – I did it. Someone raided the pantry – it was me. Door left unlocked so that one of them could sneak out – you're looking at her. They'd hide their stash in my drawers – molly capsules and acid strips and pot brownies. Talk about a gateway drug. Chocolate that gets you stoned, mmmm. The oldest was a girl named Danny who was like thirteen but could pass for sixteen, easy. Filched our house mom's stodgy makeup – the maroon lipstick, beige concealer, the cherry blush – and turned herself into a pinup girl. Get this, she used to put sugar sprinkles on the corners of her eyes to look like a pixie. Would coat her lips with Pop Rocks and have boys lick them off. I loved her; she was super twisted. If our mom noticed anything missing, though.... You guessed it, all me!"

Good story, but I was starting to get fidgety. This felt like a stall. "Oh man, Pop Rocks," I deadpanned, taking a closer look at the room with its two doors. The one we'd entered and the one on the other side that I was expecting to crash open any minute now – that acid-spitting homunculus thing to storm through.

"Actually, I took ecstasy before I ate a pot brownie. I was eleven, maybe? Snuck out with Danny and we rode our bikes to one of her boyfriend's basements. A bunch of high-school boys eating acid under black lights while listening to rap. It was the best I'd ever felt in my life. The first time I felt like I fit in somewhere and wasn't afraid of the world. The first time I ever felt like I deserved to live. Like I wasn't some dirty bug or something. I just danced the whole time while Danny made out with her boyfriend on the couch, and I was so happy for her. My wide, floaty smile glowing in the dark like all the others. Dancing until I was drenched with sweat to songs about pain and retribution that I could feel with all my being. All of us lost and confused in this little dank room sensing we belonged to something bigger, connected in ways I couldn't understand. But then it wore off, and I couldn't handle the come-down."

Been there, I thought. *Better to stay high or not fly at all.*

"Coming back to reality was like dying. I was a raw nerve. I've never felt more abandoned and unwanted. Not even worthy of my own love. But the ecstasy brought it all back. And the acid changed my reality. And the pot made me happy. The boys made me feel wanted. And the booze numbed the pain. Until the house mom found me wasted one night, puking in my sleep – passed out, actually. And it was the last straw, despite being the first time I'd been busted for something I'd actually done. They shipped me off to Spring River the following week."

The air-conditioning cut off and the room fell so silent it must have been soundproofed. Malia's voice was wet with emotion. I could hear the saliva trickle down her throat when she swallowed and splash in her gut.

"It was such a joke how they scheduled our offsite counselling at the same time as that Love Week retreat." She wasn't smiling, though.

And neither was I. "I was just thinking the same thing."

"Every single girl at Spring River had a fucked-up childhood. Abusive parents. Girls who were bullied at school for being gay or strange. Some were just straight-up psychos. And we're put in a camp with these goody-two-shoe Sunday Schoolers from the suburbs who can't even appreciate how privileged they are."

I wanted to tell her that my childhood was far from ideal, but my absent dad and petty rebellions paled in comparison to what she had been through, assuming she was telling the truth. And I assumed she wasn't.

"But that wasn't the worst part. It was the hypocrisy. They'd talk about how good your group was. All you innocent boys and girls with your kind and forgiving God. Tell us about how far we'd fallen in sin and that our only redemption was through Christ. And we'd get to believing it, seeing how you all seemed to be so decent and happy. The counsellors so kind and caring. You were the kids we wanted to be. The counsellors were the parents we wished we had. Which made us crave their approval so much, we were willing to do anything to get it. And then the counsellors would come around and talk to us, invite us back to their cabins. We were happy to be chosen. Thought that what they wanted us to do was normal among your group."

I never saw the church counsellors as conduits to God. But they had seemed like decent enough dudes. Guys who truly cared about preaching the gospel and setting a good example. "You're saying the counsellors came on to you?"

Malia smirked. "That's a polite way of putting it." You could see the memory hurt. "It's more like they came *in* us."

"Fuck...." Wrong word choice, but rarely is it used literally. "That's awful. That's disgusting, I'm sorry. I can't imagine the counsellors from my group doing that, though."

There I was, skewered again by her eyes. "They did, trust me. Nothing about that was coincidental. If anything, it was tradition."

I'd been brought up to believe God had a plan for each of us. Looking at Malia, in her slutty nurse costume with her nightmare childhood, I wondered what He'd been huffing when He concocted His plan for her.

"Still, I'm not sure I see the connection," I said.

Her hand had turned hot on my thigh. "Don't you see? We encountered the same evil, at around the same age."

My heart hammered as I eyed the closed door. That had sounded way too much like a cue. Something was coming, and I wanted to be gone when it arrived.

ᚱ

It was time to bounce from this room. I peered into my cup and saw coffee grounds floating in the dregs. Swallowed them down for a final boost of energy.

"So, what? You work with this outfit, now? This freak show?"

"Work is not the term I'd use. No."

"But you're a part of this somehow, aren't you?"

"Sure. Same as you."

I stood. "Well, I want out. I'll be happy to trade horror stories on the other side, but not here. It feels like a setup. You said you were here to help. Then please, help me. What comes next? Where do I go?"

"Only one way out," she said, motioning towards the far door.

That settled it, then. Trust no one in a house of lies.

I gripped the back of my chair, rolled it to test the weight. They had these same chairs at the studio where I record commercial tunes for toilet paper companies. The base unit is a good twenty-five pounds, solid. I grabbed the seat in one hand and the back of the chair in the other, hefted it like a battering ram.

"What are you doing?" Malia asked, scooting backwards towards the wall.

"The opposite," I said – sugar, caffeine, and adrenaline traversing my veins – "of whatever you tell me to." I charged the wall mirror, unleashing a war cry that sounded more like a wounded hawk, and crashed the base of the chair against the glass window, creating a fractured dent.

I heard Malia yelp behind me. "You can't do that," she said, but she didn't sound authoritative. She sounded scared.

"The fuck I can't." The fear in her voice told me this was the right move. "Watch me."

I slammed the base of the chair in the same spot, squinting against the shards of glass that stung my face and neck. I reared back and slammed it again, like chopping wood, grunting from the impact. Ignoring the pain in my back. Again, WHAM, and the top-right wheel broke through into the recess beyond. It was a two-way mirror after all. Which meant someone was sitting on the other side, likely staring in shock. I paused to peer through the hole but it was too dark to see anything. Two more slams and the base of the chair broke through. It hung suspended in the air as I let it go. I paused to steady my breath, my heart thudding so hard it hurt.

"Stop, look at me," Malia said. Her reflection was fragmented in the shattered glass. A crack ran down the centre of her face, splitting it in two. "Come with me, and I promise I'll get you out of here. Do this, and they'll kill you. Plain and simple. There's no looking behind the curtain."

The chair was stuck in the mirrored window like a cork. I could leave it there, follow whatever path they'd laid out for me and the horrors that awaited. Like a cow being led to slaughter. Or I could go off script and try to rewrite the ending.

Most likely it was the sugar high, but I felt invincible at that moment. "What, have you never seen *The Wizard of Oz*?" If this was being recorded, I wanted a tape. Proof of this mini-rebellion. "It's fear of the unknown that keeps us in check."

My reflection was fractured, too. A maniacal jigsaw of jagged features. I looked in my many eyes, the pain receding. They had pushed me too far. I grabbed the chair and used it to widen the hole, rounding off the sharp edges. Then I pulled it out and threw it behind me, staring into the dark hole I had made, waiting for a face to emerge. Or the barrel of a gun.

The room was about the same size as this one. A terminal of video monitors rose from a desk against the far wall. Otherwise the room appeared empty. Unless there was someone hunched under the mirror, something I wouldn't know without peering inside. Exposing my head, which had been severed on wallpaper and mounted on a wall. Jesus, maybe this *was* part of the script. My act of rebellion anticipated and accounted for.

The lights went out, and a door slammed closed behind me. Malia had fled the room. Off to warn the others, I assumed. Which meant I had to hurry.

I poked my head through the hole before paralysis rooted me in place. Looked down and saw an angry face peering up at me from the floor. I screamed and so did he, rising up towards me as I retracted my head. My neck caught on the underside of the window, slicing the skin, and trapping my head in place. I screamed in panic and pain, and so did my attacker, mirroring my expression. It took another second to realise I was looking at my own reflection, captured on a pane of glass that had landed on the floor. Here I'd almost decapitated myself from self-inflicted fear. So much for rewriting the script.

There was no time to sigh with relief. An empty chair was still swivelling from whoever had just been sitting in it. And was now off to gather weapons or reinforcements, or both. I quickly removed more of the broken glass until I had a hole large enough to step through, then I climbed inside.

The room was a surveillance station featuring a desk with a control panel and about twenty monitors stacked four rows high. In one, I saw the operating room where I had awakened. A light-skinned man with dark hair was spraying cleaning solution on the operating table and wiping it down with a rag. To the right of this monitor was one showing the empty hallway I had just walked through. Next, the trophy room, which was now being dismantled. Several men, all similar if not identical-looking, were busy removing the animal busts from the walls, wiping off the dark spots where fluid had seeped from the deer's decomposing necks. My eyes flashed across the monitor screens, stopping when I recognised a face.

It was Caspian. His idiotic head intact. Sitting with his hands cuffed to a small table pushed against a wall. A man in a police uniform sat across from him, and they appeared to be arguing. Caspian's head was shaking as he spoke, gesticulating with his cuffed hands. The officer leaned back and crossed his arms, looking sceptical at best. I searched and found an audio panel with buttons corresponding to each monitor. I pressed the one for Caspian's room, and caught the cop midsentence.

"—yourself any favours, here. You were the last person to see him. Your prints are in the car and on the gun found inside the culvert."

"What gun? What fucking gun?" Caspian's voice was hoarse, his words still slurred. "I didn't have any gun."

"Then how'd your prints get on it?"

"I have no idea! Planted somehow. I was fucking passed out, you know. Jesus!" I stopped listening as I scanned the other screens. My stomach sank when I saw other rooms I recognised. My master bathroom back home, looking out through the mirror covering the medicine cabinet. My bedroom, looking down from the ceiling fan over the bed. My living room, from the television towards the couch. Each of these rooms was empty.

Where was Cassie? Where was Rox? It would help if I knew what time it was, but I didn't have my phone and wasn't wearing a watch.

"Being blackout drunk doesn't count as an alibi, Lance," the cop was saying.

"Fuck this, I'm done. I'm not saying nothing else without a lawyer."

He had been watching us. There were cameras in every room of my house. Even one in Rox's bedroom, looking down from a mobile of planes that we had constructed together. The instructions said it would take an hour to assemble, but it had taken us the better part of a week. Kid had really wanted to help, so I'd let him, breaking it up into manageable chunks that could hold his attention, reconfiguring pieces over and over and over again until we got them just right, calming his tantrums and encouraging him to keep trying. His eyes were beaming with pride when I hoisted him up to hang it from a hook on the ceiling. He gave one of his rare smiles – that smile more precious than any material in the world – as the planes took flight, circling one another in the formation we had created. And this psycho fuck had turned my son's most prized possession into a spy camera. Watching who knows what, as he lay in bed alone.

Of all the fucked-up things I had seen so far, this was the worst. This demanded retaliation. I'd find the freak behind this and hurt him. Hurt him bad. You don't fuck with a man's family. You especially don't mess with a father's son.

My mind had drifted away from the monitors to thoughts of revenge, so I was slow to see the change. The simultaneous pause. When my attention returned, I saw that the men had stopped cleaning up their respective rooms and were now standing underneath the cameras looking directly into them. Staring straight at me. Identical faces all expressionless. Then, as though on cue, they all turned to leave their rooms. The man who had been cleaning the operating room entered the hallway I'd just come from, walking briskly towards the break room I was just in. There was no time to leap back through the double mirror and barricade the door. Others were filing down separate hallways that I assumed led towards this room. I looked around for a weapon and found nothing except for the swivel chair, which wouldn't do much. The door to the break room opened, briefly backlighting the man in dim light before he closed it and entered the dark.

All I could hear was the cop talking. "What kind of lawyer do you think will take on your case, huh? The evidence we have on you?" I reached for the audio button, but didn't want to turn my back on the hole in the mirror. Before I could find it, the man stepped into view. His face obscured in shadow.

"Why don't you help us out and maybe there's something we can do for you?"

I backed up against the table, checked the door.

"You're in a bad situation here, you know? Why make things worse?"

The man stood still, light glinted off his eyes. Watching me.

"It's only a matter of time until we find the body. What then? Come clean now and I can get you life with early release for good behaviour. Keep this up and you'll be facing death."

I lifted the chair and jabbed it at the man like some lion tamer. He didn't flinch.

"You're in a bad situation here, you know?" the man standing before me said in a dull monotone, echoing the policeman's words. "Why make things worse?"

"Shut the fuck up," I said.

The man smiled. "Why don't you help us out and maybe there's something we can do. Keep this up and you'll be facing—"

I slammed the base of the chair into the man's face and upper body, feeling a satisfying thunk as it made solid contact. I used the chair to barricade the hole and hustled towards the door.

"You were the last person to see him alive, Lance," the cop said. Caspian was hanging his head, that lank hair covering his face. I almost felt bad for him. Then I realised the cop had suggested I was dead.

The man removed the chair and began climbing through. *I should have stayed with Malia,* I thought, as I began my blind run.

᛫

No one wants to admit they're dumb. In fact, one of the central aspects of stupidity is a complete lack of self-awareness. I'm just smart enough to know how stupid I am. Which means I'm mostly harmless to others, but a menace to myself.

How many mistakes had led to my present predicament? Poor choice in friends. Inconsistent compromises. Unwarranted bravado that led me to read that book.

The culvert. Sticking my head in the wall. Ditching the only person who claimed to have my back. Dumb! Dumb! Dumb!

I'm fucking dumb.

The hallway was wide enough to fit a car and lined with concrete, like a bunker. Fluorescent bulbs spaced every few feet separated by shadow. My shoes made a clapping sound as I ran. My sprained ass hurt. The air smelled like abandonment.

This was stupid. Another dumb mistake, one I now truly feared could get me killed. They had already framed a suspect for my murder. My dumb mistakes would land Caspian in prison, maybe death row. Damn, if only I'd suffered through *Moby Dick* instead of provoking this crazy asshole.

Running blind like this would get me nowhere fast. So I stopped; listened. Heard a faint buzzing sound, the hush of trapped air. No footsteps, though. Yet.

Six sets of doors branched off the hallway, three on each side. Placards were hung beside each door but I didn't pause to read them. A roll-up garage door was at the very end of the walkway – a gaping eye drawn on its front like on the back of a dollar bill. Always watching. This Professor O was a Peeping Tom.

I heard the door from the surveillance room open and close. Saw the man I had hit with the chair enter the hallway. He had a purple lump on his forehead and blood was leaking from his nose. Our eyes met – my body was prepared to fight or flee, but I wanted a third option – then he reached out towards the wall and everything went dark. Coffin dark. So dark I had to hunker down and hold my arms out for balance.

His shoes clapped against the concrete as he stalked towards me, not worrying about stealth. A calm, steady pace. I told my body to move, but it wouldn't. My signals were misfiring. Advance? Retreat? Attack? Flee? To where?

Meanwhile the man kept coming, closing the distance by half, his footsteps growing louder. Silently, I shuffled sideways and flattened my back against the wall, holding my breath as I slid towards the man coming my way, hoping to sneak past him and.... Well, I didn't know what. I was acting on pure survival instincts. Same as prey.

When I was just a few steps from him I stopped and became one with the wall, holding my breath, not even wanting to disrupt the air. He stepped right in front of me and continued walking past at the same steady pace. I had no idea if he was holding his arms out, or doing anything at all to detect me or defend against a potential attack.

Should I attack him from behind or sneak back into the surveillance room? My legs were shaking so hard I feared he'd sense the vibrations. All I'd wanted was to play some rock tunes and here I'm being hunted by some stranger in a game with rules I don't understand.

He was about ten feet past me when he stopped. The air attained an electric charge. Several seconds passed, maybe a minute. I'd hold my breath until I fainted if I had to. Then he started making a hollow clicking sound. A clucking of his tongue against the roof of his mouth, or some convulsing of his throat, and I desperately wished for the silence to return.

The noise echoed in the silent tunnel, reverberating off the concrete walls. It had a sonar quality to it, and then I realised what it was. Echolocation. Like that clone from the foster home who turned all his roommates into mush.

I heard him turn, the echolocations now coming towards me. A mechanical sound, inhuman. Penetrating. A light forming in the darkness – a blurry ball of red between my eyes. Inside my mind, expanding. A shadow shape, a tall, slender man in a suit, or an owl on a limb. Images transposing, shifting, merging. Two inverted triangles spinning, stark lines flashing like a strobe. He's no longer in the hall, or no longer outside my mind. I can't hear his footfalls, or the location of his clucking tongue. The sound originates inside me, the base source, calling me home in a backwards tongue. Blood throbs through my veins. Animal heat, rising. Hunger, lust. Hate. Standing now before me. My mirror image. One mind; all. I can see without eyes. Feel his neck in my hands, his throat cave under my fingers. The squeeze. Our blood pumping as one. The clucking sound becomes a gurgle, and my mind returns.

What the fuck? I'm panting, strangling this man in the dark. Not me, though. Whatever that was before. Him, or someone else who had become me. I'm not a killer. Not like this. I relax my grip and the inhuman echoing returns, first separate, then burrowing, becoming. Me becoming it. A violence that birthed the world. Pulled towards a singular point, a crimson dot, the final void. Destroyer. The Anti. Hate like a black rose.

When I return, I'm in a dark hallway with a dead man in my arms. Strangled, I presume, although I don't remember doing it. I had disappeared. Time stopped. I had lost all sense of self and become less a thing than a sick emotion. I felt soiled. Abused. I released the man and slumped back against the wall. My insides scooped out.

There was no way to take that back, and it had happened without my consent. My body had been hijacked somehow and forced to conduct the most heinous of acts. The ultimate sin. Even if it had been in self-defence, which I do believe it was, that didn't change the fact that I was now, and would forever be, a killer. Tainted for having taken a life. All for what? Why was this happening?

Data? That's what the woman had told me while I'd been stuck in that head. Was this an extension of Professor O's perverted research?

The thought of continuing on, of actually trying to find my way out of this place, was overwhelming. I just wanted to sleep and wake up somewhere else. Wake up *someone* else. Start over again. Do it all differently. Every bit of it, even Cassie. Even Rox. Erase it all from history.

Or was this remnant thinking from the pall that had overcome my mind? Had maybe possessed my mind. That effervescent hate.

They weren't just going to let me out of here, that much was clear. So, what? Was I just going to give up and die? No, I was the victim here. I hadn't asked for any of this, even if I had been warned it could happen. I hadn't believed it. But it was happening, and it would continue happening to me and others unless I could get out of here and expose it somehow. Besides, my family was still being watched. I couldn't let them become part of this in any way.

I checked for the man's pulse. His skin was still warm, his head limp in my hands. Not like I'm some fucking EMT or anything. In fact, the only pulse I'd ever checked was my own after almost overdosing on coke. He was flatlined, as far as I could tell. Wasn't breathing. Nothing more than decaying meat, same as I had felt while under the influence of his hypnotism, or whatever. A pointless bag of squishy things.

I got back to my feet. My eyes had adjusted as much as they were going to and I still couldn't see shit. I needed to find Malia. There was no way I could do this on my own. Those other men in the video monitors had looked identical to the one I had just strangled. They all, I presumed, would be capable of putting me under that murderous spell. She had said she could help, and I had no better option than to believe her.

The same mad curiosity that got me to stick my head in the trap wall tempted me to look behind one of the doors in this hallway, but I resisted. Who knew what I'd find, which was part of the allure, of course. Instead, I shuffled back towards the surveillance room, grasping out in the dark until I reached the door. All the video monitors were now blank, so this room was dark as well. I groped for a light switch and found one, squinting against the glare. I climbed back over to the empty break room. Considered chowing another Krispy Kreme donut, but killing a man had murdered my appetite.

The twisted images from that hypnotic trance still wormed through my mind. Serrated words turned my thoughts into confetti. Letters swapping places to distort the meaning of my internal monologue. I no longer recognised my inner voice. Maybe the damage was permanent and they'd made me a schizophrenic.

But the mirror had been an illusion. As had Caspian's decapitated head. The rooms had been fabricated. This experience was richly detailed, but fake. So, too, was this mental condition. A momentary fog caused by some kind of hypnosis. Had the fight in the dark been staged? The dead man a dummy?

I staggered towards the far do0r. Stopped, and shook my head. Not do0r, *door*. Imposter words invaded my mind, spoken through a mental ventriloquist. Hijacking my helium. I mean, my he4d.

Too much was happening t0o fast. I gripped the back of a chair and tried to calm myself. My cavernous mind was filled with bats. Seeking flies with sonar chirps. Scrambling my thoughts into jumbled burrs. And I knew whatever was happening would never stop, that my mind would never be normal again. Just like this friend I'd had in high scho6l – Carlton Mass. Or Moss, like on a log at a swamp. The son of a frog, I mean his mom was a sculptor. Dad a computer guy. Sales guy or technician or filch or something. Fuck, it was hard to blink. Think. Kid drew these hilarious comic strips about a world that was the opposite of ours. Where bacteria were the apex species and people were lowly germs. Our bowels were verdant gardens and the earth was a piece of turd in a petri dish. Birds were still the same, but were so embarrassed by their dinosaur heritage they hid in shame. We used to get stoned and pass his comics a4ound. Laugh our asses off at the hapless humans who fought wars over dung piles while the germs built utopian societies. Carlton's drawings became increasingly jagged, I mean intricate. The plotlines, circular. Humans lived in the intestines of bacteria that lived in the intestines of humans. Twelve-page comics soon turned into two-hundred-page compendiums. His nails got dirty, I remember; Carlton's did. And his pubescent whiskers looked like s0ot. The comics bled out into his reality, and he became convinced we were all germs harbouring the ultimate form of intelligence in our colons. His eyes got big and round and he talked real fast and he stopped eating and his smile stopped being nice. And the so0t – the *soot* – on his face spread down onto his neck and chest that got so skinny you could count his ribs. And then his parents sent him away to a place we weren't allowed to visit and we never saw him again. And I knew right then that the same thing that had happened to Carlton was happening to me, right here and now. That my brain had been scrambled and wouldn't work the same way anymore. And it didn't even matter if I made it out of here, because I'd just be sent away to someplace that people couldn't visit. Locked in a room with a stranger in my head. Herding – *hearing* – words that weren't quite right and didn't mean what they were supposed to.

My body moved independently from my mind. Like the shadow on a sundial. And I was looking through a door I couldn't recall opening. The one Lamia had walked through. I mean, Malia. It looked like the entrance to a service elevator. Cream-coloured linoleum floor with green flecks. Textured wallpaper. The elevator doors were scoured steel and wide enough to drive through. There was only one call button – maybe up, maybe down, I didn't know. I pushed it seconds before the thought entered my mind. The bell dinged like a revelation.

The doors slid open and I shuffled inside. The cabin was the size of a Manhattan studio apartment. Mirrors lined the walls – Him watching me watching me watch Him, like the circular logic of Carlton's comics as he went insane. My eyes were big and round like his had been and I couldn't make them look normal. The Krispy Kremes had likely been my last meal and soon my face would be a skeleton covered by a thin layer of skin.

The cabin lurched and began to vibrate, but I couldn't tell if I was ascending or descending. Alone in this elevator that could hold a hundred people or more. No emergency phone. No buttons. Just spotless panes of mirrored glass spanning the walls, ceiling, and floor. Three hundred and sixty degrees of me, and I looked like an extra in some slasher film. The cabin slowed, and jolted to a stop. The doors whisked open.

Shock scrambles the mind, shock clears it.

Staring out through the open doors, I felt equal parts horror and relief.

I'd know this place with my eyes closed. Name it by smell alone. Any bar regular learns the scent of their favourite watering hole. A blend of the beers they keep on tap, the fry oil from the kitchen, brands of cigarette smoke absorbed in the walls, wood oil for the bar top, vinegar for the floor, dishwasher steam, urinal cakes, and wallpaper glue. The elevator let out into the hallway leading to the restrooms in my old favourite bar, The Mule Kick. The place I'd gotten blackout drunk the night Rox fell from his crib. The last place I'd tasted booze.

The same old cigarette machine stood between the bathrooms, though I know the place banned smoking several years ago and had it removed. I peered in on the rows of Marlboros, Winstons, Camels, Camel Wides, and gripped the pulley knob. I'd been a Marlboro Red man, myself. The deadliest of them all. When I go for something, I go all in. Or, at least, I used to. I can't say I put the same amount of soul into my commercial music as I did playing for the Rising Dead.

I recognised the wood-panelled walls covered in peeling posters for local clubs and music fests. Saw the show calendar for Smith's Olde Bar featuring dates from June 2010. I'd fucking been to the Rebirth Brass Band concert the first Saturday of that month. Couldn't tell you what they'd played past the second song, but I'd shown up.

A halved papaya marked the women's restroom, a banana marked the men's. On the opposite wall, a tarnished mirror advertised a barbershop called High & Tight where you could get loaded while having your hair cut and face shaved. I'd been many times, once woken up surprised to find myself sporting a Mohawk and Fu Manchu, which had been hilarious until the buzz wore off.

I heard the general bustle of activity from the barroom at the end of the hallway. A low babble of conversation, shuffling footsteps, the clink of glassware. The shock of finding myself in a place I recognised seemed to have cleared my mind some, at least temporarily. But I knew this had to be another elaborate fabrication designed to torture me, and I wasn't especially eager to find out what was in store. I shouldered open the guy's bathroom door, entered a restroom I'd had sex in more than once and snorted more coke in than I could haul in a truck.

It was empty. Or I thought it was until I heard a toilet flush from the one covered stall. Followed by a loud sniffing sound. Before I could turn to exit, the stall door opened and a stocky, bald man wearing a plaid shirt with the sleeves rolled up walked out. He placed a knuckle against his left nostril and snorted, sucking up snot or whatever else happened to be in there.

"All yours, bub," he said, holding the stall door open for me.

I shook my head, too stunned to speak.

He shrugged and walked to the sink and opened the faucet, scrubbing his hands as he eyed himself in the mirror. Checked his nostrils for debris. "Fucking hell, man," he said, either to himself or me. He was a magnet for my eyes. "Bub, keep looking and I'm going to have to charge," he said. A tribal tattoo spanned the base of his bald head. His perfect ivory teeth had to be dentures.

"Right, sorry," I said. An OCD doctor would appreciate how thoroughly he was washing his hands. Scrub any harder and he'd slough off skin. "Wow," I said, without meaning to.

"Fucking-A." His smile suggested we were in agreement, there. "You got any juice, bro? Need any?"

For a moment I thought he meant grape juice or something like that. Fatherhood and sobriety strike again. Then I realised he meant cocaine, and that I indeed wanted some, badly.

"Nah, man. I'm good."

Steam was rising from the tap, fogging the mirror. His hands were turning into lobster claws. "You don't look so good, there, pal. Come on, let me set you up. One toot."

If there was a single germ left on his hands I'd have been surprised. My nostrils were dilating in some Pavlovian response to his offer.

"Friend, come on! Earth to pally, pal. You're like in a stupor, there."

His forearms were covered in a blur of blue ink, except for the underside of his right arm where the green blob from *Ghostbusters* looked like he was about to slime Dr. Venkman. The rising steam slowly revealed the clear outline of a word drawn on the mirror: OBSIDEO.

"What are you, brain-dead, pal?"

I looked in the mirror. My hair was still caked in fake blood. It was streaked down the sides of my face and dotted my shoulders. Were this man a normal person he'd be calling me an ambulance, not offering narcotics.

"Anyone needs a toot, it's you. Trust me there, pal."

"No, thanks," I said, surprised my voice still worked. I pointed to the word on the mirror in front of him.

He grunted laughter. "Kind of bathroom shit is that?" he said. "Back in the stall there someone wrote, *Looking For a Little Joke? It's In Your Hands.* Now that's funny shit."

It took a couple of seconds for the joke to sink in, then a dull, dopey laugh tumbled past my lips. Damn, if laughing didn't feel good. Doesn't it always?

"Heh, there you go. Lighten up, pal. You ain't in no church, you know. Try and have a little fun."

Finally, the man decided he'd nuked all the germs on his hands and cut the water. Ripped several paper towels from the dispenser and dried off. Balled the beige paper and shot it into the trashcan. Swish!

"Get after it, killer," he said, clapping a steamy hand on my shoulder as he walked past, those phoney teeth flashing through his smile. I waited for the door to shut behind him, then approached the sink he'd been using and cranked the heat. It wasn't quite scalding, but it was close. I cupped my hands underneath the tap and splashed water on my face. Dunked my head under the faucet and washed out the blood. Crimson water coloured hairline fractures in the basin of the old porcelain sink, turning it into a bloodshot eye. I wetted a paper towel and began to dab the spots on my shirt.

Use COLD water, JESSE, or you'll lock the stain in. This was my mother's advice, which I ignored, as usual. Maybe if she'd tried punishing me once I'd have paid her more attention. I don't know. Maybe if she'd offered more than trite witticisms handed down from dummies.

Wish in one hand, spit in the other.

If God wanted you to have a hole in your tongue he'd have put one there.

Don't eat that, you'll get worms!

That word had resurfaced in the steam on the mirror: OBSIDEO.

Don't mind if I do, I thought absurdly, and then came that dopey laugh again. The brain-dead chortle that comes from sniffing too much glue. As though there's such a thing as moderation when it comes to sniffing glue.

Who knows how long I'd been gone at this point? Was it still technically Saturday night? Or had I been missing long enough for Cassie to file a police report? Was that what had landed Caspian in the interrogation room? And, if so, what did that say about my odds of getting out of here? Would the psycho behind all this be willing to release me when he already had a suspect for my disappearance? My death?

What was it Malia had said? *I'm still stuck in this thing. I don't even know how long now.*

Well, this had gone on long enough for me. I turned the water from hot to cold, waited for it to go frigid, then splashed my face, bracing against the shock. Again and again and again and again, my clouded mind clearing with each application. I felt my anger rising, breathing heavily now. This was the rage I'd once manufactured before taking the stage as a member of the Rising Dead. Pumping it from a well I thought had dried up. A vile organ gone dormant. Regressing to a primal state. Slathering aggression – wide eyes, strained neck, snarling. The twenty-something-year-old me who had smashed his balled fist into his best friend's face. Kicked holes in hotel walls for no reason. Worked crowds into swarms of frenzied chaos. I wouldn't lie down. Would not be cowed. It was time to rise.

Water dripped from my chin as I pushed through the door. Nearly bumping into Malia, who was standing in the hallway. She had retired the nurse costume and was now in street clothes. Blue platform shoes, sheer black hose, plaid kilt, Black Sabbath concert tee, hair parted and tied in pigtails.

"There you are." A steel tongue stud glinted through her wide smile. "What, did you take a bath?"

I shoved past her, marched towards the bar ready to bloody whoever I found there. Wouldn't be the first time I'd thrown fists in this place. Won some, lost some. Not that anyone really wins that fool's game.

Five people were staggered at intervals along the L-shaped bar. The floor tables were empty, booths along the wall were too. The room looked just as I remembered it – dark like an ocean storm. The wood scuffed, chairs wobbly. Every little knickknack was in its rightful place, which would have required Hollywood's most meticulous set designer. The horseshoes bearing the names of regulars that circled the banister above the bar. The photo of Ronald Reagan sunbathing in a cowboy hat and boots by a pool. The topless lamp lady with her radiant boobs.

My eyes shifted to the front door, the stencil of that poor man getting mule kicked in the face on its frosted glass. Symbolic of how you feel after a full night at this place. I started towards it and no one stopped me. Grabbed the brass handle and shoved.

It didn't give. The door – assuming it was an actual door, and not some perfectly rendered prop – was jammed.

"Hey, where you think you're going, Jess?" I recognised that jovial voice. "You're not trying to drink and dash, are you?" Scott Razetti. The man who'd never cried 'last call'. "Get your sorry ass back over here, you scoundrel."

It couldn't be. Fucking Razz. The Mule Kick's bar manager for as long as I'd been a regular. But his sister had been diagnosed with pancreatic cancer a couple years back and he'd gone home to Long Island to help her die. Shit was supposed to take you quick, but Lisa was a feisty woman. Tough as her brother, if not tougher. I'd partied with her a half-dozen times and she was a wrecking ball. Loud and brash. Shots every half-hour. Beer and coke after the bar closed. Bloody Marys in the morning. She was bald now, but still breathing. At least, last I'd heard. But Razz no longer worked the bar.

When I turned, though, there he was. That stupid Hawaiian shirt like he was at some sunset luau, not a slum bar in West Midtown. Shock of black curls sprouting through the open collar in front. Thing is, this was the Razz from when I used to come here. Forty-something-year-old Razz from when his sweaty black hair still came together in a widow's peak, not the sixty-year-old diabetic bald man he'd become.

Hard to know how to play this. Like being on the outside of an inside joke where you don't want to look stupid. But, here, I didn't want to get hurt. Or worse.

Water dripped from my chin. My hair was soaked. I looked like I'd just walked in from a rainstorm while everyone else was bone dry.

The cokehead from the bathroom turned in his stool. "This guy," he said, smiling, like I was there for comic relief. "Get him one on me, will you?"

"Sure thing," Razz said, turning to the liquor rack behind the bar, grabbing tequila, vodka, rum, gin. I instinctively checked the daily special chalkboard by the host stand, felt the blood drain from my face.

2 for 1 Long Island Iced Tea!!

The Ultimate Tea Party!

I can't tell you how many times I've wished I could take that night back. Wished I'd just stayed home with Cassie, made box pasta with jarred sauce and gone to bed sober enough to hear

Rox's cries before he flipped out of his crib. It looked like this was my second chance.

Malia came from the back hallway and grabbed a stool a couple over from the guy intent on getting me lit. She pulled one out beside her as an invitation.

"Thanks, buddy," I said to the guy from the bathroom, then took the stool by Malia. Would it surprise you to learn it was the same one I was sitting at that fateful night?

"Don't mention it, pal. Next round's on you!"

Malia grabbed a handful of cocktail napkins and used them to pat dry my hair. She gently brushed my face with the damp tissue and then dabbed my nose, like I was a toddler with a messy face. "Better?" she said.

I caffed. That's a mix between a cough and a laugh. "Much."

Razz was no mixologist. He was a drunkologist. Fuck the liqueurs and fruit rind; just serve 'em strong enough to strip paint. He topped off the two pint glasses with a splash of cola, stirred the drinks lazily with a spoon.

"Cheers, guys," he said, setting my drink on top of a coaster picturing a performance seal drinking a Guinness.

"The girl can have the other one," the guy from the bathroom said. "Want it?"

"Did Jeffrey Dahmer have good taste in men?" she said.

"Hey-ho! In more ways than one," the man said. "You catch that one, Razz?"

"Yeah, hilarious," Razz deadpanned. "Nothing funnier than cannibalism, as my dear mother used to say."

The resemblance was uncanny. His voice, his mannerisms. This wasn't someone pretending to be Razz. This was the man himself. Which, of course, was impossible. Unless we'd travelled back in time.

"Cheers," Malia said, tilting a pint glass towards me that held enough booze to get a gorilla buzzed, and on that night I'd had a minimum of four.

This wasn't funny. It was an insult. A deliberate attempt to reenact the worst night of my life. I'd leave my head in that sweltering wall for a week if I could get that evening back.

To be able to take Rox to Little League ball games instead of life-skill centres. Play my guitar without giving him a migraine.

"No, thanks," I said. This time I skewered her eyes with mine. "I don't drink."

Malia dipped her head and whispered through lips that hardly moved. "You want out of here, don't you?"

I don't answer rhetorical questions.

"This is the only way," she said, moving her glass closer to mine. "It doesn't get easier than this, trust me."

I could smell the liquor. After seven years of sobriety, it still had its draw. Its promise of sweet oblivion. The most assured escape from my querulous mind. But it comes with a cost that is steeper for some, especially me. Stealing my memories and leaving me with a moral debt.

"Not going to happen," I said.

The jukebox kicked on, or maybe it just changed songs and I hadn't been listening. I heard the melodic opening to 'Sweet Melissa' by the Allman Brothers. The sound of those gifted brothers whose own demons had resulted in this angelic tune. Why is it that choir boys can't seem to write heavenly music?

"Then you're stuck here with me, I'm afraid," Malia said, then sipped her drink through a straw.

How theatrical.

"Hey, Razz," I said.

"Yessir." He rested his arms on the bar and leaned towards me. That old chain-link bracelet with the Virgin Mary medallion clinked against the wood. It had been his grandfather's good luck charm in the First World War. A story I'd heard at least two dozen times.

I studied his face, looking for signs of makeup. Searched his eyes for deception. "What's the story here, man?"

He frowned. "With what?"

I said the first thing that came to mind. "Your sister. Lisa."

The two teeth to either side of his incisors were silver, which made him look like Jaws from *Moonraker* when he smiled. Call him that, though, and you'd find your next drink watered down. That's if he knew you. Spit in it, if he didn't. He armed sweat from his brow, which was always damp. "That fucking crazy broad," he said. "Took her kids, my nephews, you know, out to Cedar Beach the other day. The boy, the little one, Tommy, he swims into a jellyfish or something, gets stung all up on his shoulder and the side of his chest. He's hollering like a maniac. Fucking kid can yell like you've never heard."

I've heard worse, I wanted to say. That night, after I left here.

"You've told me this one before," I tell him.

"What?" He looked genuinely puzzled. "Nah, there's no way. It just happened. And you haven't been in here in, what? A while."

I shrugged. There was actually something comforting about the situation. Like falling back into a familiar role. The dim lighting, Allman Brothers on the box, Razz with his Hawaiian shirt and dense thicket of chest hair. Something about it felt ceremonial, even. *All of this for me.*

"Okay, then," Razz said. "You heard it already, what happened?"

Vapours rose from the glass of booze below my face like some witch's brew. I leaned across the bar, locked eyes. "She pulled him out of the water, squatted over him, and took a piss on his chest right there on the shore."

A beat passed where 'Sweet Melissa' ended and 'Gimme Three Steps' by Lynyrd Skynyrd started to play. I had time to think, *Gimme three steps towards the door.* Then the bald guy from the bathroom started howling laughter. Razz looked perplexed, but started laughing too, that donkey's bray that brought back fond, yet fuzzy memories. One of the signature sounds of The Mule Kick. Beside me, Malia, who had just taken a sip from her drink, snorted and cupped her mouth.

The laughter fed on itself like fire on oxygen. Spread like a disease. This was madness. I may have just murdered a man engaged in this senseless escapade and here we were telling funny stories. And then I was laughing, myself. Couldn't help it. The absurdity of it all washed over me. Razz's streaming eyes, saliva stringing from his steel teeth. The man in the plaid shirt slamming his hand on the bar like a judge calling for order.

Malia hunched over, her face turning red as she struggled to keep from spraying Long Island Iced Tea across the bar.

"Fucking Tommy...." Razz says, pausing between bursts of laughter. "Christ...his mom's peeing on.... Peeing on him right there...in front of...all his friends and shit." His back is arched, eyes closed, screaming laughter at the ceiling, gripping the bar with one hand for balance. The other guy has gone silent, laughing so hard he can't breathe. Malia can't hold it any longer and booze goes spewing through her fingers like puke. I catch some on my shoulder, and it makes me laugh that much harder. I can't help myself. This is madness, plain and simple. I'm going insane.

I don't know where we are. A warehouse? Underground in a bunker somewhere, like the lab Doctor O used to hatch his clones? Is this part of some deranged experiment, or just a senseless hoax? And what's the difference, anyways?

"The fucking thing is..." Razz says when he can breathe, "it just makes...the stinging worse! Like rubbing...salt in... a wound!"

There are functions beyond our control. Sneezing in the sun. Yawning during a lecture. Laughing in church. I couldn't have stopped laughing had someone stuck a gun in my mouth. Which, in a way, is what this felt like.

We were howling, gasping. God, it felt good. Of all the horrors I'd seen that night, the only thing I could picture at that moment was Lisa in her tacky one-piece with the frilly skirt squatting over her son and squirting stinging pee onto his torso while he squirmed in front of all his best friends.

Then it hit me. There was no way they would have this info unless they'd gotten it from Razz himself. Did that mean he was in danger? Had he been abducted? Was this some fucking replicant created in Doctor O's classified lab?

"Oh, God!" cried the guy at the end of the bar, holding his ribs like they hurt. "I can't take it!" He stumbled from his stool and staggered towards the restroom, clutching his body, his face a sweating radish. Probably going back to blow another line of coke.

The first sip was a reflex. A conditioned response triggered by the ambience as a whole. The stool, the setting, the sounds, the smells, the scene. Taking a drink for an alcoholic is no different than drawing breath. It's just as vital. And that first sip was more refreshing than clean air after inhaling smoke. It was like being reunited with a lover you thought had died. Worse, one you thought you'd killed. And she's not even mad. In fact, she still loves you. Is ready to forget all about the breakup and go right back to the way things were.

Every morning, I wake up wanting more than anything to have a drink. Just one. Just one small, simple drink to take the edge off. To help me relax. To numb the pain just enough to tolerate it. I see my seven-year-old son's look of confusion when I tie his shoes and want a sip of whiskey – just one – so that I don't have to feel my heart break. Again and again and again. To dull the sound of his cries that I can't soothe. Something, anything, to free me from this life of suffering, this coffin of skin and bones. But I bear it. And thank God every night I go to sleep sober that I made it another day without hurting anyone other than myself.

Alcoholism isn't a disease; it's a possession. That's why we fight it with faith. In that moment of weakness, my faith had left me. I tell myself now that my body betrayed me. That the demon scaled the wall and slipped past my sentry men while they were busy piddling their dicks. But I know better. It was weakness, plain and simple. We look for any and every excuse that will validate our desire to use our drug of choice. And, in this instance, I allowed myself to cave. Perhaps even subconsciously, I told myself this was good enough of an excuse. I mean, fuck, what was the alternative?

And I didn't just take a little sip and stop to assess my decision. The second I felt the sting of liquor on my tongue, that cleansing heat, I started gulping it down like a man dying of thirst. Half a pint went down in that first pull, the ice settling towards the bottom of the glass with a musical tinkle that tells bartenders like Razz it's time for another round. Sure enough, I saw him wipe his streaming eyes and begin mixing me another one. Heard

Malia's straw slurping on the dregs of her own and signal for a second as well.

And I won't lie. At that very moment, there was no other place I would rather have been. I didn't want to drink. I was being forced to drink. Against my will. This was the ultimate excuse. One so convincing, there was no way anyone could dispute it. Not Cassie. Not my sponsor, Al Tanner at AA. No one. I had to do this, or I might never make it back home. Drink or die. Drink or never see my family again. How could I refuse?

I liked it, though. Especially once the potent blend of vodka, gin, and tequila hit the receptors in my brain. BOOM. Malia knew better than to smile, or show any sign of victory that would stiffen my resolve. She let me stew in my shame until the booze could steal that away. Replace it with false bravado. Remember me? I'm the fucking guy chicks used to throw panties at on stage. Had a whole crew of leathernecks hauling my gear across the world so that I could scorch earholes with my electric guitar.

I felt the ice cubes clink against my teeth as I strained for every last drop. There was a brief moment of sorrow. Not for breaking my sobriety, though. Rather, remorse over the empty glass. But it was short lived as I looked down and saw its replacement already waiting for me on the warped coaster. Razz took the empty glass and removed it from sight, so that there was only the one in front of me. Always just the one.

Seven years of restraint sloughed from my shoulders, leaving me light and buoyant. Time became irrelevant. The extras blurred into the background, as the world narrowed down to the three of us in this make-believe tavern. Our little coven of deceit. And the smile that cleaved my face was so large it made my cheeks ache, as though engaging muscles that had atrophied.

Finally, our laughter began to fade. 'Fortunate Son' by CCR was now rocking the juke box. The Mule Kick didn't have TVs mounted, so it was just Malia and me sitting at the bar without anything else to stare at. I took another long, delicious pull from my fresh drink to prevent second thoughts from sinking in. My mind felt wide and open like the blue sky over the gulf shore on a perfect summer's day.

Razz plopped his heavy arms back atop the bar. "Huh," he said. "Guess I had told that one already. Hell with it. Shit like that don't ever get old. I'll tell it at Tommy's wedding, and beside Lisa's grave, assuming I don't go first, that is. Way that broad gets after it, I don't see how that's possible, though."

Addressing Malia, I aimed my thumb at Razz. "You're looking at the pinnacle of health right here. Guy wouldn't touch a vegetable if it made his back hair crawl onto his balding head."

"Not true. I ate one of those artichokie things once. Hair started falling out the very next day."

That was another of his old stand-bys, *It may have choked Artie, but it ain't gonna choke me!*

I chuckled by way of habit. Then noticed the one detail they'd left out from this place. "Hey, where are the pork rinds?" I asked. Instead of peanuts, The Mule Kick offered complimentary bowls of fried pork skin to snack on while sipping booze.

Razz, or whoever was pretending to be Razz, squinted in puzzlement. "Uh...all out, I guess," he said.

"Shame," I said. "That was like the rug in Lebowski's room. Pulled the whole place together, you know?"

Malia gave me a 'hush up' elbow to my arm. I turned towards her, my head like a balloon on a string. "So." I drew the vowel out into a low vibration. "What comes next?"

If she had been pretty before, she was beautiful now. Raven braids with streaks of blue. Lips painted glossy red. Skin so flawless it looked fake, and might have been. That's another form of intoxication right there: rebellious beauty. One I was addicted to as well.

"That's up to you," she said, her cheeks dimpling when she sucked her straw. Staring at me with eyes that twinkled with mischief.

Regular people savour their drinks. Alcoholics guzzle them. Two gulps and I saw Razz ready another round. "You know, I always wondered what became of the Spring River chicks." That was true, too. Some say life is an even playing field, but that's bullshit. Some people are fucked from the jump. Place a trust-fund baby in the ghetto and see how far she gets. Some of the most worthless people I know own the most stuff. "Guess they wind up here, huh?"

Malia shrugged. "Don't know." She took another sip. Damn if she wasn't pacing me on my path to oblivion. "This one did."

I surveyed the room, soaking it all in. "Not such a bad gig. Catch a rock show, grab a few drinks, fuck with someone's head. Sure beats cleaning toilets, or blowing smelly fat men for cash."

"Oh, yeah? Speaking from experience?"

"No, not quite," I said, then held up my hands defensively. "Not that there's anything wrong with that."

"'Course not," she said. "Wrong gets a bad rap."

That made me choke. "Right on," I said when I'd cleared my throat. "That's trademark-worthy."

She chuckled like I was the most charming man in the world. "Right. I'll make it my next tattoo."

I turned my hand palm up. Saw the word 'Rox' tattooed in black ink above the top horizontal crease. Along the vena amoris. The love line. God, how Caspian had made fun of me for getting that. For good reason. Not only was it cheesy, it was contrived. Like trying to manufacture love for my son by staining his name into my skin. Make it a reality on the surface, if nowhere else. But I've learned to truly love him by now. Haven't I?

"What's that?" she said when she saw me staring.

I balled my hand into a fist. "Nothing." My foot started bouncing, feeling that restless energy that comes with getting drunk. The need to move from place to place until you find something that's never been seen before. Chasing that one mystifying experience that will make the whole night worthwhile. The chance encounter that will set life on a new trajectory of adventure. We'll achieve world peace before we discover salvation at the bottom of a bottle. But we'll never stop trying.

"Nothing, huh?" Her knee touched mine. "You've got nothing tattooed along the love line of your palm?"

What's that old nursery song? First comes love, then comes marriage, then comes a baby in a baby carriage. Here's me on booze. First comes buzz, then comes bluster, then comes me bleeding from my nose because I got pissed for no reason and bashed my face against the wall. Halfway through my third Long Island Iced Tea I was feeling the bluster and making the turn towards senseless rage.

"None of your business, is what it is."

She propped her elbow on the bar and rested her head in her hand. Maybe the booze was getting to her. Then again, she could win an Academy Award for acting drunk. I reached out and grabbed her half-full drink and smelled it. Yep, it was the real thing. Strong enough to fuel a passenger jet.

"Go ahead, taste it," she said. "Think I'd let you drink alone?"

"Yes, I do." So I did. And there was no denying the burn.

I slid the glass back towards her, picked up mine and raised it. "Cheers."

"Cheers," she said, clinking her glass against mine, fighting to keep the smugness from her smile.

We both finished the rest of our drinks in four deep gulps. I slammed my glass down, and the room turned fuzzy. My tolerance was not what it used to be. Was it really wise to get hammered while in this hellhole? Couldn't get any worse, I figured. This was one experience I'd be happy to black out.

I raised a finger to request another drink, which wasn't necessary. Razz was already making the next round. Here was seven years of sobriety going up in smoke. *Fuck it*, I thought. *Might as well burn it to the ground.*

ᚠ

"On the house," Razz said, placing a fresh drink in front of me. It was mostly liquor with just a scrim of melting ice at the top.

"You're a good man, Roxy," I said, my words beginning to slur.

"Tell me something I don't know," he said, taking away our empties. Leaving just the one.

Malia leaned close. "Is that your girl?" she said.

"Huh?"

She pried open my hand and pointed. "Rox. You just called Razz Roxy."

"Oh. Nuh-uh." I shook my head, and had to grip the bar for balance. Stifled a burp. "My boy."

"As in, boyfriend?"

Shaking my head was making me dizzy so I stopped. "No, my boy. My son."

"Ah...." she said, like she'd just found a puzzle piece that had slipped under the rug. I expected more, but she returned to her drink.

"Ah...?" I said sarcastically. "What's 'Ah...' mean? You figure some shit out or something?"

She pushed her bottom lip out in a pout. Like I was being mean. Like she hadn't fucking choked me and slammed my head against a table an hour or so ago. "Just another connective thread."

I could feel my body swaying. Maybe another sip would straighten things out. "What, you got a son named Rox, too?"

She shook her head. Nice and steady, unlike mine. This girl was putting me to shame. "Never reached full term. Miscarriage. It was a boy, though. Or would have been. I bet you can guess when."

I felt like the intellectual equivalent of Einstein, but my brain was sharp as a ball of soggy wool. "I give up," I said.

"Love Week," she said. "Fitting, right?"

It dawned on me then. "You mean one of the minister dudes?"

She nodded, eyes glistening. Whether from tears or triple-distilled vodka, I couldn't tell. "Yep, I guess you can say he filled me with the Holy Spirit. I gave birth to a ghost."

I dig dark humour when stone-cold sober. Get me drunk and I'll dance on the gallows and wedgie the poor sap swinging from the rope. "That's messed up," I said, which sounded witty in my mind, but simply matter of fact when spoken. "Fuck." My exclamation point.

You'd think I'd just recited a poem by Rumi by the way she was looking at me. "I bet you're a good father," she said. I may have been drunk going on smashed but that still rang my bullshit bell.

"The fuck gives you that idea?"

She shrugged. "I've met lots of other ones."

I waited for more, but that's all she gave me. I took another drink and hardly tasted it. My tongue had been anaesthetised. 'Fortunate Son' gave way to 'Thorazine Shuffle' by Gov't Mule, the de-facto house band for the bar.

"Line up a couple shots here, Razz-O," I said, wanting a change of taste. "Jamesons," I specified. Caspian and I had consumed so much of the stuff we should be stockholders.

We slammed those, then two more. Then my bladder signalled the alarm – piss is imminent, proceed to the docking station immediately and prepare to unload. I slid off the stool and performed my own Thorazine Shuffle, staggering like a newborn fawn on ice as the booze rushed to my head.

"Buckle up, buttercup!" Razz heckled. Malia offered her arm for balance, and I used it to steady myself. The floor canted as I walked to the bathroom, sending me stumbling into the hallway wall. My shoulder crashed into a framed poster from the '06 Wannee Festival, and cracked the glass. I heard Razz yell something from behind, but couldn't make it out. *Hurray for that,* I think. The bar had become a cruise ship in high swells, forcing me to hold my arms out for balance. I pushed through the door and cast forward, stumbling until I hit the far wall. *A good place to rest*, I thought, placing my forehead against the cream tile. Nice and cool.

"Whoa, Nelly. All fucked up there good." It sounded like the man from earlier. What is he, like the bathroom concierge?

"Nah," I mumbled, peeling myself off the wall. Now I was on a tilt-a-whirl, could feel the earth spinning through space. Hurtling 20,000 miles per hour through the void. "I'm the rocket man," I said, as though that made any sense. Then belted out the old Elton John tune. "Rocket Man!"

I vaguely remember performing a heartfelt duo with that guy in the bathroom, and that's where my mind started to shut down, capturing snippets of imagery in snapshot memories. Grainy scenes with soft borders, faint copies of copies shot through a kaleidoscope lens, attempts at bringing coherence to babble. I reject these, mostly. Pretend they didn't happen, and pray that's true. There's me, snorting lines off the toilet lid. That dude with the bald head right in my face. We're laughing or yelling at each other or both. Crashing against the stall walls like rodeo bulls in a cage, wrestling or fighting I'm not sure. My shirt's off. Shoes, gone. Zipper down. Dancing in the barroom, on the bar. Malia stuffing dollars down my waistline and through my open fly. Kicking glasses, falling. Razz slapping me on the floor. Laughing, yelling, both. Grabbing his face, the latex yielding in my fingers, tearing along the neckline, gapping around the eyes. So much jostling, stumbling. A camera held in palsied hands. The bathroom – Malia on her knees, maybe bent over the counter. I pray that's a dream, not a memory. OBSIDEO in steam. Kicking the cigarette machine, staring at the elevator, wanting to kill. Wanting to die. Razz's braying laughter on a broken record.

Minutes, hours, days, who knows? Oblivion achieved.

⋆　　⋆　　⋆

"Sir." I'm being hauled up by my feet from the depths of a bottomless well. Diffused light comes hazy to my eyes, gilding the closed lids with an amber glow. "Sir." Someone is shaking my arm. Hard wood under my head. I lift it and gape through burning eyes.

"Sorry, sir. This isn't a hotel. You'll have to go." The man saying this is dressed like a barkeep from an old saloon. White frill shirt with long sleeves. Black armbands and bowtie. A groomed beard that comes down past his neckline. Round spectacles.

I straighten, still drunk, but back from my blackout. In a bar I don't recognise. My mind struggles to establish context, to answer the questions racing through my head: *What happened? Where am I? How did I get here?*

My first flash memory – false or not, I'm not sure – is my finger tearing the latex mask on the man masquerading as Razz. I try to see more, connect that moment to this one, but I come up blank.

"Sir, please." The man is trying to be polite. Man being a generous term. This hipster barely looks old enough to serve liquor. I look around and see another guy down at the corner of the bar. His banker's shirt is straining against the avalanche of his belly. Red-rimmed eyes glare at me through inch-thick lenses. He shakes his head in disgust and returns his attention to his watered-down scotch the colour of my morning piss.

Then it hits me. I'm being asked to leave. Does that mean I'm done? Have I been released?

I quickly survey myself, assessing my condition. My shirt is inside out and on backwards with the tag sticking out in front like a Roman collar. My zipper is down, and my shoes are untied. My whole head is pounding in sync with my beating heart, but I can't tell if I'm injured or just terribly hungover. There's a tarnished mirror behind the bar that shows red splotches on my face that look like rust. Definitely injured then, just a matter of how bad.

"Sorry," I croak like a talking walrus. I can taste cigarette smoke on my breath and my throat is lined with shards of glass. I pat my pockets. My keys are in the front and that's all. Wallet's gone.

"Your friend paid the tab," the hipster says, frowning and crossing his arms. His dwindling patience is almost depleted.

"You need to go."

My friend. Right. *My good pal.* Must have given a hell of a tip in order to leave me here.

"Need to go." Wait, is that the same as, *"Free to go?"*

Every nerve ending screamed in agony as I stood. I used to drink enough flammable liquid to torch a building and wonder why I felt so bad the following day. The door was just ten or so steps to my right. Its frosted windowpane glowing with daylight, RED ROOM written across the front in gold lettering. But what if it's just another fabrication? A lamp casting artificial light within a room filled with abominations and echolocating clones? What if I'm stuck in a never-ending series of torments for a crime I've already atoned for? Or maybe I'm mad and I'm imagining the whole thing. Maybe I'm dead and this is hell.

I braced myself as I reached for the brass door handle, expecting someone to grab me from behind. I pushed forward and the door held, either locked or jammed or fake. My shoulders slumped, and I nearly cried out in desperation. Then I pulled and the door swung easily on loose hinges, almost bashing me in the nose. Sunlight stabbed my eyes, causing me to squint, to sneeze. I staggered out into the ripe afternoon heat, the sun wavering directly overhead, and scanned the mid-size parking lot containing half a dozen cars, including mine. I could hear the whoosh of traffic on a nearby road. Could smell hot asphalt and tyre rubber, scents more pleasing in their promise of freedom than a field of sunflowers. I may have been whimpering as I scampered towards my car, prying my keys from my pocket. I may have been weeping like a kid after a schoolyard scuffle, but I'd never admit to it outside of this confession to you.

Heat fumes rose from the car as I opened the door, followed closely by a hot stench. Holy shit, that smell. My grandpa used to fish with chopped chicken livers. Kept them in a fridge he had out in a work shed by the pond behind his house. The power cut out during a lightning storm once and everything in the fridge spoiled. When we came out the next day, the work shed was buzzing with flies. Insect buzzards looking to lay baby worms. When we opened that cooler in the dank summer heat of Alabama, the meaty smell that bloomed out caused my eyes to water and made me heave so hard I nearly got a hernia. My grandfather made me help him dump those coagulated containers of chicken guts into a garbage bag and the smell stayed with me for days, like it had soaked into my skin.

This was that smell. Rank and beefy. I closed the door and looked around, making sure I was alone. Then I cupped my hands around my eyes and peered in through the window. It was too dark inside to make out much. But I didn't see what I was looking for. Namely, a dead body, or parts of one. I moved to the back and looked inside. Empty seats; empty foot wells. Which meant the smell must be coming from the trunk. My key fob had a trunk release button, but I didn't know if I wanted to see what was making that smell. Stuck in there stewing in the summer heat. Couldn't be Caspian. The decapitated head I had seen in the drainage culvert must have been a prop, because I had seen him alive and well – well maybe not well – in the police interrogation room, being grilled about my disappearance. Which I would soon clear up. Maybe Kevin, then?

Surely not someone more familiar. Not Cassie or Rox.

I checked my pockets again, hoping to find my phone, but they were empty. Even if I'd had my phone, I'm not sure calling the cops would have been such a good idea. How would I explain a dead body in my trunk? Where would I start and how much would they believe? None of it, most likely.

Cringing, I popped the trunk, holding my breath as heat waves rolled out. I lifted the lid, and expelled all my air in a gust of relief. Aside from my guitar case, a flat soccer ball that had never been used, and a torn camping tent I'd been meaning to return to REI, the trunk was empty.

I could feel the clock ticking. Surely, escape would not be as simple as getting drunk in a replica of my old haunt, waking up hungover and driving away. Something was coming for me. I had to get out in public where I would be safer than in this secluded parking lot while I figured things out. I opened the driver's side door and slid in. And that's when I saw the source of the smell. The cloth passenger seat was soaked in a viscous maroon liquid that had to be blood. Red splashes coated the door panel and a puddle was pooled in the floor mat. The passenger window had faint maroon smears that came from a hasty attempt to wipe it clean.

I quickly looked for my phone but couldn't find it. Nor did I see anything left behind by Caspian. I slid the key in the ignition and groaned as the engine failed to start. *Please,* I prayed. Something you'll want to start doing, if you haven't already. *Please don't break down on me now.* The engine caught on the third attempt and I didn't wait for it to warm. Just threw it into gear and peeled out towards the lot exit. Pulled out on some road I didn't recognise and took a right without bothering to check for traffic. A horn blasted as a car swerved to avoid clipping my front bumper and I tolerated the man's middle finger with unaccustomed grace. I'd take road rage over homunculus spit every day of the week and kindly ask for more.

The light up ahead turned yellow and I stomped on the accelerator, not wanting to get stuck at a light, but it turned red way before I was close enough to run it. I eased up behind the car in front of me and stopped. Got boxed in from behind. The guy I cut off was on my left and staring me down. When I looked at him, he grimaced and averted his eyes, moving his car up as close to the one in front of him as he could. That couldn't be a good sign.

I checked my reflection in the rearview mirror and barely recognised the face staring back at me. My right cheek was swollen and scraped, my eye purple going on black. My skin had a crimson hue as though it has been covered in blood and roughly scrubbed with a washcloth. My goatee was stained red. A trickle of dried blood ran from my ear down the side of my neck.

Sadly, this was not an image entirely unfamiliar to me. The look of surprise on my battered face over injuries incurred mysteriously during a blackout. How the fuck would I explain this to Cassie? Hell, I didn't understand it myself.

The light turned green and I followed the cars through. Two lanes ran in opposite directions, a string of strip malls on either side. Franchise shops found in every town, spreading like a virus. Billions served into ubiquity. But this familiar scene was now cast in a sinister light. A series of cheesy façades camouflaging the interconnected hell dens where innocent people were taken and subjected to unexplainable terrors. My world had irrevocably changed and I didn't know how I could possibly acclimate to this new reality. There is no end to our veils of innocence, and life gets worse as each one falls away.

Two miles farther down the road and I saw a sign for I-85, a highway that I knew would lead me home. Took the on ramp and found my bearings after a few exits. I was near Macon, about sixty miles outside Atlanta. There's nothing in these parts, which made them perfect for this psycho's sadistic tricks. Assuming I had been out here the whole time. Could be they drove me out here while I was passed out to cover their tracks. Either way, it didn't matter. I'd be home in an hour and could start the process of finding out who had done this and how. Which would be tricky, as I had no evidence aside from the condition of my face. My first call would be to Solomon. Why he would recommend this book in the first place made no sense to me. Why he'd subject me to this.

Mile markers flashed by as I considered my next steps. Step one would be to appease Cassie, which would be no easy task. She had almost certainly wandered past worried into the realm of pissed off. My eighty-proof breath fumes wouldn't help my case much. It would almost be easier to tell a lie than it would the truth. Just say I relapsed and went on a bender. Once in seven years wasn't too bad, and it wouldn't happen again. Write this whole sordid episode off the ledger of my life and move on. Lock the trauma away and lose the key, which was how I'd traditionally dealt with such things. Not that there's a model for how to handle what I'd just been through. No word for the type of PTSD certain to plague my future. And to think of the other unfortunate souls going through their own version of this right now. We live in a psychotic world and the only way out is death. Jesus, the car reeked of blood.

I arrived at the city limits, watched downtown crawl by on my left. Took the 14th Street exit and turned towards West

Midtown, where we live. I was about five miles out when the stereo popped on – I hadn't been listening to anything other than the frantic ramblings of my mind, and were those to be recorded I'd wind up in a padded room. Probably will anyway. If so, I'll save a cot for you and count us both lucky.

The broadcast began with the same grumbling laughter I'd heard in the car with Caspian while driving home from the Full Moon Saloon. I looked down and saw the clock was still stuck on 12:00. Longest damn hour in recorded history. Then that gravelly voice came through – the DJ at the dingiest strip bar on the bad side of hell.

"Welcome back to The Midnight Hour, ladies and gentlemen. Heh, who am I kidding? We have an audience of one tonight. And I so hope he's enjoyed the programming we prepared especially for him. But all good things must come to an end, even hours as fun as this. Beware what comes after midnight, Jesse. Do like the song says, and let it all hang out. Don't hold nothing in. And maybe we'll see you around. Until then, enjoy your walk home."

The clock turned 12:01 at the precise moment my right front tyre blew with the sound of an M80, surely detonated by whoever was behind this. Pulling to the side of the road, I promised myself right then that if I ever found this guy, I was going to put him through as much pain as humanly possible.

That's a promise I wish I could take back.

∧

No phone, no cash for a cab. Thankfully I was only a couple miles from home. Still, August in Atlanta is no time for a walk. And my throat felt like a vacuum filter. If our bodies are mostly water I should have evaporated before I reached my front door.

I still had no idea what day it was. I assumed Sunday, but wasn't sure. The lack of cars lining my street, and the empty driveways, led me to believe it was a weekday and that my neighbours were at work. Not that I knew what they did or where it took them. Many of my neighbours pal around, but we keep mostly to ourselves. Recovering addicts are like that, I guess. Don't want to tell our story outside of sanctioned rooms. Explain why we're refusing the cold beer offered by the hospitable neighbour who doesn't trust people that don't drink. Listen, friend. I'm liable to fuck your wife after a few whiskeys. But you can take my sober word to the bank.

Dear God, I was hungover. Vision blurry. Stomach queasy. Every nerve ending frayed. Justifiably paranoid. My grainy eyes craved sleep. Muddled thoughts needed psychiatry. Life-sustaining molecules required H_2O. Here I am stumbling down this residential street like the first zombie of the apocalypse, and I have no idea what I'm going to tell Cassie when I see her. Turns out I didn't have to worry about that. Her car was missing from the driveway, and when I went to unlock the front door, someone else opened it from the other side.

"Jesus Christ, Jess." Standing in the doorway was Al Tanner, my sponsor from AA, shaking his head with a look of such concern I would have shed tears had I moisture to spare. "Thank God you're okay."

"I'm far from fucking okay," I said, pushing past him. That two-mile walk had felt like a marathon. My feet were stuck in

South Dublin County Libraries
Tallaght Library

Issue Summary

Loaned today

Item: SD100000031799
Title: Mr Mercedes / Stephen King.
Due back: 21-03-22

Item: SD100000031874
Title: The sun dog / Stephen King.
Due back: 21-03-22

Item: SD100000031985
Title: Will haunt you / Brian Kirk.
Due back: 21-03-22

Thank you for using self service

concrete blocks. Seeing Al here was equal parts comforting and disconcerting mixed in a bowl of confusion. "Where's Cassie?"

The house was blessedly cool, air-conditioning being among the greatest of mankind's inventions. I was less than twenty-something steps from my Sleep Number bed, which was up near the top as well. The door closed behind me. I stumbled a few steps and collapsed onto the couch in the main living room. Turns out my bed was too far away.

Al walked over and looked down on me. "Was it worth it?" I heard him say.

The last thing I needed right then was condescension, but it was to be expected. "It's not what it looks like, Al. I was fucking kidnapped. Held against my will. They made me do it, I swear."

Rather than pull out his phone and call the police, Al crossed his arms and sighed. "Fuck," he said. "Okay, look. Sleep it off. We'll talk when your head's clear."

I wanted to get it all out right then and there. I had questions of my own, and time was of the essence. But the couch cushions had the gravity pull of a black hole, dragging me towards unknown depths. This pending sleep was a singularity beyond which I could not see. "Where's Cassie?" I asked again, but my eyes had already closed and I could feel myself drifting away.

Al, that sweet bastard, laid a blanket over me, and placed a pillow under my head. "Shhh," he said, and that was all the encouragement I needed. The house could have been burning down and it wouldn't have mattered. I fell into a nightmarish sleep where dark seeds planted during that terrible experience began to take root.

★   ★   ★

I woke up feeling like a new man, but not in a good way. Not new as in shiny and refreshed, but new as in different and changed. Alien and strange. My consciousness altered and implanted in a surrogate host. The first thing I noticed was pain. Agonised throbbing inside my fragile skull. *You are in your son's head.* That lovely voice, my head stuck in that sweat chamber, staring into that room of senseless carnage. Then came sickly heat, radiating from the inside out as I lay in a puddle of toxic sweat. My throat on fire, forehead burning. Stomach a roiling stew.

My breath was ragged and sour-tasting. Thoughts laced with shame. A mental state conditioned by countless morning-afters where I'd had to atone for ill decisions from the night before. I grasped at wispy memories that broke apart before coming into full view. The ones featuring Malia in what seemed like sexual interplay troubled me the most.

The room was dark. I squinted at the windows and saw that it was night outside. I startled when I saw the silhouette of a figure sitting in the chair beside me. Its head swivelled when it saw me move, heard me groan. And in that brief instant I braced for the clicking sound of echolocations I was sure would come. Penetrating my mind and implanting those marauding thoughts. Leading me to murder. Marching me to my padded room.

"Have some water," the shadow man said, and I relaxed when I recognised the voice as Al's. Saw the glass in his outstretched hand. The water was room temperature but I'd never tasted anything more refreshing. It lubricated my cracked lips and soothed my parched throat like a balm.

Oh, but I was home. Safe. That hellacious night was over. I'd survived, and there was something in that realisation that eased the hangover. Even produced a little pride – the most seductive of all sins.

"More," I said, holding out the empty cup. "Please."

Al returned with a fresh glass. This one far more nourishing than those replenished by Razz. Or whoever had been pretending to be him. I could faintly recall tearing at his latex mask while thrashing in some drunken delirium. Him cackling with laughter while pinning me against the ground. Christ, what a disaster. What a mess.

I sat up, waited for my throbbing head to subside, then repeated the last thing I had said before passing out. "Where's Cassie?" Adding, this time, "Where's Rox?"

It must have been somewhere in the twilight hours between

two a.m. and five a.m. I could tell by the depth of silence, the breathless hush. Those few hours when, on any given day, half the planet is experiencing a mass hallucination entered into during sleep. I used to think half the world was dreaming the other half into existence. Sometimes I still do.

The recliner squeaked when Al reached over to turn on the table lamp. I squinted against the soft light diffused by the corrugated shade. Fucking Al. Sometimes AA feels like a game of who can one-up the other with the terrible shit they've done during the throes of addiction. No one can one-up Al. He's the only reason I'm sober. Or was. I didn't think sobriety was possible until I heard how bad he'd had it. Then I knew, if Al could get sober, so could I.

"She's fine, Jess," Al said in his gruff voice from decades of torment. That man right there had blown more coke than Escobar ever trafficked from Columbia. "She's upset's, all. Called me when you didn't come home after your show. Then, well, when you sent that stuff. Man, Jess. What can you expect?"

The light grew brighter as the bulb warmed. And then I remembered that the room was bugged, and that we were almost certainly being watched.

"Watch what you say," I said. "Our conversation is being recorded right now."

Al leaned towards me. "What the hell are you talking about?"

I pointed towards the ceiling fan like that explained everything. "Room's bugged."

He relaxed back in his chair and shook his head. That three a.m. silence returned.

"What do you remember?" Al said.

I proceeded to tell him everything I remembered up until the moment in The Mule Kick's men's room when things got fuzzy. The gig, the radio station, waking up to the doctor with the walrus teeth, Malia, Professor O's experiments, the reenactment of the night my son fell from his crib. I left out the bit about strangling the man in the dark hallway. I didn't know what had happened back there and wasn't ready to confess to murder. Especially when it had most likely been a hoax. Like all the rest.

That was a lot for anyone to take in, even Al, who has heard it all. He sat with his arms crossed, thinking. Then he turned towards me. Scrutinising my backwards shirt. My bloody and swollen face. Vindication was coming, I was sure of it.

"Don't bullshit me, Jess," he said. "The fuck did you take?"

So much for salvation. "That is the truth," I said. My croaking voice was less than convincing. "Crazy as I know it sounds. I swear it."

He stood. A task that seemed heroic to me right then. Gravity had increased tenfold while I slept. He walked over to an office nook we have off the kitchen on the way to the garage. Flipped on another light there and ruffled through some papers stacked on the countertop. He grimaced, and I knew that wasn't good. Al is the guy who will pull you naked from a puddle of puke without batting an eye. He's like a janitor for junkies. Cleans the clogged-up shitters in the seediest of bars. But whatever was printed on those sheets of paper revolted him. He tapped them straight and returned to his chair without meeting my eyes, which was another bad sign.

"Here," he said, handing me the stack of papers face down. Then he stared at his empty hands as though they were coated in some residual filth.

I turned the stack over. Saw printed screenshots from a phone. Texts sent to Cassie's phone from mine.

I thought my nightmare had ended. Clearly, I was wrong.

ᚱ

Here's how the first text read, sent Sunday morning, around two fifteen a.m.

Hey Casx!! Show wuz great!! Made sum new fans!!

This was followed by fuzzy pictures of Malia flashing me on stage at the Full Moon Saloon. My eyes are locked on her exposed breasts – her baby feeders as I'd called them at the time. Then pictures of me talking to her by the bar with our arms entangled. My head is tipped towards hers like I'm whispering sweet nothings, not politely asking her to get lost like I was. A drunken smile is smeared on her face.

Beneath this was another.

Got more than the dead to rise t0night!!

Below the text box was a picture of my erect penis with a female hand wrapped around it. Nails flecked with turquoise paint. I guess it could have been another man's cock; my face isn't in the photo. But you know what your own dick looks like. So does your wife.

Lik3 old times!! Remember?
Tug 2x for a backstage pass!

Oh, God. It wasn't a false memory. There's Malia on her knees. I'm in her mouth. I have a beer in my hand that I don't remember drinking. A stupid, wasted look on my face. Now I know why Cassie's not here. There's no explaining my way out of this.

D0n't b3 mad. You kno3 who I am.

That's not me in these photos. Not the man I now represent. I put that shit behind me years ago. Walked away from that way of life. Sacrificed everything that made me happy to do what I thought was right. To own up to my mistakes and make things better. I was on my way home, goddamn it. Had made it through a night filled with the worst of my temptations. Had rebuffed the willing groupie. Had turned down the free booze. Caspian belongs in those photos, not me. And yet, there I am. No denying it. But, fuck, that's why I don't drink. That's why I quit. Because it turns me into someone I'm not. Replaces my conscious self with some self-absorbed monster who doesn't consider consequences. It's like a possession. Like some puny demon taking my body for a joy ride while I'm asleep at the wheel. I beat it, though. AA was my exorcism. Al my Catholic priest. Rox's confused tears my fucking holy water. And now that's all going to be taken from me? For what? What possible reason could the person behind this have for ruining my life in this way?

Some questions, I've learned, are best left unanswered.

The images on these pages shamed me deeply. And Al had seen them. Worse, Cassie had. How many hours had she spent wondering when I'd be home, worrying about whether or not I'd relapsed? And then to receive these texts like I'm taunting her. Rubbing my relapse and crude infidelity in her face.

I talk about the sacrifices I've made for Cassie, like she hasn't sacrificed for me. Like this was the life she dreamed about as a little girl. Me with my shit job and selfish tendencies, her Prince Charming. Us with our crippled kid.

Al was still staring at his hands. I was still staring at my dick.

And it's not like Cassie had to settle, either. No, we made our bed together, but she sleeps in it more soundly than I. Grew into this life with its limitations like a rose through a cracked sidewalk, while I grind my teeth and stew with resentment and ponder the what-ifs and fantasise alternate scenarios like I deserve them more than her. She doesn't even fault me for the night Rox had his accident, although she could. He fell during my shift. And there's no way it would have happened had I not been obliterated. I know that inside my heart, even if I'm not able to admit it. Hell, she's capable of making more money using her talents than I am with my crap tunes, but she's never once pressed that issue. We'd have a better life if she worked and I stayed home, but I know – we both know – I'm not capable of doing it. It's a sacrifice I'm not willing to make.

So maybe this is what I deserve. Maybe this is karma baring its jagged fangs. Worse happens to people less deserving than me, that's for sure. Rox did nothing to deserve me as his father. The stumbling dummy in these photos with a beer in his hand and dick in the mouth of some strange woman who had helped set him up.

"This isn't what it looks like," I said to Al.

If there's one thing addicts do better than anyone else, aside from stretch out benders, it's lie. Al knows this. Expects it, actually.

"Looks pretty cut and dried to me, Jess. What am I missing?"

"What you're missing," I said, realising how ridiculous this would sound, "is the part where I was chased off the road by a couple of hillbilly twins, and where my life was threatened unless I did what you see here. I didn't send those texts, Al. I don't even have my phone."

"Not sure I see a gun pointed at your head, there," Al said.

"No, it's wasn't like that," I said. "But the threat was there, trust me."

Had it been, though? Had I ever really had my life threatened? Everything, it seemed, had been an illusion of sorts. Except for these damn pictures. Even these, though, were the result of my own actions, and hadn't been explicitly coerced. In fact, hadn't I enjoyed being at that bar once I'd accepted my fate?

Al nodded, took the empty glass from my hands. "Coffee?" he said.

"Time is it?"

Al checked his watch. "Bit after five a.m."

"Jesus, okay." I said. My most concise prayer.

I patted my pockets as he walked back towards the kitchen, felt something that hadn't been there before, and pulled it out. It was a business card. Stiff, with sharp edges. Quality stock. The image of an eye was on the front. The same eye I'd seen on the garage door in the hallway where I'd choked that man. Below was that same obscure word I'd seen on the bathroom mirror: OBSIDEO. I flipped it over and read the words ALWAYS WATCHING centred on the card. I was surprised to find a web address listed underneath this statement: www.eyeofobsideo.com. We've come to a time where criminals have their own URLs. Have to budget server costs into their illicit business expenses.

I never visited that website, and would avoid it if I were you as well.

The early bird chirped outside – damned overachiever – and the first grey light of dawn coloured the window shades. This side of the world was waking, the other side bedding down. Soon the streets would be filled with men and women bustling to work, children scrambling to class, everyone riding that one-way conveyor belt to the coffin. Engaged in a day of sublime normality while I struggled to reorient my worldview to fit the events of the past couple of days. Strive to understand what purpose I served this total stranger, what data set I represented to Professor Fuckbutt. How I could possibly go on without scanning every room I entered for hidden cameras and looking over my shoulder every few steps for echolocating clones. Not to mention convince Cassie to return home and allow me to see my son again.

I heard the coffee machine gurgle, then Al walked out with two steaming cups. Handed me one and sat on the edge of his chair. I gave him the business card, if that's what you'd call it, and he turned it over a couple of times.

"What's this?" he said.

"Found it in my pocket. Saw that same picture, and that word OBSIDEO, back at the place they took me."

Al scowled. "Always watching?"

"Think I'd make that thing, have it printed as some kind of premeditated alibi in case I got caught cheating on my wife? Come on, Al. That's crazy."

He sipped his coffee, and I sipped mine. Better than the brew in that random break room, but not by much. I'll never touch another Krispy Kreme donut, though. And that's a damn shame.

Al stuffed the card in his front pocket. For how quiet he was, I knew his mind was working overtime. Al looks like he operates a forklift for a living but he was once one of the more successful commercial builders in the southeast. Lost out on a bid to build the old Atlanta Braves stadium by a ball hair due to shady backdoor dealings. Everything Al does is above table and face to face. "You've got one thing right," he said, turning so that he and I were now dealing face to face. "This is crazy as fuck. Craziest shit I've ever heard, and I've heard it all."

"You and me both," I said. Despite how hard my head was pounding. Despite how ashamed I felt by what I'd seen in those pictures, I forced myself to meet Al's eyes and hold them. My ability to have him believe me depended on what he saw there, squiggly bloodlines or not. "Hell, I'd be better off lying, Al. But I'm not. Someone is fucking with me. Still. Or maybe this is the end of it, I don't know. But I would never do this had I not felt like I was being forced to. I give you my word as a friend and a brother. I need you to believe me, man. Because if you don't, then I'm stuck dealing with this all alone and I don't know if I can do that." That was the pure truth right there. Without Cassie and Rox, there would be nothing left to live for. And fear would follow me every day. "I really don't."

Al reached out and took my hand in his. Rough and strong and made for fixing things, building them from scratch. "I'm on your side, Jess. No matter what. Okay?"

It hit me, then. Relief from unvented stress, comfort in the face of fear and shame. My eyes prickled and burned, my vision turned blurry. Every time I've fallen, he's been there to pick me up. "Thank you," I said, and he squeezed my hand. That pushed me over the edge. A wave of emotion hit me. Broke me like the flood walls that failed New Orleans. And I unleashed an ugly wail, crying tears that burned like hydrofluoric acid, chest heaving like I'm having a seizure. This took some time to pass, and Al waited patiently, holding my hand through it all.

When I was finally able to get ahold of myself, I felt fifty pounds lighter and cleansed. Not clean, but no longer mired in filth. I had been repressing those tears for the past several years and they had grown toxic.

"Drink some coffee," Al said, and I did. It had cooled, but still had a kick. He had made it AA strong.

"Jesus," I said again. Repeating it like I knew I'd need the son of God in the days ahead. "What a mess."

"You're not alone."

We released hands and sat up. Insecure men consider emotion a weakness. Men who have faced their demons and survived think different. "So, where's Cassie?" I asked for the third time. "I need to know she's safe."

"She's safe," Al said. "Just needs some distance right now. Time and space to think."

I nodded. "What the fuck am I going to do, Al? How do I make this right?"

This conversation would have been easier in the dark, in the shadows. The morning sunlight streaming through the window made me feel vulnerable and exposed.

"Same way you got sober, Jess. Be honest, have faith, and take it one day at a time. This ain't going away overnight." I realised I'd have to trash my sobriety chip; I was back to day one.

Physically, I felt horrible. But that paled compared to the pain of knowing I had made things harder for Cassie. I couldn't accept complete responsibility, though. Yes, I was complicit to a degree. Technically, no one had forced me to take those drinks. But I was also a victim in some elaborate scheme that I still couldn't comprehend. And the person behind this needed to be caught and punished. I hope that happens before he comes for you.

"Someone's out there doing this shit. Planned this whole thing, starting back before Saturday night. That girl in those pictures?" Who had taken those pictures? How had they gotten on my phone? "I told her to fuck off back at the bar. Those pictures don't show what was actually going on. Later? Man, I don't even know. I was in the black, man. All the way gone, you know?"

He nodded. That he did know. Al had gone from being a partner in a commercial building firm that designed and constructed luxury resorts to homeless in record time. Like sleeping in underpasses homeless. Eating out of trashcans. Al, the most trustworthy man I know, had, at one time, robbed colleagues, customers, and family members for coke money. Al, the smartest man I've ever met, had been mugged multiple times while buying crack from shady dealers. These were two men sharing the same meat suit: one living in the light of sobriety, the other lost in the black. For Al, there had been no final straw, no bottom. Just one perpetual free fall in a dark void until he stumbled upon a book that popped his parachute open. *The Book*, actually, by Alan Watts, which he had found on a park bench like some totem of divine intervention. Strange that a book had saved him, while a book was destroying me.

I noticed he had yet to suggest alerting the cops. "You don't believe me," I said.

Long inhale, slow exhale. "Right now, I'm just taking it all in. Rest assured, we'll get everything sorted out. What's important is that you're home, safe. Let's just start from there."

Al had once told me the only difference between building a tree house and a thousand-acre resort is time. Pragmatic, Al.

The coffee was waking me up, clearing the cobwebs from my hangover. And I realised that I stank. The mixture of fear sweat, body odour, and whatever sewer water had been in that drainage culvert. "Fair enough," I said. It wasn't what I had wanted to hear, but it was the best I was going to get. "I'm going to take a shower."

Al offered a sheepish grin. "I was going to suggest that. You smell like roadkill."

I flipped him off and it felt good. Felt normal. Like I was regaining control. I went back to my bedroom and undressed. I would be incinerating these clothes. Walked naked to the shower and got it steaming hot. So hot it hurt, which is what I wanted. I wanted to feel pain. I needed purification. I wanted to punish myself, even though I knew this situation wasn't entirely my fault. Right then, it felt like it was. Felt just like all the other times I'd done something completely fucked up during a night of partying – that guilty sensation programmed into my psyche like a Pavlovian response.

I would have preferred to bathe in bleach instead of the organic glop Cassie buys from the hippy health store. I needed more than green tea extract to scrub this grime off my skin. But whatever. That's Cassie's thing. Won't kill roaches, fucking loves spiders. All our indoor plants are fake because she can't stand the thought of placing live flowers in a vase and watching them die. Considers it sadistic. I thought she was ridiculous at first, but her logic has a way of asserting itself over time. She likens house pets to prisoners, and that's where I draw the line. I'd probably bitch more about the baking soda toothpaste if I weren't too lazy to go to the store. Colgate, that's my great compromise.

I could have stayed in the shower for an hour or more had I not heard Al call for me from the living room. Not quite panicked, but definitely concerned. Which grated my frayed nerves. I quickly rinsed and wrapped myself in a towel, dripping water as I hurried back towards the living room.

"Yeah, what is it?"

He'd turned on the TV and paused it. The picture was frozen on a talking head for a local news station. I don't watch the news, so I didn't know which one. Watch an hour of news and you're living in Armageddon. Look out your window and you'll find songbirds and smiling people. The two don't add up. The difference, I guess, is that nature isn't an advertising platform for oil companies. At least, not yet.

"Take a seat," Al said.

I've learned it's typically best to do as Al says, so I did.

He rewound the feed and stopped it. "You're sure you told me everything you remember from the last couple of days?" he asked. "I'm serious. You need to shoot straight right now."

"Al, I swear, man." The frozen image on the TV screen was foreboding. "I've told you all I know."

Al sighed. "Okay, watch this." He hit play.

Looking closely now, I recognised the news anchor, but not because I'd watched his program. It was the same guy I'd seen on the monitor screens in the surveillance room. Or *guys* I should say, plural.

Blue blazer, white shirt, grey striped tie. The polished oak desk appeared authentic, as did the professional backdrop. The station logo was stamped in the lower right-hand corner of the screen like you'd expect. The anchor started talking and a photo of my car on the side of the highway where I had been abducted appeared in a box next to his head.

"Police are still looking for the whereabouts of local rock musician Lance Caspian, who was last seen performing a reunion concert in a small club outside of Atlanta Saturday night. He is reported to have left the club with his bandmate, Jesse Wheeler, who has gone missing as well. Wheeler's car was found abandoned on the side of I-20, and appears to have been the scene of foul play. While responding officers are withholding specifics at this time, we do know that blood was discovered on location, and that it is currently being analysed to determine whether it matches either man. Anyone with information regarding the whereabouts of Lance Caspian or Jesse Wheeler is asked to please contact their local police officials with details."

It was then that I honestly wondered if I was suffering some kind of delirium. If my shattered mind, in an attempt to establish context and identity, had concocted this conspiracy and placed me at its centre. This was padded-room-grade paranoia. Nothing else made sense. "That's not real," I said.

Al stared thoughtfully at the TV screen. "What isn't real?"

"The news report. That guy there is one of this psycho's henchmen. I—" Strangled him to death, I almost said. "Recognise him from the place where they took me. And I saw video of Caspian being questioned in an interrogation room about my whereabouts. Like he was a suspect in my disappearance. It's a hoax. This whole thing is."

The fake news anchor began shuffling papers and the picture changed to an ad for Captain Morgan's Spiced Rum. Some C-List actor wearing a ruffled pirate suit struck the one-legged pose from the bottle's label. I had recorded the song for this commercial. Had made five thousand dollars for the score that was mostly synthesised steel drum.

I unwrapped the towel and used it to dry my hair. We had to get out of here, and there was no time for modesty. Al had seen worse in those pictures. Had sure as hell seen worse in the roadside grottoes where he used to get high.

"You're in deep shit," Al said. Pragmatic, Al.

"Over my head in T-Rex shit. And I need some help."

Al stood, came towards me, grabbed the towel and used it to cover both of our heads. We were close enough to kiss under our cotton hood. "You said your house is bugged. You're sure?" he whispered. His breath smelled like rust.

I nodded. Thank God, he believed me.

"Okay," he said. "Get dressed. I know a place we can go."

I nodded.

"Do it quick," he said, and then dipped out from under the towel, leaving it draped over my head. I felt like a naked buffoon. Like a child in need of an adult. I scrambled back to my room and began throwing clothes in a cloth travel bag I keep in the closet. Pulled on a Cannibal Corpse T-shirt I'd gotten during the '93 tour and a pair of camouflage cargo shorts. For the sake of stealth, you know? Tugged on my low-top Converse and was ready to roll. Assuming I'd be gone at least twenty-four hours, I swiped my toiletries off the bathroom countertop into the open bag and zipped it closed. Glanced in the mirror, and regretted it. The face staring back at me looked terrified. And appeared years older than last time I'd seen it. Frail, even. Pale and sick with haunted eyes. I would not trust this man to protect me, and he's all I had.

No, not true. I had Al. Sucking him back into my dramatic bullshit. Taking it, this time, to a whole new level of fuckery. I've never seen an angel with wings, but I've seen plenty wearing trucker hats. Okay, time to go.

When I came out, Al was hunched over my desktop computer in the alcove off the kitchen. White light flashed from the screen onto his face, reflecting off his eyes. I scanned the room for things I would need. Difficult, as I didn't know where I was going or how long I'd be gone. Not long, I hoped. There was one thing I knew would come in handy, regardless of where we went.

"One minute, Al," I said and rushed out to the garage without hearing a reply. The knife was in a dusty sheath under a pile of garden tools I've never used. Fake plants don't require much maintenance. I clipped it to my waistband and rushed back inside. Al was standing there waiting.

"All set?" he said.

"I guess," I said, shrugging. "Follow you."

He led the way out to his car, a maroon '98 Oldsmobile with satin seat covers that smelled like old cigarettes and attic mould. Al had quit smoking when he got sober, something most addicts never achieve, but his car still harboured the habit's ghost. This close to leaving, I grew anxious, certain that we were about to be boxed in. That a squad of phoney policemen would turn up to arrest me and take me to some fake station imprisoned with more abstract horrors. Or with those, like my son's head, that presented a kind of logic I didn't want to contemplate. I started tapping my foot and drumming against my leg.

"We're going," Al said, triggering the ignition. Like everything else in Al's life, the car, although old, was well maintained. He pulled the gearshift into drive and slid away from the curb. He could floor the accelerator and it would still take a full minute to reach highway speed. My stomach began to somersault. I saw one of my neighbours walk out in his business suit, carrying his briefcase in one hand and a portable coffee mug in another. It was the first time in my life I had envied anyone remotely like him. He smiled and raised his briefcase in some kind of friendly salute. I waved while wondering if that news report had been broadcast widely or to an audience of one. Two, counting Al.

Soon we were free of my neighbourhood and taking random turns in order to spot a tail. Not that either of us had experience in that field. Al and me, fugitives on the run from a mystery.

"The hell were you doing on the computer?" I asked, turned in my seat so that I could look out the back window.

"Checking that website, from the card you had."

"What, eye-of-obsideo-dot-com?"

He nodded, and I leaned sideways as he took a sudden turn. I was feeling better with the adrenaline spiking my system and now craved another drink. Wanted to be back in The Mule Kick on a one-way trip to oblivion, not the path towards heartache I was on right now. Even in my best-case scenario, I'd still have to address the hurt and broken trust my infidelity had caused. Part of me wanted to quit right then. Surrender. Raise the white flag to whatever god had given me this life. Ask for it to end, or begin again with a clean slate. The first part of my life had been played on the Easy setting, but at some point in my twenties it had switched to Advanced. I now lacked the skills required to play.

"What was on it?" I asked. We had been driving randomly for over twenty minutes now. If we were being followed, it was via GPS, so I turned forward in my seat and buckled my belt.

"Nothing," Al said, eyes alternating between the road and the rearview mirror.

But I'd seen light from flashing images. Something had been on that screen.

"What do you mean, nothing?"

He shrugged. "Just a placeholder page, or something. It wasn't operational. Nothing there to see."

Like my rock career, this was a dead-end road. I reached for the stereo, then stopped myself. Last thing I needed was to tune back into The Midnight Hour. I'd much prefer to drive in silence.

"Where are we going?" I asked.

Al scowled, thinking. Scanned the dash, the steering wheel, the roof, looking for a surveillance device, I figured. He lowered his window to allow air to whoosh in, providing cover for us to talk.

He leaned towards me, and I towards him.

"I got a quiet little place in the mountains of east Tennessee. In the middle of nowhere. A secluded spot outside this small town that's all but abandoned. It's where I take people who need somewhere safe and away from temptation to dry out and clear their mind. Call it The Purge Palace," he said with a wry smile. "It's absorbed more sweat and puke than most methadone clinics."

The idea of drying out was overwhelming. To think I'd let that devil's brew back in my body again. Risked what I'd worked so hard for the past several years to achieve. All ruined in one night. Last time had ended with Cassie taking Rox away from me. Rushing him to the hospital. Me, too drunk to drive. Desperately trying to stay awake but passing out anyway. Waking in the morning wondering where everyone had gone before the memory hit me like a flash of lightning. Cassie clutching my son's limp body to her chest. Not sure if he was alive or dead. Trying to revive him with the beating of her heart. A silent scream. Eyes bulging and blinded by panic. Paralysed, while I stumbled and tried to comprehend the severity of the situation. Then they were gone, just like now, and I was alone, never to see my son in the same condition again. I wondered what explanation Cassie had given for the need to leave so suddenly. Routine was important to Rox. He did not transition well.

Unlike Al, I had hit rock bottom. That morning, waking up in our apartment alone with the fragments of a nightmare surfacing that I knew was no dream. Seeking relief from the only reliable source I had, the frosty bottle of Smirnoff I kept in the freezer. Guzzling from the neck until I could muster the courage to make the call. Considering my numb response to the news being relayed by my wife as a show of strength and resolve.

Swelling of the brain

"It'll be okay."

Fractured skull

"He's in good hands."

Permanent damage

"Don't worry."

Half listening as I calculated how much liquor was left.

Sobriety had seemed like personality suicide. Killing my amorphous, rebellious self to assume the predictable shape of a square. No one writes rock songs about tap water or spontaneously drives to Vegas for the breakfast buffet. Despite my best efforts, I was being forced into the life I'd always protested. Because you can't be a good guy who does bad things. That just makes you a liar. A fraud. And in my heart, I'm a good guy. Or want to be, anyway. Am willing to go square, if that's what it takes.

If only Cassie had left me after that first night, like I'd wanted to leave her. If only I'd never met Al. Caspian and I would still be out on that road somewhere. Indulging our selfish hearts without harming anyone else. Either that, or dead. And I'd be okay with that.

Purge Palace, here I come. Please take the toxins from me. Make me worthy of my son, my wife. Please help make me whole again.

We passed a few miles in silence, then I looked down and saw something that eclipsed every horrible thing that had happened so far. The tattoo of my son's name – the one along my vena amoris – had been inked over with three sixes. Part of me was still clinging to hope that this was all some elaborate prank. Not anymore. No one sane would consider this a joke. I balled my vandalised hand into a fist. Squeezed until it hurt.

"You see them before they left?" I asked. "Rox, Cassie?"

He shook his head. "No, she just called. Said she was leaving and why. Asked if I'd watch the house. Wait for you to come home. Assuming you would. Left those pictures for you to find, I guess."

We had a couple of hours before we hit the roads leading up into the Smoky Mountains. Plenty of time to think. Too bad my pickled brain was operating at half capacity. Busy burying dead brain cells and consoling the bereaved. I didn't have the luxury of idle relaxation, though. I had to get ahead of this thing, quick. I was already so far behind.

"How much of what I've told you do you believe?" I asked, expecting to hear 'none'.

Unlike me, Al takes time to think before he speaks. As a result, he rarely has to apologise for something he says. "I'm still working that out," he said. "But, for now, let's assume that everything you told me is true."

"I'll take that as a starting place," I said. I thought about showing him my defaced tattoo, but that type of self-sabotage wouldn't be completely out of character for me while wasted. It proved little. "The question is, when will it end?"

"And you'd never met any of these people before?"

I borrowed a page from Al's playbook, leaned my head back,

closed my eyes, and remained quiet while reflecting on the faces I'd seen. The first image I saw was the puckered scar traversing Solomon's neck. My eyes snapped open. "Let me borrow your phone," I said.

Al dug it out of his front pocket and handed it to me. There was a time I knew the phone numbers for close to twenty people. Now I don't even remember my own. But Solomon had requested a vanity number, DEAD RISING, and that was hard to forget. I dialled it and waited, certain he'd ignore the call due to the unrecognised number, but he answered on the third ring.

"Holy shit, Solomon!" I said.

I'm not sure what I expected, but not laughter. Certainly not the cold, humourless laughter I was hearing now. "Ah, the new initiate. You having a good time?"

"Jesus Christ, man. You knew this shit would happen? What the hell is going on?"

More of that joyless, automaton laughter. "This is the best thing that could ever happen to you. You've been chosen. And the world will praise your name." The Solomon I know speaks with a nervous stammer. He's an anxious little slug. The person I was talking to now sounded like Solomon, but it was as though his voice box had been borrowed and was being used by someone else.

My mouth opened, but I couldn't conjure a word.

"Surrender yourself," Solomon said. "Your identity. Let it go. The more you resist, the worse you will suffer. You've already died. Now be reborn."

Solomon is the only member of the band who has never written a song. He's much more eloquent banging on drums. And here he was reciting some Eastern spiritual nonsense like a wannabe mystic.

That goddamn, soulless laugh. So close and intimate it felt wet inside my ear. "Sacrifice for the greater self," he said. "Release."

I could hear him breathing. Hear the smugness of his breath. A vacancy of humour. Then I heard what I wanted to believe was static interference, a clicking on the line as we drove farther away from the cell towers of the city. But it was an organic sound, born of vocal chords. A clucking of tongue within a cavernous mouth.

A red ball of light formed in the centre of my mind and began to expand. Eating my awareness as it grew. Devouring my thoughts like a dwarf star. Sucking me through a worm tunnel to a graveyard in space. Time dilated as I left my body behind, and I felt something enter from the other side. My vacated mind a receptacle for it. An overwhelming sense of murderous rage that—

My head rocked to the side as Al struck my face with the back of his hand. He had already slapped the phone to the ground, where it now lay.

"Hand it to me," he said, once I'd come around. I could still hear that mechanical clucking sound emanating from the speaker, faint and impotent from its place on the floor. My body felt brutish. A cumbersome anchor for my conscious mind that had just wandered to who knows where. "Shut it off, first. And don't bring it anywhere close to your ear."

And that other presence I'd sensed, replacing my conscious awareness as it drifted off. Coming, it seemed, to inhabit my body. The voice on the phone had been Solomon's, but that wasn't his personality.

I reached down, holding my head as far from my hand as possible. Grabbed the phone and ended the call, silencing that perverse noise.

What had we just been talking about? Where the hell were we going?

"Friend of yours?" Al said, taking the phone from me and making sure it was shut off.

"I don't know who that was."

God, I was tired. My face sore. Al's slap had broken the trance while giving my bruises a bruise. Injury on top of insult on top of insanity.

Al's eyes were on the road, but I felt him watching me. "You fell into a trance there while talking. What happened?"

There was still a residual fog in my brain. Like someone had taken an eraser to my mind. Or removed matter to clear space.

Shaking my head didn't help, as I'd hoped. Maybe I needed another slap from Al. "I don't know, Al. It happened back at the place they took me to as well. Was part of this crazy-ass story they told. Some kind of hypnosis, or something. Some kind of mind control. That's what it feels like, anyway." Take this train of logic any further and I'd need a tin-foil hat to ride. "This is so fucked up," felt like a proper summary.

We had left the city an hour before and had the two-lane highway mostly to ourselves, which worried me. I would have preferred the company of others. Would have felt more comfortable in gridlock than out on the open road.

"You said this started with a book?"

"Kind of," I said. "The dude I was just on the phone with, Solomon. Our drummer. Was our drummer, I mean. For the Rising Dead. He told me about it. A book about someone who haunts the people who read it. I figured it was bullshit. I mean, you can buy the fucking thing at bookstores. Who knows how many people have read it; this shit can't be happening to all of them."

"So why you, then?"

Connective threads. That's what Malia had been implying. That somehow our histories were related in a way that singled us out.

"I have no idea," I said. But what I really meant to say was, I have no idea what to say that won't sound insane. "At first I thought it was the other guys putting this on as some sort of stunt to add excitement to my mundane life. Punishment for succumbing to domestication, or something. But that's not it. I don't know what this is."

"That was your friend on the phone? The one who told you about the book?"

"Yes and no," I said, sighing in frustration. "Sounded like him, but it wasn't him. Shit he was saying isn't shit he would say. Then, that hypnosis thing. He doesn't know how to do anything like that, and would have no reason to try it on me. Solomon's a softy. The guy I know would do anything to help a friend. He wouldn't fuck with me like this."

The fog lifted and the hangover returned, causing my brain to throb. Amazing, the swings in life. A couple nights ago I was experiencing the highest of highs – a golden crown on the achievements of the past ten years. And here I am now at the lowest point since I started down this path towards recovery.

"Think they might have slipped something into one of your drinks? Something dissociative or hallucinogenic?"

"I'm not hallucinating this, Al. My face, those pictures, that newscast, that call. You tell me which of those isn't real."

Al nodded. "No, I don't mean like that. Not like an acid trip, or anything. Back when I was using, I once train hopped down past Alabama towards New Orleans. Got mixed up with a pack of ramblers into some twisted shit. Occult-type shit. Would conduct these rituals while taking these designer drugs they cooked up on their own. Called bath salts now, I guess. Which is basically a catchall term for drugs of unknown composition. The shit they cooked up? Man, it just took their minds away, made them all zombie-like. Vacant eyes, nobody home. Feral, kind of. Like an animal."

Doctor O knew a thing or two about feral humans. Another connective thread?

"I never took any of the stuff they were cooking," Al continued. "I was a tad more discerning. Junky, sure. But of the more pretentious variety. I liked to know where my crack came from. Before there was farm to table, there was lab to vein for fastidious fuckups like me.

"It made for top-shelf entertainment, though. Camped out in an underpass for some dilapidated road. Decorated with the most lurid shit you've ever seen drawn in graffiti. Demons with pitchfork dicks. Cannibal farms with bodies lined up like crops, limbs for the picking like ears of corn. Had a secret-society feel to it. Dangerous and taboo. I'm so high I'm just wanting to see what's next. Eat from the forbidden fruit, you know. They'd get into their rituals. Painted up in soot. Chanting these incantations while taking their zombie powder, then some of them would space out. Some of them wouldn't. These ones, they'd get quiet and super focused. Mouthing those incantations. Making noises like I heard coming out of your phone. And then I swear, crazy as it sounds, they'd enter the minds of those all zoned out. Parade them around like puppets. Whispering words that came out of their puppet's mouth, making gestures that the puppet would mime. And not like it was scripted out. Fucking spontaneous. At least, that's how it seemed. Again, I was flying back then and realise my perception was skewed. But, you know me. I'm a sceptic if there ever was one. Which I guess is why I never told anyone about that before. But there was something going on then that has the feel of what's going on here. You looked like those people under the underpass before they got paraded around."

And it had felt like something invading my consciousness, both times I'd been under that bizarre spell. "So, mind control," I said.

"Something like that, yeah."

"But why? And why all the other freakshow shit surrounding it?"

Al patted his front pocket, reaching for the pack of cigarettes he'd quit years ago. A look of mourning passed his face. He grabbed a pack of Trident from the front console, offered me a piece, which I declined, and then popped one in his mouth. He breathed heavily while trying to chew the stick of gum to paste. "Wish I had the answer, my friend. I don't. Just theories and observations. I say we hunker down in the mountains for a few days and see how things feel then. Allow some time for whatever may be in your system to flush out, then reassess. Meanwhile, figure out what kind of olive branch we'll need to get Cassie back."

"Shit," I said. "I could have a flock of doves deliver diamond-encrusted olives and she'd shoot them out of the air."

Al smiled. Tried to stifle it, and failed. Instead he chuckled. "Fucking dove hunter. That's some cranky shit."

I chuckled, too. Not much, but enough to ease some of the tension in my chest. As my Nanna used to say, "A chuckle a day will do ya." And she lived ninety-eight spirited years, so I'm inclined to follow her advice. Meanwhile, my days are few and numbered. So are yours.

"This place you got, what's it like?" I said, wanting to avoid any and all potential surprises.

"It's a shit shack," he said. "Small and drafty with residual smells of toxic sweat and puke. But it's private and safe, and fairly cosy once you get a fire going. Which I don't suppose we'll be doing this time of year."

After having my head stuck above the mantel of a fireplace I doubt I'll ever appreciate a hearth fire again.

"It got a view?" I said.

"Trees. Dirt. Fallen leaves." Al smiled when I slouched in my seat. "Don't fret, though. Prettiest damned dirt you've ever seen."

No, friend. That's reserved for the six feet of soil that will cover my grave.

I

I nodded off at some point. Restless, anxious sleep. My body was a doorway. Like in that movie, *Being John Malkovich*, but I was the star in this film. The back of my head would swing open and this murky light would pour through, filling the open cavity of my skull with a noxious substance like curdled milk. A maroon veil fell over my eyes, filtering my perception through a lens of rage, turning friends and neighbours into objects of hate. I had become a killing machine. An avatar for deviant thrill seekers wanting to spill blood while keeping their hands clean. My core self was bound and gagged and kept in a cage as the invaders manoeuvered my pliant body through a senseless killing spree, delirious child-like laughter echoing in my ear canals as I became drenched in gore. My hands were wrapped around Al's neck, grunting as my muscles were commanded to squeeze with all their strength, and I jerked awake when his oesophagus collapsed under my rigid thumbs. That feeling of falling back into your body.

We were driving through a plume of dust, off the highway now, travelling down some dirt road. Al had the windows up; the interior reeked of last night's liquor oozing from my pores. Looks like I was purging early.

"Where are we?" I asked, and Al shushed me with a finger against his mouth. The trunks of birch trees lined the road. White and spindly. Maple and spruce created the canopy of darkness deeper in the woods. Al removed the finger from his mouth and pointed up the mountain, suggesting we were close.

My shirt was damp, the collar stuck to my chest. My hair plastered to my head. But my headache had subsided some. And my stomach was less queasy. In fact, I felt the first pangs of hunger, which I considered to be a good sign. After all the fried sugar I'd consumed, I could use a vegetable or two. Okay, maybe just one.

The dirt road was narrow and rocky with a line of tall grass running up the centre that scraped the undercarriage. Al's Oldsmobile kicked rocks and rolled over the uneven terrain like a boat through swells, my head flopping on a flaccid neck. A gap in the dense foliage outside my window caught my eye, and I turned to look. Saw sporadic cabins set deep in the woods. Haphazardly placed as though someone had thrown them against a game board like dice. One had a pine tree crashed in through its caved-in roof. Another was collapsed in on itself like an upside-down crab. Through the blurring stretch of pine and birch I saw a leaf-strewn dirt road, disconnected from the one we were on now. An abandoned depot with incomplete sign letters cast askew. A larger building with a tall spire that I glimpsed before it became obstructed by a dense uprising of wood. Perhaps a church. Then the road turned uphill and the little village was lost behind us.

We went maybe another mile before reaching a clearing on the side of the road barely wide enough to squeeze the car through. A trapezoid of cut wood was stacked in front of a cabin coated in weathered red paint. It was dark back here. Tall, thin trees crowded the house, leaning towards it as though conspiring. The windows were screened over and coated in small branches and spiderwebs.

Al continued past the house and parked on the far side, hiding the car from the road. The car gave a tired cough and quit as soon as Al cut the engine. Old man was as exhausted as me.

We listened to the ticking engine and cry of outraged insects. "You lied about the view," I said.

Al peered through the windows. "How's that?"

I pointed at the web-strewn window screens backing the house. "Spiders."

"Ah, right. Out here we call that mosquito repellent."

"Clever," I said. "I've always called that necrosis."

"Leave them alone and they'll leave you alone. Just remember, you'll be sharing the bed."

I shuddered despite the damp heat turning the car into a sauna. My forehead felt like an oil slick, and a little pool had formed in my clavicle. "Where's the bellhop?" I said.

"I'll show you." Al reached over and pulled down my sun visor. All I could see in the narrow mirror on the backside were my bruised and bloodshot eyes. "You're looking at him," Al said.

God help me, then. A futile prayer, for the land out here is Godless.

I opened the door and cringed against the heat as I exited the car. Dank and gooey with a scent like the inside of a barn. A lumbering fly landed on my neck and buzzed away. Drunk after tasting my sweat. Al popped the trunk and I retrieved my travel bag. Looked down and saw at least four mosquitos sucking my blood. Ticks were probably scaling my shoelaces, looking for a tender place to clamp on. I shook my legs while turning in a circle. The cabin was sturdier than Al had described, which didn't surprise me. The roof was in good condition, with a small gabled uprising that I assumed was a loft. There was a large propane tank on this side, which was clean and appeared well maintained. The woods surrounding the lot were dense with a gentle downhill slope that became steeper about ten yards past the property line. A good defensive position, I thought. Which I hoped would not come into play. Quiet, aside for the constant background chatter of bugs.

"Yeah?" Al said, stepping beside me.

"Sure," I said. "I mean, thanks." We met eyes for a brief instant and Al clapped me on my back.

He led me around. Four slate rocks formed a walkway to the front porch. He lifted the second one closest to the house. Dug in the dirt until he found a key, then spit-shined it with his thumb. Two rocking chairs were to the right of the door on a small wood plank porch. An ashtray on the railing held a cigar butt. Al doesn't smoke cigars. A placard above the door showed the street address, 15, which seemed unnecessary. It's not like the post office delivered out here. Al inserted the key and it turned easily. The door was stuck, but opened with a crack after a couple of shoves. A musty scent wafted out, but at least I didn't smell puke. I slapped at a mosquito buzzing my ear and stepped inside.

"What's that town we passed on the way up here?" I asked as I surveyed the interior. A small sitting room with furniture straight out of an LL Bean catalogue. Wood frames and rustic fabrics featuring bears and trout. No TV, but bookshelves along the walls. A small kitchenette with a fridge, a stove, and a four-top poker table to dine on. A spiral staircase led to a small open loft. I could handle a couple of days here, no problem. More than that, though, and this place would start to close in.

"Mostly abandoned," Al said, referring to the village I'd inquired about. "Couple of folks keep a place there, I think. Depot's shut down, though. Truth is, I haven't explored it much. You hear gunshots sometimes during deer season."

"You got any guns here?"

Al shook his head. "This is rehab, remember. Firearms and detox don't mix."

He had a point. "Can you get me one? You know, just in case."

Al closed the door, cutting off the sound of insects, and locked it. "You plan on shooting someone?"

I thought of the man I may have strangled. "I plan on defending myself."

He walked to the kitchen and I followed. "Let's just sit tight for a day or so before we worry about arming ourselves, all right? Hold a hammer, you find a nail. Guns wind up going off, and I don't think we want to make things worse."

I squeezed by Al and opened the fridge. Was relieved to feel cold air. A half-full litre of Coke Zero was standing next to a box of baking soda. I opened the freezer and saw a collapsed carton of ice-cream sandwiches encased in frosted ice.

"I'll make a run into town and get us stocked up. Want anything in particular?"

A bottle of Jameson would hit the spot. "Just, whatever," I said. I wasn't interested in living as some survivalist out in the woods. I wanted my family back. My self-respect. "Stuff for sandwiches and stuff. Some coffee would be nice."

"Got plenty of that," he said, opening a cupboard to reveal cereal boxes, Teddy Grahams, and a large container of Folgers coffee. I grabbed the box of Teddy Grahams and started eating. They were stale, and the honey flavour had dissolved, but it was better than nothing.

"Stove works," Al said, igniting the gas flame to prove it. "Water." He lifted the faucet handle and it shuddered for a few seconds before pouring brown water that eventually cleared. "Let that run for a little bit," he said.

"I'm boiling that shit."

He smiled. "Shower has hot water. Just keep it short. No disposal. No dishwasher. Watch what you flush."

"Dude, I'm not moving in."

"Just saying. Takes a while to get a plumber out this way, you know."

I popped another Teddy Graham, saw a framed letter by the door leading to the bathroom and went for a closer look. "How come you never told me about this place?" I said, starting to read the scripted verse.

Normal Day....
Let me be aware of the treasure you are.
Let me learn from you, savour you,
bless you before you depart.

"Place is private, man," Al said. "Reserved for people who need a private place to go."

Let me hold you while I may,
for it will not always be so.
One day, my nails shall dig into the earth,
or bury into the pillow,
or I shall stretch myself taut
or raise my hands to the sky...
and want more than
all the world
your return.

"Some deep shit, there, Al."

"Mantra of sobriety," Al said.

I turned. Al was in the kitchenette, the water running behind him. Tan, weathered face, greying hair, sturdy frame. A man who had survived hell but still fought the devil every day. "What the fuck am I going to do?" I asked him.

He came towards me, opened his arms. We embraced. This man, like a father to me. He pressed his grizzled cheek against mine, hugged me so tight it was hard to breathe. Tears stung my eyes and I gulped saliva that had thickened.

"You're going to kick ass, man. Like you always do. And I'm going to be here to help you."

I squeezed so hard I could have cracked a rib. Al always knew exactly what to say. And always followed through on his word.

"Okay," I said.

He released me and there was none of that awkwardness that often comes after two men show honest affection. His eyes were steady on mine, and they gave me strength. Confidence that I lacked.

"We fall down, we get back up," he said.

I nodded. "Yep, okay." Like it was decided.

"Unpack, or whatever. Settle in. I'll run back down to the store and stock up. Be back in an hour or so."

"Got a resort guide here? List of amenities?"

"Yep, it's real short. There's reading, and there's thinking."

He twirled his keys as he walked towards the door.

"I appreciate this, Al," I said.

He paused at the door. "I know," he said, then left and closed it behind him.

I stood there and listened to the engine start and the crunch of tyres as he drove away. Thinking about the letter on the wall, and all the normal days I'd taken for granted.

I haven't seen Al since.

And the son-of-a-bitch took my knife.

✝

Alone, again. Out in some place in the middle of the fucking woods. An isolated lodge made to rehabilitate train wrecks like me. Get us back up and running. Back on the rails.

The cabin had electricity, but no phone. Not that I was ready to give Cassie a call. I figured Al would let her know I had made it home safely and that he was helping me get straightened out.

I dropped my travel bag on the couch and browsed the bookshelves. There wasn't much that I recognised. No Tom Robbins, Tim Dorsey, John D. Macdonald, Carl Hiaasen, Harry Crews. Hell, not even Stephen King. Most of the spines looked old and academic. A couple by Crowley. Shit that I was into when I was in my early twenties, trying to appear dark and complex. Books on sobriety, philosophy, New Age spirituality, which Cassie would have loved, Goetia something. I saw one sticking out an inch from the rest, a book with a Russian title, *Мáстер и Маcaрúта*, and discovered loose pages tucked inside. Flipped through them and saw that it was a journal of some kind, handwritten in blue ink. Recently, it seemed.

I put the book back on the shelf and carried the loose pages to the couch. I set the box of Teddy Grahams between my legs and ate stale crackers while reading the following account. My mouth becoming increasingly dry as the story evolved.

★   ★   ★

April 22

I used to keep a diary when I was younger. Around the time I began to fancy boys, if memory serves. My entries were not so much chronicles on my daily activities as they were love poems. Exaltations from my eleven-year-old heart on what it meant to long for another. Some snotty-nose prat, most like, who had pulled my hair on the playground, or bruised my shin. Remember that? Courtship as a child was like warfare. Survive the pinches and name calling, the hair pulling and gossip, and you became a couple. For a few weeks, yeah? Then it got too scary for the boy, or too boring for the girl, and one or the other would break it off. Go back to being sworn enemies.

But how the heart would buzz for those few weeks. The head swoon. A dizzying rush of unbridled emotion, like a drowning, it was. The centre of the world. The star in one's own love story. At least that's how it felt to me. And I wrote it all down in this little book with a simple, unnecessary lock, for I had no one to protect it from. No one who would have cared to read it. And I'd smear the pages with perfume I pinched from my mum. Some dusty glass bottle meant to look like crystal, but cast in a plastic factory and kept on her dresser as ornamentation. A show of sophistication that produced the opposite effect. Poor Mum.

Scribbling words in the flowery cursive I've since abandoned, like giddy and throbbing and gushing and forever. Sealed with cheap factory perfume. An eleven-year-old's ode to love.

Ha! I'd love to read that now, I would. I mourn that little girl. Dead and gone and buried in the largely forgotten past. Ever lie in bed at night and think back upon a childhood memory and it's like you return to that place in time? And it's sweet for a moment. Because you remember you were once sweet and innocent. And then you realise you have entered the body of a ghost. A version of you that no longer exists and never will again. And you wonder if you got from that precious time what you were meant to. Or if you took for granted that things would always be that way. And then the pain of nostalgia hits your heart so hard it's like you wish you didn't remember it at all.

Life is a bit like that. So sweet until you remember you only have a little bit of time and then it's like you wish you'd never been born so you wouldn't have to die.

Here I am, then. Starting another diary, it seems. Many years later (I won't say how many). The clock ticking. Nearing its end, in fact, I think.

Lost in love like warfare. In the most unlikely of places. The only thing missing is my mum's perfume.

★   ★   ★

April 23

I don't know to whom I'm writing this. If, indeed, anybody. Who is my audience, here? Me, I suppose. Or the eleven-year-old me still inside somewhere. Not lost, not dead. Right here with me now.

It's been nearly ten days since I've been out here. Left here, I mean. Whether Tracey was taken or part of this whole sordid affair from the start I don't rightly know. "Back in an hour," she says. And at the time I believed her. Settled right in, I did. Got good and cosy. No clocks here so I couldn't tell when an hour had passed. Or two. I became worried when my hunger became more than just a tingle in my stomach. Didn't really want to eat the stale crackers in that dusty cupboard. We had a whole menu planned. It was all that was keeping my spirits up after all that has happened. Still happening, I guess. So much for books being good for your mind, and all! Load of rubbish, that. Not that I wasn't warned.

So, no. I haven't had my Caprese salad. Haven't had my linguine and prawns. The chilled bottles of Pinot Grigio. Not even my Dulce de Leche ice cream or fried tater tots (Mmmmm!) Not that the nearest Piggly Wiggly was apt to carry such things, but we would have made do. Tracey knows her way around a kitchen. She once dated a sous chef at a fancy French bistro who gave her chlamydia, but also taught her how to make a fantastic roux. Ha! Tracey, my love. I hope you're somewhere safe tonight, far away from here.

My safety is in question, that much is for sure. Those animals are out there. I can't bring myself to call them men. Even if that's what they look like. Professor O's feral minions. Those soulless beasts. Stalking the perimeter of the cabin. Peering in through the windows. Keeping watch, I suppose. If they even comprehend their purpose, which I'm not convinced they do. Not all of them, anyway.

There's one, though, that seems different. And believe you me I'm being cautious here. Keeping my scepticism high. Mr. O is nothing if not clever, I'll give him that. Psychopathic, sure. But brilliant, too.

I caught him lingering at the window. The different one. Scared the bejeesus out of me. It was dusk, and the bathroom window is on the south-eastern side. I couldn't see him with the lights on; could only see my reflection in the windowpane as I stepped out from the shower. And I probably wouldn't have seen him at all had he not placed his hand on the glass, making a knocking sound. Not aggressive or anything. Gentle in fact. But it startled me, and I shut off the lights to kill the reflection and there he was standing right outside in the shadows.

There's the two types. The clone ones like a large pack of identical twins. And then the wild ones, as though raised by wolves, or worse. This was one of the wild ones. But less so than others I've seen. His long hair was fairly neat and pulled back over a shoulder, not strewn with sticks and leaves. He was upright, not all hunched over. Not as skittish, or senselessly aggressive. A look of curiosity in his eyes. Maybe even wonder at seeing me naked like that, his hand on the glass as though seeking contact, not shying from it or trying to scare it away.

Frozen like a statue, I was, naked or not. And so we stood there like that for a good thirty seconds, just staring at one another. His hand held out towards me. My heart pounding against my chest. Nearly hyperventilating I was so afraid.

He turned a second before I heard the crack of a branch from a fair distance away. He began to growl, then. Not at me, but at whatever else was out there. A growl unlike any I've ever heard. Like a tractor engine or something. A big diesel truck. He puffed his chest out and extended his arms, his back turned towards me now. I heard a halting step out in the brush, then a second growl from out that way. But more timid, like. Then he walked away from the window towards whatever was out in the woods.

All the others I had seen outside the cabin had felt predatory. This one, though, even in that one brief encounter, had felt protective towards me. Displaying a more human-like intelligence than I had seen before. Curiosity, if nothing else. But I thought it was more than that. Call it vanity, but it had felt like attraction. Bloody hell if that he-beast didn't fancy me!

I can't say that

*　　*　　*

April 24

My poor hand keeps cramping. I'm not used to writing longhand like this. Good thing they spared my good hand. Left hand is squashed right up. Oh how it hurts. So much of me hurts and has yet to heal. I do wonder how much pain I have left to endure. I'd rather just end it, yeah? And might yet.

Whether or not I do depends on my would-be rescuer. My last chance out of here, I think.

I slept little that night I first encountered the man at the window. There are no blinds here, so I feel exposed. Like a hamster in a cage. On exhibit, or something. I heard people, animals, whatever all is out there doing their nightly patrol. The crack of branches, footsteps through leaves, the occasional growl or lonesome howl. I tried reading a book, but Lord what frightening literature they keep out here. I'm done reading, I'll tell you that. Were I to live another hundred years I'd never touch another book. I'll watch reruns of Downton Abbey till I die, if I must. Ha!

It had been a week at this point. I'd resorted to eating the dreadful mush in the cupboards by then. Like chewing dust, that was. Whose idea was it to make crackers in the shape of adorable teddy bears, anyway? Like I find that appetising, chomping off the head of a teddy bear?

And the boredom had become excruciating. Alternating between boredom and paralysing fear. Enough to make me want to play with that Ouija board stashed in the trunk just for the diversion, but I think that's better left alone. My mind hasn't felt right since that bit of voodoo they put on me. Thoughts rise that don't feel like my own. Seeing things, like those words in the mirror that make my mind go blank. Like clearing a flat for someone new to move in is how it feels. The confusion is terrible. All of it is, really. A waking nightmare.

Why me, is the question, isn't it? I'm nobody, really. Live alone. Keep to myself. Don't bother anybody. And I'm content with that, yeah? I mean, not always. But who is content all the time, anyways? Regrets, sure. We all have those, yeah? I would like to have loved more. Barry was the one great love, and it wasn't much at that. Hot at first, but lukewarm before we could ring the wedding bells. Cool by the time I broke it off, downright frigid afterwards. They said I was family, that they'd love me forever and always. Then I'm a tramp and a tease and all the other things they said about me all because of feelings outside my control. Like they wanted Barry to live his whole life with someone who no longer loved him. Or couldn't abide with someone not loving him as much as they felt he deserved. Prats.

There are billions of people in this world, you'd think there'd be just one for me. If so, we never met. Place I work, everyone keeps to their cubicles like ostriches with their heads buried in sand. Life seems so exciting on the telly, but it's dreadfully boring in reality. That boring life seems pretty good now, yeah?

I saw him again that next day. The one with the groomed hair and intelligent eyes who had come up and touched the window. Scared off whatever had been advancing from the woods. He was standing at the edge of the clearing, staring in through the kitchen window, watching me ruffle through the cupboards as though hoping to find something I know is not there. With that shaggy beard it's hard to guess his age, but he's a young man for sure. Early twenties, I'd guess, but maybe even more like nineteen. His body is like what you see in a textbook on anatomy. Honed muscles all perfectly proportional and aligned. He wears cloth pants with a drawstring and that's all. He's handsome, I'll admit, in a savage, primal sort of way. Like a cave man, yeah? But there's a tenderness there that I thought I might have been projecting but now know I'm not.

A stage of evolution that dear Doctor O hadn't prepared for, or part of his plan, I don't know.

I watched him watching me. He seemed frightened at first. HIM frightened by ME! Cowering behind a tree for a bit. Then he came around. We stood there, him about five metres from the window. And I don't know why I did it, or where the courage or stupidity came from, I think I was just numb by that point, but I put my hand on the glass like he'd done the night before. Pressed it so that my palm turned white and a little fog formed around my fingers. I felt a feverish sort of desperation. My heart rose into my throat and I began to cry. Thought I was all cried out, but I guess you never are. I wanted contact so badly. His expression changed as he watched my display. His eyes softened and his shoulders slumped as he took a step towards me, an arm reaching out. He could see my pain and it touched him, I think. There was no way he was putting on an act, for he's not that sophisticated. I began sobbing then, and I placed my other hand on the window, the mangled one. Bracing as my broken bones burned like fire. Reaching towards him as he reached towards me.

Another few steps and he'd closed the distance by half and was still coming. To do what, I had no idea and didn't care. Then I heard and saw a crashing in the woods behind him. He turned as a couple of the wilder ones came through, hopping with their arms out wide like chimps do when playing or about to fight. My protector, as I think of him now, unleashed that growl of his again. Like a throttling engine, puffing his chest and holding his arms out wide. And they had a little standoff, like. Seeing which would back down first, but none of them would. The two wilder ones, hair like a bramble on their heads, naked except for a little thong over their genitals that seemed more for protection than modesty, advanced. So did my protector. And then they clashed in a ferocious battle, a noise like you hear when a pack of dogs engage in a real fight, not a pretend one. A fight for death or survival.

It was two against one, and the other two looked bulkier and more animal-like in the way they were hunched over with hands curled in like apes. But then I saw my protector pull a stick or something from a pocket in his pants and begin hitting them with it. And the two wild ones yelped in pain as blood began to spout from injuries and I realised that it wasn't a stick he was holding, but a makeshift knife he'd fashioned from wood and stone. And he kept swinging it and poking them with it, stabbing and slicing them open, that guttural roar eclipsing all sound until the two finally turned and scrambled away, staggering back through the woods, defeated.

He turned back towards me, but I was so frightened by what I had just witnessed that I cowered away from the window. And I could see the hurt and confusion in my protector's eyes as I backed away, but I couldn't help it. The walls were closing in on this little cabin isolated from all the world and surrounded by things that would do me harm as they'd done already. And I just wanted to be left alone, for the rest of my life if they'd leave me to it. But that's not how this game is played, yeah? I don't know what the end game is, but I know there is one. I just want some control over the outcome.

All the rest of that day I spent in hiding, huddled under a blanket that I spread out from the couch to the coffee table like a kiddie-fort. My stomach grumbling from hunger. Thinking, quite earnestly now, about taking the ending into my own hands. My options are quite limited, though, I'm afraid. There are no knives here, which shouldn't come as much surprise. Wouldn't do to give me a weapon now, would it? No bath, so drowning's out. Oh, but the thought of that gives me shivers. So desperate to die that I drown myself. Is that even possible? Hanging's the only way I can figure. Tie one end to a closet rod and the other to my neck and sag into it until the world fades to black. Dreary, dreary thoughts. But they come as a kind of relief, too. A way to escape this constant pain and suffering. My loveless life that I took for granted until it was too late.

But there's hope now, yeah? Faint and stranger than a flying turtle, but there all the same. I'll tell about it once my hand stops cramping. If I'm still here, that is.

★   ★   ★

April 24, cont.

Not much time left. I'll be leaving soon, tomorrow if all goes to plan. Dare I believe this is my plan, and not one concocted by clever Professor O? So I have to write this down even if my one good hand feels like it's turning to stone.

That day I spent huddled under the canopy of my fort, growing hungrier while thinking my dreadful thoughts. I heard footsteps later in the afternoon, coming closer to the cabin than they typically *would. Then I heard footsteps approaching the door right next to where I was hiding in my fort. I heard a kind of chuffing, snuffling sound, beast-like on the front landing. Then a violent banging on the door followed by the sound of footsteps running away.*

My heart was up in my throat. Forget the bloody noose, I was going to die of fright right then and there. I tucked myself into a little ball like one of those roly-poly bugs while listening to the footsteps fall out of range. Eventually I uncurled and waited to see if my heart would settle down or seize right up. My head was tingling from holding my breath for who knows how long. And my vision was blurry. So maybe it was the lack of blood and oxygen in my brain that drove me out from my hiding spot towards the door and commanded my hand to turn the knob. Of all the things I thought I might see on the front doorstep, the skinned and fire-roasted rabbit was furthest from my mind. The fragrant aroma rising up from the steaming rabbit caught me by surprise and caused my stomach to grumble. This cooked meal left here by my protector, I presumed. I hardly remember retrieving the plate and scooping the rabbit onto it. I was drooling, if you can believe it! Feeling like one of those blasted castaways on that silly Survivor show. And it's with more than a little shame that I'll admit ripping into that succulent flesh with my bare hands, gnawing on ligaments and bone much like the beast that cooked it for me undoubtedly would.

It was among the most delicious meals I have ever eaten, and that's the plain truth. Partly, I think, because I was so hungry. But also because of the odd circumstances in which it was served. The intensity of the situation I find myself in. All of my senses on high alert. Fighting for my very survival. Being protected, if not courted (lord, what a curious existence!) by a feral man who fancies me. Showing more valour in his defence of me in this isolated cabin than any other man ever has. Preparing a cooked meal that he hunted and killed on his own. Show me a man like that in the city who doesn't expect a proper shag in return. Ha!

It still worried me that this unlikely interaction was being orchestrated by the psychopath behind this whole mad experiment. Still worries me, in fact. But the time has come to take action, and that's what I plan to do, for better or worse. That's all we can do, yeah? Keep moving forward and pray for the best.

I'm not sure how much of the next part to share, assuming anyone will find and read this. These are the juicy bits my eleven-year-old self never got to write into her diary dotted with Mum's perfume. Not that the adult me has all that many entries to offer, either, truth be told. I can't say my exploits with Barry would have done much to make Aphrodite blush. And romance seemed much like a wasted pursuit after those flames of passion fizzled out. Like an illusion, really. People confuse love with the biological need to make babies, then become stuck with someone they hardly like once the hormonal fog has cleared.

I took a cool shower after finishing that scrumptious meal. No perfume here, but there's a body powder with a pretty smell I put to good use. Donned my terrycloth robe – lord, how my mum would kill me! – and carried the plate of rabbit scraps out onto the front porch. I set the plate on the railing and sat myself on the front steps, keeping my legs open just a bit, yeah? Enough to where I could feel the spring breeze against my bare skin that was still damp from the shower. And I became wet between the legs, too. Scared, yeah, but excited by the sensuality of my intended provocation. More than anything, I needed a protector, and now had one, and intended to lure him in. Not much for me to lose, yeah? Except my life, which I've about given up on anyway. Once you've accepted the noose, not much else matters. Might as well go out in a way that would make my inner child proud.

The others came first, and that was something I hadn't planned for. Two of them, young ones, though it's hard to tell with how filthy they are, but I'd say early teens. Crouched by the ground, peering between a thicket of leaves. Grunting and breathing heavily. Mewling almost. Oh God, Tracey, I'd been flashing a couple of wild boys, what has become of my life? Ha! And then one of them breaks through the brush and comes towards me. The other quickly following behind. Eyes like dinner plates. Twin peckers poking out like dowsing rods leading the way to....

I clamped my legs tight and closed the robe. I didn't think I could make it back inside before they were upon me. This was not the seduction my irrational mind had envisioned while showering in the afterglow of that glorious meal. Instead of luring that handsome, half-man back into the cabin with promises of romance, I was to be raped out in the woods by a couple of prepubescent cave boys.

Perhaps fearing he would lose out on the conquest, the boy in back raced forward, passing the one in the lead. Then they were both scrambling towards me, running on all fours like chimps. I stood and turned back to the cabin, but only made it a step before one of them clutched the collar of my robe from behind and yanked backwards. The strain pulled my belt lose and I felt the robe sliding free from my body. The boy stumbled back with the robe in his hand, leaving me naked as a sunflower on the front landing. Then the other boy was upon me, grabbing me in a bear hug, grunting with his face against my shoulder, his pecker grinding against my thigh, smelling worse than week-old garbage.

He lifted me and carried me down the steps away from the cabin as though I didn't weigh a thing. Then his companion came and began grabbing at me, too. And they started snarling at each other, gnashing teeth. And there I was, caught in the middle. Bicycling my feet in the air like I thought that could get me somewhere. Screaming myself now, and it was the first time I'd heard my voice in over a week and it was terrifying to hear. A hoarse roar of raw panic, as beastly as the feral boys. My eyes closed so it's just dark jostling and war cries and the musk of pending sex taken by force. This looks like the end of things – I'll make sure it is – and here I'm destined to leave this earth more frightened and confused than I entered it.

There was such a ruckus I hardly registered the first blow. Next thing I knew the boy carrying me had let go and when I looked down he was folded back on himself with half his head caved in from where my protector had bludgeoned him. The other boy began flailing his arms, piss spraying from his shrinking pecker as my protector – my saviour – advanced, swinging his club. The first blow hit the boy on one of his flailing forearms and I heard it break like a tree branch. You could see it bend in the middle with the hand-end dangling and that arm was useless to him now. He screamed in pain and fell to the ground and rolled himself into a *ball. My protector stepped forward, raising his club in the air. And I closed my eyes against the pending violence — I'd seen too much already. But it never came. Instead, my protector kicked the boy in the backside and half-said, half-grunted, "Go!" The boy was up and running for the woods as fast as an Olympic sprinter, I can tell you that.*

Sorry, but my hand is cramping.... I must rest. Hopefully I'll have time to finish.

★   ★   ★

Cont.

Argh! My hand is so tight and sore from writing, but I want to get this down before I go. I'll do my best.

My protector had saved me from the two attackers, killing one and sparing the other. "Go, go," he grunted, watching the woods and guarding my back as he pushed me towards the cabin. We got to the open door and he turned at the threshold to guard me as I shut myself inside. Without thinking — I'd have done none of this had I been using my head — I grabbed his arm and tried to pull him in. Even using both hands and pulling with all my strength, I couldn't budge him. He turned and saw what I intended. "Please!" I said, pulling on this statue of a man. "Please, come!" And then he did, coming inside with a shocked and confused look in his eyes. I shut the door behind him and locked it, put my back against it and tried to slow my runaway breath.

My protector took one look at my naked body heaving breathlessly against the doorframe and averted his eyes. He balled up the blanket I'd been using as the canopy for my fort and handed it to me with his head turned. Chivalry may be dead in the metros, but it's alive and well in modern cavemen! I wrapped the blanket around me like a toga. Feeling a bit like Aphrodite now, yeah? Perhaps that's who's been borrowing my mind these last several days. If so, I'll give her something to blush about, yet.

He's still holding the club. Blood and strands of hair cling to the edge. I'm looking at him in profile and he's like a picture from a history book. Block face hidden behind a rangy beard. Roman nose. Long, thick luxurious hair any woman would die for flowing down and spilling over his shoulders. Maybe I'm sprucing it up some, yeah, but not much.

All thoughts of using him as some pack animal vanish as I see the gentle sensitivity behind his fearsome and brutish face. He looks at me now, and I've never felt so lovely in all my life. I'm like a goddess to him, some divine being. And I know this because he begins shaking from head to toe as though standing in a freezing rain. I come towards him, his earthy smell fills the room like flood water, and notice the pale and shiny scars that appear latched to his arms and upper body like skin-tone leaches. His face is older than his eyes. Aged by the sun and stress of living outdoors. And I know he's never felt the gentle caress of a woman. At least, not one like me.

I take the club from his hand and set it down. He's taller than me by a foot, shoulders wider by half. Chest matted in wet curls of black. I place my hands on his hips and run them up the length of his slick torso, and he shudders beneath my touch. He's watching me, but won't meet my eyes at first, until I force him to, and then he won't look anywhere else. A charge has formed between our two bodies, a tractor beam drawing us close. We embrace, his body carved from stone, and I whisper into his ears as I let my toga fall to a puddle at my feet, "My protector."

"Mother," he breathes into my hair, the only word he knows for woman. Not maternal, though. More like Mother Earth.

"Yes," I say, guiding his hands across my body. My neck, my breasts, slick now with his sweat and mine, my stomach, the crease between my legs. Here he shudders again, and so do I. And then I pull him with me onto the couch, move his granite body between my open legs. Push his cloth trousers down with my feet and feel the throbbing hardness extending out, directing it towards my opening. I come within moments of him entering me – Oh God, I can't believe I'm writing this – and then so does he, arching and gasping as though fighting for air. And then he collapses on top of me and I wrap him up with my arms and legs, holding him close and keeping him inside.

"Mother," he says.

"*Yes.*"

He is less shy afterwards. I cling to him like a concubine. Like a meek woman he's clubbed and dragged back to his cave. Though it's the other way around, more like, yeah? I am his, entirely. My life literally in his hands. And he knows this. Oh if Barry could see me now! Or his mum, my God! That two-faced twat.

We use a kind of sign language to talk. I point to myself and then point outside. "Go far," I say.

He nods. "Me," he says, and holds the club to his chest.

"My protector, yes."

He left to gather supplies, and I clung to him desperately and cried, begging him not to leave without me. Fearful he'd get hurt and I'd be left alone out here all over again. I began this journal to occupy my mind, but then, thank God, he did come back, and now we must go. To where, I don't know and hardly care.

The thing about that book is that it doesn't end. The story begins when you set it down, I think. And now I'm the heroine in some unlikely love story with a plot I can't follow. My destiny unknown.

Once again swept up in a dangerous, warlike love here at what may be the end of my life, or perhaps a new beginning.

I've seen death and rejected it. I choose life, and whatever it may bring.

And now I'm no longer afraid.

Love to whomever is reading this. May you find a protector to lead you back home.

xoxo,

Priscilla Y.

P.S. Tracey, you owe me a fancy meal if I ever see you again, my love!

★   ★   ★

Were I to try to swallow the coagulated paste in my mouth, I'd have choked. I stood from the couch and stared at its stained cushions as though they were contaminated. The same spot those two unlikely lovers had first fucked. Arsenic could have been flowing from the water tap and it wouldn't have mattered. I had to lube the pipes in order to breathe. Christ, what had I got myself mixed up in?

Here was when I began to worry Al wasn't going to return. Same as that chick's friend Tracey from the journal. Whether it's real or not, I don't know. But I assume it is. The fucking cabin is being patrolled, that's for sure. Those feral fuckwads out there looking in. So what, am I going to have to mate with some half-human she-mutt to escape this place? Priscilla was right about one thing, the plot in my personal story had thickened. I don't think mine's a love story, though.

By nightfall I'd come to terms with the fact that Al wasn't returning and I was out here on my own. I'd woken up on the mountain road leading up here, so had no idea how long it was or how far away from civilisation. Surrounded by woods of unknown depths that are filled with Professor O's feral goons. They started patrolling as soon as the sun went down. I heard branches cracking just past the perimeter of the clearing surrounding the house. Peered through the kitchen window, and didn't see anything at first. Stood there and let my eyes lose focus like I was looking at one of those hidden-image pictures or trying to find Waldo or something. And then I saw them. Shadowed outlines crouched low to the ground, blending into the brush. Watching me.

That bullshit was not going to fly. Some Peeping Tom may have saved Priscilla, but I wasn't about to strut around naked like some fucking live sex stream for these creeps outside. The bathroom has two large towels that I used to cover a couple of the windows. Tore one of the bedsheets apart to create blinds for the others. Made the place dark and even more claustrophobic, but at least I have my privacy and can move around without being monitored. Assuming the place isn't wired for surveillance, which it must be. Fucking Purge Palace my ass. How the hell did they get Al to set me up like this? The only thing I can think of is that website from the card in my pocket. Those images flashing across his face. Who knows what he was subjected to, either directly or subliminally. More likely, though, they got to him earlier and threatened him in some way. It *had* to have been some dire shit, that's for sure. Or hell, maybe they convinced him this was some elaborate role-playing game I had signed up for and he was doing me a favour. Priscilla was right about another thing: Professor O is one clever fuck.

I spent that first night tearing the place apart. Looking for surveillance equipment, supplies, or anything else useful I could find. Aside from the creepy books and stale crackers in the cupboard, there wasn't much out there. Found the Ouija board Priscilla had referenced in her journal in a trunk by the front door. That and the board game LIFE, which seems like some inside joke. Hardy har, Professor O! What a card you are.

There's a double edge to having the windows covered. It makes the night sounds that much more ominous. Especially when you know you're not imagining the things you hear. The cracking branches and crunching leaves really are the footsteps of strange men stalking the perimeter. It frustrated them, too, I think, not being able to see me. Probably short-circuited some directive hardwired into their DNA. I could hear them grumbling on the edge of the forest. Grunting in some brutish tongue. It wasn't long before they began to approach the house. A couple of the bolder ones even banged on the windows, almost hard enough to break them. Maybe my blinds weren't the best idea after all, but at least it gave me some control, and I'll take all I can get.

The stress of fear and anxiety, the lack of sleep, the lingering hangover, it was all too much for my body to take. Falling asleep felt suicidal, but I had little choice. I could have mainlined the whole container of coffee grounds and would still have conked out. It was a deep sleep, too. No dreams, at least that I remember. The blank slate before birth. The empty void I hope follows death, though now am not so sure.

I felt a bit rejuvenated that next morning. Sore from my drunken exploits, but clearer in the head and not as sick to my stomach. A mellow haze was filtering through the sheets covering the windows. Birds chirped outside. I heard branches cracking, but from smaller beasts. Squirrels and chipmunks and rabbits, foraging for breakfast. It was almost pleasant, actually. I thought about that fire-roasted rabbit Priscilla's protector had cooked, and it got my saliva working. I doubted I'd be doing much hunting, though. No weapons with which to kill.

I brewed some coffee and munched on stale crackers. Breakfast of Prisoners. Started a shower, getting the tea-colour water scalding hot. Scrubbed my skin until the water turned cold. Then I stood under the cold stream for a while, too. I had repurposed the two towels as window blinds, so I had to air dry. I stepped out of the shower and froze when I saw what was on the mirror. Greek letters or runes or some shit scrawled in the fog. Water streaks in the lettering as though someone had recently used a finger to draw them.

$$ \text{ᚠᛒᚼᛁᛥᛘᚠ} $$

This must be the writing in the mirror Priscilla had mentioned in her journal. I stood quietly, listening for the sound of movement within the cabin. Staring at those runes in the steam. Whether from fright or stress or the words themselves, I began to hear a voice whispering inside my head. A seductive male voice. Soothing with a slithering lisp. So soft I had to strain to hear it, using a language I couldn't understand.

You are the carrier. The vessel. Through you we speak to the world. Spreading our message. Entering the mind of all with ears to hear and eyes to see. You have a space inside for us to fill. Through these acts it has opened. The time for us to enter has come.

The voice grew louder the longer I looked, and I felt myself falling back into that trance-like state. I rushed forward and cleared the mirror with my hand, muting the voice like a radio signal going out of range. Something about mirrors. Mirrors had been used to activate the clones in Professor O's early studies.

Mirrors in almost every room, beware of them. Well, that decided my next move. I grabbed the towel from the bathroom window, thank God there wasn't some cave dude on the other side staring in, and wrapped it around my elbow. After a few deep preparatory breaths, I smashed the mirror to pieces. Collected the shards and threw them in the trash. I can still see the image I saw reflected back in that mirror as I prepared to strike it. Grey whiskers filling in the beard around my goatee. Wide eyes more scared than angry. Puffy cheeks with purple bruising that would soon turn yellow and green. Age that I hadn't noticed before. Weakness. Lack of conviction. Cowardice.

I trembled from that brief act of violence. My elbow hurt. You think you're the same testosterone-fueled maniac you were as an early man until you experience the fear of failing muscles. The atrophy spiral towards death. Nature abhors weakness, and here I am out in the wild. How the hell am I supposed to save myself, much less win back my wife and son?

By becoming the man capable of doing it, is how. Pretend like I'm in some ill-conceived movie where a hero is needed and fulfil that role. What would Batman do? Maybe that should be my new mantra whenever faced with one of this maniac's twisted tricks. Trouble is, Batman has a billion-dollar utility belt and washboard abs, and all's I've got is a saggy gut and an aching back.

I spent that day reading back through Priscilla's journal, looking, perhaps, for connective threads. There was some comfort in knowing another person had been out here, alone, under the same circumstances. And she had prevailed, presumably. She had at least gone out swinging. Or fucking, rather. Either way, she'd gone out on a high.

Got me thinking about Malia. Had she been my protector as she claimed or just another bit actor in this...what? Game? Experiment? Punishment?

Would she be coming here to rescue me, or lead me to my next temptation? My redeemer or destroyer? Here, I'm assigning external blame for my fate as though I don't control my own thoughts and actions. It's time to stop looking for someone to save me; I'll save my goddamn self.

As though conjured, I heard a woman's voice. High-pitched and hysterical. Sobbing and pleading and screaming for me. Too distant to tell if it was Malia or not, but coming closer. Someone on a death march, by the sound of it. The long walk to the gallows.

"Jesse!"

My heart seized when I heard that cry. My breath evaporated. People in passionate relationships know what it sounds like to hear their lover scream their name. That was Cassie out there.

"Jesse!"

I scrambled towards the front door, threw it open without considering the likelihood of this being a trap. A trick to get eyes on me since I'd barricaded myself inside. It was dusk and the shadows were thick under the canopy of trees. Hulking shapes shifted near the tree line. I heard the excited rasp of feral boys. The alien light from a firefly shined a flash bulb on a bushy face and blinked out. Footsteps came crashing through the brush. Cassie screaming my name, "Jesse!"

"Here!" I shouted, eliciting a hoarse murmur among our feral audience. I reached inside and flipped on the porch light, sending those closest to the perimeter shuffling back into the receding shadows. The forest was rich with the blinking lights of fireflies flashing on the faces of the men hidden in the trees. The night loud with insect chatter. A whole ceremony out here beyond my understanding. The boys or men or whatever those things were cleared a path for Cassie to stumble through. If I'd had a weapon, maybe I would have run to her. But I was so damn startled and confused I stood frozen in place, still not completely convinced this wasn't some kind of a setup. They had presented a convincing Razz, after all.

She came to the clearing, flinching in fear every time she passed by a feral scout as though expecting one of them to grab her. Then there was nothing between her and the cabin and when she realised this she broke into a frenzied sprint towards the door, unleashing a scream like a runaway train. Eyes wild, mouth stretched in a panicked grimace. My animal wife.

She crashed into me without slowing, knocking us both back through the door. I tripped and fell onto the couch.

"Oh God, close it! God, close it!" she was yelling hysterically, jumping and flailing her arms as though freeing them from spiderwebs. "Oh God. Oh God. Oh God God God."

I had to move around her to get to the door and she grabbed me, holding me in place. Sobbing into my neck, pumelling my arms and back and everything. I could see three loin-cloth-wearing whack jobs sneaking towards the cabin. If Cassie didn't release me in a few seconds, they'd be inside. I flung her onto the couch and raced towards the door. The men outside froze when they saw me approach and actually retreated, which was an encouraging sign. Emboldened, I shouted, "Get the fuck out of here!" Trying to project my voice to the far side of earth. Then I slammed the door and threw the lock. Growling a bit myself, surprised to find my dick getting hard like it would at the apex of a crushing guitar solo. I'll go feral if I have to. Raise the fucking dead.

Cassie was not dressed for a trail hike. Her rayon sundress only came down to mid-thigh, exposing legs – beautiful legs, I must admit, God it was good to see her – that were striped red with scrapes and abrasions. Naked arms smeared in mud with angry welts from insect bites. Dirt tracks lined her flushed and sweaty face. Black hair was tangled and littered with briars and twigs. She had never looked more beautiful to me. I fell to my knees before her.

"Jesus, what the fuck?" I said. A question, I guess, directed towards Christ and his maniac father. Then, "Where's Rox?"

"She has him," she said, still hysterical but trying to calm down. Slow her breathing, slow her racing heart. She lowered her head, shook it. Attempting, it seemed, to bring coherence back to a world that had turned insane. "He's safe for now, I think. They sent me to come get you."

Her hands were on my shoulders, mine on her ribcage. Her sundress was damp with sweat and she smelled like garden soil. A million questions fought for supremacy in my mind, leaving me speechless. Okay, keep it simple. "Where?" I said.

She swallowed heavily, her eyes closed. Almost back to baseline already. "A few miles from here," she said. "Some abandoned town in the woods. I don't know where. I was blindfolded coming out here."

Those fucking monsters. It's not enough to wreck my marriage, they had to terrorise my family, too. "He's safe?"

A shuddering breath exhaled through pursed lips, centring her. She opened her eyes and they were clear and focused. I always knew she was good under pressure, but goddamn. She looked at me now for the first time. Running her fingertips lightly across my face as though reading my bruises in braille. Scanned my body, my arms and legs, checking for injuries or proof that I was real, wincing when her eyes returned to my face. She cupped the back of my neck and pulled me towards her. Our hug was an attempt to merge two bodies into one. It hurt in a vital way that proved we were both together and alive.

After a minute or two we separated. "I don't know," she said. "I think he is, for now. What happened to you?"

"I was taken," I said. "Kidnapped after the show on Saturday night."

She was nodding like this made sense or was somehow expected. What about the pictures, then?

"Taken to some place and...tortured," I said. "Just fucked with like you couldn't believe." I didn't know how much to say or what to describe. "That book I read, I don't know if you remember. Solomon gave it to me. They've been watching us. Wiretapped our house, everything. In the mirrors. Fucking ceiling fans. I have no idea what's going on or why. But they got Al. Everyone, I don't even know who else. They sent you here? Who?"

That Cassie was absorbing this information so calmly was astounding. But, then again, this is the woman who dropped everything to care for our disabled son without skipping a beat. Women are tougher than men, I'll tell you that right now.

"Saturday. Rox had been down for a few hours and I'd just gone to bed myself. I was drifting off when someone started banging on the door. Just after midnight, maybe."

Of course, The Midnight Hour.

"Said it was the police. Asked me to open up, it was an emergency. So I did and there were these two police officers out there. Like, identical twins or something. They told me that you'd been in a bad car accident. They said you'd been critically injured and were in intensive care and that you may not last the night." She started to tear up now, and it felt like someone grabbed hold of my heart and squeezed. "They said that I needed to come right away, that you may not last another hour. They were like rushing me. Rushing me so fast I almost left Rox behind, I was so groggy and just not thinking clearly. They actually had to remind me to go back and get him, and I should have realised something was wrong right then, because how would they know about him? But I was just so upset that I'd almost left him alone and worried about whether I'd get to the hospital in time and what I'd find when I got there."

Clever, clever man, that psychotic doctor or professor or whoever he is.

"They put us in the back of their cruiser. All I put on was this dress that I picked up off the floor. Rox was still in his pyjamas. They looked exactly the same sitting up front and it set off alarms, but I couldn't tell if I was picking up signals or just completely out of my mind. An hour later, though, and I knew something was definitely wrong. It shouldn't have taken half that long to get to the station or hospital or wherever they said we were going while I was only half listening because I was so focused on keeping Rox calm. Then I realised we'd left the city and were virtually alone on some quiet highway heading out here and I started to freak out, but I had to stay calm for Rox. They wouldn't tell me where we were going. What we were doing. Anything about you. Then I realised we were locked in the back of the cruiser with that barrier between the front and back seats and that I'd done something very stupid by getting in that car."

Tears carved tracks through the dirt on her face as she talked, looking down at her hands as though ashamed. I lifted her chin so that she could see me. I needed to see her. "It's not your fault," I said. "You did nothing wrong. These people, it's a whole system. They're smart, fucking crazy smart. They got me, too. Got Caspian. Got Al. Got Solomon. Who knows who else. Thank God you're okay, though. And you say Rox is okay?"

She nodded. "For now. Who are they? What do they want?"

Might as well ask me the meaning of life. "I have no idea. I think it's like an experiment or something. Or some sick ritual."

Though if what I'd read in that book was true – this one I warned you not to touch – then I had a vague idea of what was in store, but couldn't burden Cassie with the prospect of that happening to us.

She took another calming breath, winced when she swallowed.

"Here, let me get you something to drink," I said, and she nodded thanks.

I ran the tap until the water cleared like Al had instructed. Had he been reciting a script? I handed the water to Cassie and she sat quietly, drinking half the glass one measured sip at a time. I wanted to shake the information from her, but knew it was better to wait until she was ready.

"The cops, they pulled over to the side of the road. They made me put on a blindfold. I tried to put it on so that I could still see out the sides, but they made sure it was tight. They turned on the radio to some creepy guy who was telling these sick, like, campfire stories, but way inappropriate. Mostly stories about people getting abducted by fake cops and then raped and dismembered. Even, like, eaten. Like that's what they were going to do to us or something. Then after a few hours or so, I could tell we were off the highway and driving off-road and eventually they stopped and let us out. They let me take the blindfold off but it was so dark out in the woods I couldn't really see anything anyway."

Her face turned red and I could see a wave of emotion threaten to wash over her but she held it at bay. "They took us into this old shut-down convenience store, all the way to the back where they have a hidden hatch to these rooms underground. It looked like a hospital, kind of. Or maybe like a lab, like you said, for experiments. Just clean and sterile with plain concrete walls and two-way mirrors, I think. Or a place to interrogate people. Or maybe all of the above. One of the rooms had a bed and a desk and a toilet. Basically like a prison cell. And that's where they put us and left us overnight.

"The next day a woman came and got us. She was tall with greyish white hair, wearing a Victorian dress buttoned all the way up to the neck. Very graceful and elegant. She said she knew we were scared and that she was sorry for that and that no one wanted to hurt us, but we would have to do as they say or that they might have to. She led us up and out of the store and took us to a cabin a block or so away that looked like it had been abandoned for a while. That's where we've been staying, locked in some hidden back room without windows. Trying my best to keep Rox calm, but the whole time I've been on pins and needles wondering what they planned to do and what had happened to you.

"And then, finally, the woman came back and said you were here too and told me where to go to find you, but I said I wouldn't leave without Rox. But she said I had to. So I told her Rox could hurt himself if I left him alone. And she said Rox would be fine, that she'd take care of him. I told her she couldn't, and she approached Rox, and he didn't shy away like he normally would, and she bent down and whispered something into his ear. But I swear it sounded more like she was doing bird calls or something rather than saying anything, like an alien language or some strange code."

Tough as Cassie may be, she couldn't hold it back any longer. She covered her face and sobbed into her hands and spoke through her palms, her shoulders convulsing. "He smiled at her. Rox, he actually smiled. His eyes fluttered like he was hearing the most beautiful music ever played. Like he was feeling pleasure for the first time. He was nodding his head and he actually reached out to her like he wanted to be picked up, and she took his hand and held it and he looked at me and smiled like he does when he finally figures something out for the first time. And she told me she would take good care of Rox and that I had to go and find you and bring you back. That men in the woods would show me where to go. Those, like, animal-men."

I couldn't take her crying any longer, her pain. I pulled her into me and held her and smoothed her hair and told the most basic lie I know, that everything was going to be okay. And she pressed against me, wrapped her arms around me and placed her face in the crook of my neck, still sobbing. And then she pulled back just far enough for us to lock eyes, and then our mouths connected like we needed each other's oxygen to breathe, shedding our clothes like moulting skin. And I'd never been so hard in my entire life or her so wet and while it might have been the millionth time I'd entered her it felt like the first time. We screamed and thrashed like animals, and she clawed my back and I bit her neck, and together we came so hard the pleasure was nearly pain.

Something about this couch, I'm telling you. A place where alliances are formed and fates are sealed through the joining of flesh. I wish we could have taken it home.

We were back together. And the shit I'd done with Malia didn't matter, because that hadn't been me. Or at least not the conscious me. And while it might haunt my memory banks and give me cold sweats at odd hours, so do dozens of other fucked-up things I've done before. Can't do anything about it now, so why dwell. Deal with the shit at hand.

ᚠ

I relayed my end of the story. All of it. The whole bit about Malia, though I framed it like it had all been one big setup. Which I believe it had. Photos can be doctored. Hell, Cassie's a master of Photoshop herself. There was no need to drive the wedge of real infidelity between us at that time. It's us against them; we needed to be united.

We dined on Triscuits and had the last of the Teddy Grahams for dessert. Both of us were ravenous following the washout of adrenaline. Cassie wanted to return for Rox right away, but I knew that was a bad move. One, it was too dark to make it safely through the woods. Two, we needed a strategy, not just serve ourselves up on a silver platter.

The bit about the lady whispering in Rox's ear worried me. Hell, all of this worried me, but that part especially. It was the first piece of this strange puzzle that fit into place. Professor O's experiments all seemed to deal with implanting consciousness into unconscious minds. The homunculus, the feral kids, the clones. It was like he was trying to identify the most receptive vessel for something new to inhabit. John B in that phoney orphanage, echolocating into his roommates' ears at night. Was he creating a pathway for something to enter? Something so powerful it had turned their insides to mush. I could see Rox's damaged brain being a data set for Professor O to study – that sick bastard. One of John B's new friends.

Despite her conviction to return, Cassie's head began to sag after dinner, her eyes became bloodshot slits. I doubt she had slept much since Saturday night, and it had caught up with her, now that she had me to share the burden of stress. We showered together. I picked the twigs from her hair and massaged her body with soapy hands. I would have made love to her again if we weren't so tired. I was relieved by the lack of bruising or other injuries. Just the cuts and scrapes on her arms and legs from stumbling through the brush. I pulled one of the towels from the window – fuck the teen wolf wannabes outside – and wrapped her tight. Carried her to bed and tucked her in under the covers, shushing her slurred complaints. She was asleep before I could turn off the light. Snoring softly by the time I got in on the other side. At home, we sleep so far apart it's like we're in different time zones. This small bed forced us to spoon, something we hadn't done.... Something I'm not sure we'd ever done, come to think of it. I wouldn't call our first encounters romantic. Then came the surprise of pregnancy. The obligation of marriage. The petty resentment that followed. The self-absorbed fight for a sobriety I never really wanted, but was required after what happened to Rox.

Her hair was damp against my face. Her body moulded to mine in a state of complete acceptance and trust. All these years later, from that chance encounter that I hardly remember, to this night where we need each other to survive. What wars we'd fought together. Strength forged by the fires of our own friction. Our combustible love. And it's on nights like these where you come clean, isn't it? In the silent dark. Hidden from speculative eyes. Here's where I make my confession, then. Retract my addict's lie, the one I've told myself for seven years, and replace it with truth. That bitter fucking pill.

Rox didn't fall from that crib.

Jesus, Jesus, be with me now.

That night at The Mule Kick, I came home wasted like I said. The dark centre of a black-out drunk. That I got the car home is a miracle, but not one granted by any benevolent God. I should have died coming home, and wish I had. Driven off a cliff and become cremated in the wreckage. How's that for rock and roll?

Rox had started crying as soon as I got home. Could have been the slamming of my car door that woke him up. Or the front door. Or when I turned on all the lights. Or when I slammed the fridge door shut. He was only seven months old. Born prematurely, he only weighed fifteen pounds.

I could cradle him in my arm like a Nerf football. The junior-size kind.

Okay, if I'm going to do this, let me really do it. Here's the reenactment that plays like a bad home movie in my mind, Rox's screams the haunting soundtrack.

"Fuck," I moan from our closet-sized kitchen, shoving week-old chicken tenders into my mouth. "You kidding me?"

Watch me shuffle to the crib in the corner of the living room. I want to quiet the kid before Casssie wakes up and starts nagging me. Once the kid really got going, his wails could crack a window.

"Shh." I'm grabbing for the baby. "Little man, please. Shhh."

See me pick him up and stagger back, holding him at arm's length. Little Rox, wailing like Robert Plant singing 'Whole Lotta Love'. Then I right myself and cradle Rox like I'm some fullback looking for a hole in the D-Line. A lion couldn't roar this loud.

"Shhh!" I try and get him to gum my finger. It does nothing more than inoculate him against a host of undocumented germs.

I think I hear Cassie wake, and prepare for the pending fight. *"Jesus, Jesse! Why do you have to make so much noise! Why do you have to stay out so late! When are you going to get your shit together! How fucking selfish can you be!"* I don't want to hear any of these incriminations from her, because I already say them all to myself, and I hate being teamed up on. So I'm desperate to quiet him now. Maybe I'll just put him back in the crib and let her deal with it when she comes out to check on the noise. And it's in my rush to return to the crib that I stagger and trip, triggering my reptilian instincts for self-preservation. My arms flail out for balance, and I let Rox go. Send him flying through the air in my drunken stumble.

I sobered then, as though dunked in ice water. A curse that forces me to remember the next moment in stark detail, no matter how much I try and bury it under lies. The image of my son floating in slow motion through the air. Falling with his

arms reaching out as though wanting to be held. Silent, now.
No longer screaming.

But now I am – really bolting it out when his head hits the
ground – and in my mind I haven't stopped.

I am in my son's head, and always will be. He's damaged
because of me. And I'm the only one who knows.

It feels like my body is burning from the inside out as I
relive this night, so much of it obscured by the haze of alcohol
I have to use my imagination to fill in the blanks. And it's
not fair that I'm snuggling in bed with this woman I lied to.
I should be locked up or have had my own head bashed in
by someone equally as belligerent. And now I know I can't
sleep, because every nerve ending is sizzling and comfort is too
unsettling and it's hard to breathe and if there was a gun here
I'd use it or wish I had the courage to. What can I ever do to
atone, if anything? Put me in a room with my old self and I'd
kill the bastard. That's what I try and do every day. Bury who
I used to be.

I woke up soaked in cold sweat. My jaw ached from grinding
my teeth. More anxious than I'd been since this whole thing
got started. Snakes coiled in the stomach, spewing venom.

Sunlight streamed through the window sheets. Late
morning, judging the brightness. Cassie was still asleep, but
jerked awake when I swung my legs to the side and sat up.

"Rox!" she said, like that night she saw him on the floor,
giving me fresh resolve.

"We're going to get him today." Perhaps this is my day of
atonement.

I smelled like vinegar, but fuck showering. Fuck anything
that makes me feel good again. "I'll brew coffee and then we'll
get ready to go."

Cassie scrubbed her face with both hands, stretched, and her
spine popped. "Okay," she said.

We climbed down the spiral staircase together, me going to
the kitchen, her towards the couch. "Jesse?" she said, and her
tone made me cringe.

I turned.

"Did you take this out?" she asked, pointing to the Ouija board that was laid open on the coffee table.

I shook my head. "At least, not that I remember."

She approached it slowly, studied it, then picked up the planchette and held it towards me. "It says, 'The Key'," she said, and I could see those words written in stacked lines across the top.

"Put it down. Don't touch that shit," I said. She dropped it like it carried an electric charge.

"Someone must have come in during the night and put it there," I said. "I'm telling you, this whole thing's a mind trip. We'll get Rox, we'll get out of here, we'll go to the police and have this whole fucking place raided. This ends with us."

Cassie hugged herself, looking down at the Ouija board. Mirrors, hypnosis, now this. Call me superstitious, but there are some things better left alone. This book being one of them. But it's too late for that. Maybe it ends with you.

I started the coffee maker, peeked out the window while it warmed. The perimeter was clear. And I didn't hear the sound of anyone trekking deeper within the woods. Perhaps their purpose had been served and they'd all gone home, wherever the hell it is they live. I went to the front of the house to check that side, tried to open the door but it was locked. I turned the lock switch and tried again but it didn't budge. Turned the deadbolt back and forth but didn't hear the lever slide. I put my shoulder into the door and it was like pushing against a brick wall.

"What's the matter?" Cassie said.

"Nothing," I lied. I can't stop.

There's another door off the kitchen, but that one was locked as well. I kicked it and nearly jammed my foot. Must have been reinforced with steel. The windows were all sealed tight. We were trapped in this place, and it appeared the planchette was the key.

Why couldn't we have befriended one of the beast boys outside and gotten an escort out of here? I wonder if Priscilla was able to escape, or if her seduction had been a setup. I hope she and her Tarzan lover are living happily ever after somewhere, but doubt it somehow.

The coffee urn hissed and gurgled and I went and poured two steaming cups. Brought one to Cassie and we sipped them while staring down at the letters and numbers on the board. Here is what a Ouija board looks like if you've never seen one before, but don't stare at it too long. I'm serious.

There was this Goth chick Solomon used to hang with for a while. Black fishnet arm sleeves, pentagram pendant, platform combat boots, you know the type. We'd get high as shit and she'd break out the Ouija board. But I didn't play that game. I don't step on cracks, I don't walk under ladders, and I certainly don't attempt to conjure spirits, real or otherwise. Neither did Kevin, and Caspian's attention span wasn't long enough to suffer through it. So we'd hit the bar while Solomon held back because she was his chick and he couldn't bail.

As the story goes, they'd popped acid after the show. Back then we used to get our supply from one of Owsley Stanley's guys and the shit opened portals of its own. They'd played with it a couple of times before and had some creepy shit happen – knocking sounds, names of dead relatives – but you never know how much of that is being manipulated by one of the participants.

They were in the bus. Solomon, his girl, and maybe one of her friends and another rando. I can't remember. His girl started asking if there were any spirits in the room. And the damn planchette began scooting before anyone could even put a finger on it. But, again, people in paintings will wink at you while you're on Stanley's LSD. They rushed to put their hands on the thing and it began buzzing under their fingers. Spelled out the name A – B – A – C – U – S.

"Abacus," Solomon's girl said, reciting the word. "Where do you come from?" And then, apparently, allegedly, she stiffened and her eyes started fluttering and she began to make this mewling sound like she was scared or in pain or trying to resist something. When she spoke again her voice had become deep and gravelly, and a second face – the maniacal face of a wide-eyed man – formed like a mirage over her own. "I come from inside you," she said in a man's voice, his translucent lips imposed over hers, revealing teeth that were black and rotten. "From the backside of your eyes. The blank space in your mind. The break in your heart."

The girl's friend freaked out and crab walked away from the table. Solomon, who had a higher tolerance for fucked-up shit, leaned in to get a better look at this phantasmagoric face. His girlfriend's eyes were still closed, but the man's eyes, hovering just over her own like an aura, were wide open, the pupils scanning the room, landing on Solomon and staying there. Her breath came quicker, panting, and the man sneered.

"Yo, so how'd you die, man?" Solomon said. He snickered. "Dosed out on H or something?"

Her hand shot out and grabbed Solomon by the throat, cutting off his air, fingers curled in as though to crush his windpipe. He grabbed her wrist and tried to pry it away, but couldn't, and he was much stronger than her. Dude drums, remember. And it's not like she did barbell curls. Then that ghostly face smiled and a dry cackle came through even though the girl's lips were closed.

"I cannot die," it said. "You resurrect me. Bring me here through your emptiness."

Solomon was close to passing out when she pulled him near so that their noses were almost touching. Her eyes opened then, the man's like cataracts. When she spoke it was a discordant mix of her voice and the man's. "I eat what you grow. I am your hate."

Her mouth opened so wide the hinges popped and her lower

jaw sagged down and her neck bulged and a buzzing sound began to build from the depths of her throat. And Solomon was stuck and couldn't pull away as a swarm of locusts came flying from her gaping mouth, battering his face in a torrent rush of wings, knocking him back as she released him and the bus filled with the buzzing of locusts like a plague.

As you may imagine, mayhem ensued. Tankerson, our bus driver and stage manager – who was halfway sober and corroborated the story, at least the part about the locusts – came back and saw the bugs flying from that chick's mouth and the Ouija board on the floor, and he'd had experiences of his own, though nothing like this, so he grabbed it and took it off the bus and ripped it up the best he could and burned it soon after. Just like I wish I'd done to this godforsaken book.

The chick's jaw was all busted up. Her throat scratched to shit. Tankerson took her to the hospital and I'm not sure what happened to her from there. That was Solomon's and her last date, and I say good riddance.

I wouldn't have believed half of it if Tankerson wasn't there to validate the story. Plus, there were a bunch of broken wings and stuff in the bus when we got back, and piles of husks where Tankerson had swept them out. At least, that's what I was told. I don't really remember. The guys and I got pretty lit at the bar dealing with spirits of a different kind and when I woke up we were in another town.

So let me just say I was less than enthused by the idea of fucking around with this Ouija board supplied, as far as I knew, by Professor Fucking O in a cabin out in some nowhere woods near a mirror on which runes had mysteriously appeared that invoked the voice of some stranger in my mind. No, thanks.

"We've got to find another way," I said to Cassie.

"Another way to what?"

"Out of here," I said. "We're locked in."

We spent the next hour or so trying every MacGyver-type tactic we could come up with to pop the locks or pry open the doors. Used furniture to smash the windows, but the glass was reinforced with material that cracked but wouldn't cave. I damaged my back more than I did those windows. We scoured the rooms for hidden hatches in the floor or vents to crawl through, and found nothing. Even tried shimmying up the chimney, which resulted in nothing more than covering us in soot. At the end, it was enough to make us laugh. Sweating and smeared with soot, taking desperate measures to escape some log cabin that would have been romantic under different conditions.

"You don't have a phone, do you?" I asked.

She stared at me for a long while. "You don't think I would have tried to use it before now?"

I sighed, and so did she. I had been scared before. Terrified, in fact. But this was a different type of fear. Part claustrophobia. Part worry for Rox, with the feeling that every second we spent dicking around here put him in more danger. And a heaping pile of paranoia regarding what would happen when we played with that Ouija board. What type of portal it would rip open.

I'm not religious, but am probably more spiritual than I'll admit. I wouldn't be worried about demons or spirits or whatever may come through that Ouija board if I wasn't. Plus, so much of AA is based on having faith in something bigger and wiser than ourselves. Even if it's just our future, actualised self urging us on. Cassie, on the other hand, basically believes in all religions. She's like a smorgasbord of faith. She'll pull verses from the Bible, the Bhagavad Gita, and the I Ching in a single sitting. Mash 'em all together like some techno groove. She prays, meditates, does yoga, fasts, volunteers. Here, I lay off pizza for a few days and feel I've sanctified my body, whereas my wife is basically a holy saint. And yet I waste so much of my time wondering if I could have done better. I deserve every bit of this, I think.

Okay, how bad can it be? Fucking Hasbro makes Ouija boards, the same toy company that makes Mr. Potato Head. It's not a portal to some spirit world. Solomon and his girlfriend were tripping balls. Tankerson probably had a flashback or caught a contact high. Say Bloody Mary's name three times in front of a mirror and nothing happens. It's all superstition and manufactured fear.

"You ever played with one of these things?" I said.

"No. You?"

"No."

We squared the board and studied it. I flipped it over and inspected the back, looking for some device that would allow it to be manipulated. Other than the planchette with The Key written across the top, it seemed like a standard set.

"So, what? We just put our fingers on this thing?" I said, and she nodded, nibbling a fingernail, which I hadn't seen her do in years.

"First, let's say a prayer," she said.

This normally would have incited some sarcastic retort, but not this time. I'd have bathed in holy water if we'd had some. "Okay. Sure," I said.

We held hands. Hers were cold and damp, as were mine. We bowed our heads and closed our eyes, and she led us in prayer, because I wouldn't have the faintest idea of what to say or to whom.

"Dear God."

Whether this was a greeting or a plea, I wasn't sure.

"We thank You for this glorious day."

Starting off with a lie? Maybe I could have given this prayer after all.

"We ask that You please be with us now."

Now we're getting somewhere.

"Protect us from those who would do us harm. Shield us from whatever evil may attempt to make contact through this Ouija board, which we use under Your guiding spirit in order to rescue our son."

Hell if I didn't feel a boost of strength and energy, manufactured or not.

"And please watch over our precious son, Rox, while he is away from us. Comfort and safeguard him. Help us find our way back to him, and return us all safely home. We pray this in the name of love and all that is holy, Amen."

A-fucking-men!

The room appeared brighter when I opened my eyes, which I attributed to wishful thinking. But isn't that the same thing as prayer?

Cassie had mustered her full resolve. Was staring at the board with fierce intensity as though preparing for battle. I gripped her hand and squeezed it.

"Let's fucking do this," I said, and she squeezed back. Hard.

We placed our hands on the planchette. It was made of cheap plastic and felt light under my fingers. We waited several seconds for something to happen, our shallow breathing the only sound. Then I remembered that we had to ask questions to make it interact.

I cleared my throat. "Where is the key to unlock the door?"

My stomach dropped as the planchette began to slide on its own accord. I was not manoeuvering it in any way, and when I looked at Cassie I could tell she wasn't either. We tracked the letters it landed on, calling them out loud.

H – I – D – D – E – N

"Hidden," I said. "No shit."

"Shhh," Cassie admonished.

"Okay. Well, thanks," I said, feeling somewhat silly and smug, but no longer as afraid. "Where is the key hidden?"

Again the planchette began to move, seemingly on its own.

B – E – H – I – N – D

We looked at each other and smiled. Two questions in, and just one away from finding the key.

"Behind what?" Cassie blurted out before I had the chance.

L – I – E – S

Damnit. Our backs were both rigid from the tension of anticipation and frustration over this obscured response. If it was talking about mine, this could take a while.

"What lies?" I said, cool sweat beginning to prickle my forehead.

The planchette remained stationary.

"Whose lies?" Cassie said, which made my stomach twist. Of course it's going to be mine. And I think I know just the one. The planchette didn't move.

"A lie I told?" Cassie said, which would have been easy for her to ask. Her conscience is clear as an arctic lake.

The planchette didn't move and she looked at me, waiting. Both of us knowing it was my turn.

I cleared my throat again. "One of my lies?" Bad phrasing, as it suggested many.

The planchette moved and my heart began to thud, the oxygen in the room turned thin. Some things you want to take to your grave. Some things are best left unsaid. Some truths hurt more than they heal. The planchette was sliding towards the upper-left-hand corner of the board. It was clear where it was going, and I was tempted to remove my hands to stop the thing, or to surrender. Why rub it in my face? But I knew I had to see it through.

When the planchette stopped, it stood squarely on YES.

The key is hidden behind my lies.

I'll give Cassie credit. She kept her humour and tried to make this as easy on me as she could. "Well, hmmm," she said, her pale lips twisting into an uncertain smile. The briefest dimpling of her chin was the only indication of the dark emotion she was fighting to suppress.

"Hmmmm," I echoed. I wasn't ready for this. We needed to be united; this would break us apart.

"Looks like someone wants a confessional. Any idea what lie it's talking about?"

The room had become too small, Cassie's gaze too direct. I stood and began pacing. Went back to the door and tried it again.

"It wants to…. *He* wants to divide us," I said. "Turn us against each other. That's what this is all about."

I had no idea how he was doing this. What mechanism he was using. If it was a spirit, I didn't feel its presence. Unless it's the fucking spirit of Christmas past. Or, in my case, the last night at The Mule Kick. What if it's not the lie I'm thinking about, though, and I spew it out and we're still stuck in here, but now with a vile truth unearthed from such a deep grave we'll choke on its putrid stench? Bring it back to life like some fucking zombie that will eat our brains, if not our hearts and souls.

"You know he's watching us right now, don't you?" I said. He had to be. How else could he have made the planchette respond so concisely to our questions? How else would he know whether or not I confessed to my most damning sin?

Cassie sat there in silence, watching me, waiting. Still wearing the same dress she'd picked up off the floor in a rush to get in a car with fake cops. Arms crossed, legs scratched to hell. On the precipice of a revelation that will alter the way she looks at me forever. And she looks nonplussed. We humans are adaptable, if nothing else. Or maybe she's just a master of her emotions. Or maybe she's just so scared she's afraid to show it because then it will set off an avalanche of hysteria that will crush her and me both.

"All I care about is getting Rox back," she said.

And that should have been my only concern as well, but I was more focused on myself. Trying to prolong my past mistakes. Protect the present image I'd fabricated. The alliance we'd built on top of a lie.

"I know," I said. And I almost said, 'Me too', but I had to stop lying if I was going to start telling the truth.

I took a deep breath. "I think I know what I'm supposed to say."

She nodded, began kneading her hands.

"Or what I'm supposed to tell you."

As little as I wanted to say this, I could tell she didn't want to hear it either. The truth will set you free? Fuck that. The truth will burn you alive.

"Look, whatever it is, it's okay," she said. Goddamn, she's an angel. "I know you. I know who you are. Nobody's perfect. In fact, there's no such thing. You've done some fucked-up things, so have I. There's nothing you could do that would make me turn my back on you. What, did you cheat on me, or something? Please don't tell me you murdered someone."

"Honestly?" Because that's what this is about, isn't it? "I may have done both in the last forty-eight hours, but that's not what this is about, I don't think."

That took a chink out of her armour. She sagged and her mouth dropped open in a show of surprise. "I mean, but not like how it sounds," I said. Jesus, the counselling we'll need to reconcile all of this, if we ever can. "Look, let's get through this and I'll tell you everything. I don't know where to start, or how much of it is even real. But I'll try."

"It's okay," she said. "Come here."

I'm a man in my forties, but right then I was a boy. Cassie, my wife, but also my mom. My unconditional lover. I sat next to her on the couch of animal attraction. The cushions sagged in a way that brought us together, and she took me in her arms, held my head against her breast, ran her fingers through my remaining hairs. Creating, within her, a confessional booth.

When I was a kid I'd get scared at night alone in my room. In the dark with the sounds of the house settling, certain that someone had broken in and was creeping around, coming to my room to kidnap me or murder me in my bed. So I'd close my eyes, because I didn't want to see the face of the monster. And maybe if I couldn't see it, it couldn't see me. And then I'd wake up in the morning light and breathe a sigh of relief that the night had passed and I'd survived.

I closed my eyes and my head moved up and down to the rhythm of Cassie's breath. I listened to her heart beating.

"I guess this is for the best," I said. "Actually, that's a lie. Damn, telling the truth is hard. I don't see how saying what I'm about to say is for the best at all."

"It's okay," she said. "If it'll help us get Rox back it's for the best. Like a Band-Aid, babe."

Her heartbeat quickened. Her chest, like a pillow.

"So much of what I've been put through, a lot of it at least, seems to be punishing me for what happened to Rox. Like when I was stuck in that wall, being forced to face what it's like to live inside his head."

"Yeah?" I could feel her nodding, her hands caressing my head.

"So I'm sure that's what this is about."

More nodding.

"And the lie they're talking about is about that night."

Her heart is beating like a rabbit's. Damn, I don't want to hurt her more than I already have. Okay, like a Band-Aid. You can get through anything with your eyes closed.

"I don't think he fell out of his crib like I said."

Her hands stop stroking my hair.

"I mean, I'm sure he didn't. That night I came home. I don't remember much. But I know I picked him up out of his crib, because he was crying so loud and I didn't want him to wake you. And...." This is not so much a confessional as an exorcism. The memory wants to stay inside me like a devil. And it hurts so much coming out, a pain like fire in my chest. "I was trying to settle him down, and I tripped or stumbled. I'm not sure because I don't really remember. But I have total recall of the moment I accidentally dropped him or let him go, because I saw him in the air, and I saw him hit the ground."

She's stopped breathing, her heart is pounding against my ear.

"And I don't know why I said what I said. About him falling out. I was just so fucking horrified. And scared. And ashamed. And I just didn't want to believe it. I was lying more to myself, I think. Trying to make myself believe this other story so that I could go on living without wanting to kill myself every minute of every day."

The cabin has become a coffin. The only sound I hear is Cassie's heart. My eyes are still closed and it feels like I'm running a fever. I feel like I should say more, that there's some magical combination of words that needs to be recited in a certain order to honour the reality of what happened, or, if nothing else, unlock the front door, but there's nothing left to say.

Cassie's hand falls from my head. She still hasn't taken a breath. I sit up, open my eyes and look at her. She's staring straight ahead, but not really looking at anything. She's in her mind. Remembering, or reconstructing the narrative of our past.

"Fucking kill me, right?" Because that's what I want. "I'm so sorry." I'm done telling lies.

She looks at me and tears film her eyes. "Is that it?"

"That's everything," I said.

She reached out and grabbed my hand as the first tear fell. "That's awful," she said, her chin trembling. "But it doesn't change anything."

Please don't forgive me, I thought. *I don't think I can handle it.*

"It happened, and we can't take it back." My punishment is

staring into her eyes as she tells me this. "You were a different person, then. So was I. You," she squeezed my hand, "would not, could not have hurt Rox. The person you want me to kill is already dead. You killed him. That wild son-of-a-bitch I loved. He died and gave birth to you, a man I love even more. And you wouldn't exist if he hadn't done that terrible thing."

"Stop," I said. This was torture. "I don't deserve this."

She scooted closer to me, bringing us face to face, nose to nose. "No one deserves anything, but we get it all anyway. The good *and* the bad."

"And the ugly?" It came out before I could hold it back. I'm an idiot.

Snot bubbled from her nose when she snorted. "What are you, Clint Eastwood now?"

My choppy laugh sounded robotic, but at least it was real. Cassie and me and our gallows humour. I forgot she could laugh at anything. "Wish I was. I'd get us out of here while smoking a cigarillo and leave a row of bodies in our wake."

She smiled and fell against me, drained. Her head now on my chest, me stroking her hair. We stayed like that for a while, both of us with our eyes closed, the Ouija board forgotten, neither of us having anything left to say.

I pulled back and stood. Walked to the door and gripped the knob. If this thing didn't open, I'd burn the place down around us. The door swung in on loose hinges.

"Holy shit," Cassie said.

It was mid-afternoon. As good a time as any to reclaim our son.

"Ready?" I said.

She took a deep breath and stood. "No," she said.

I smiled. "Me either. Let's go."

Ϙ

The woods appeared empty, but I knew we were under watch. I felt confident that we'd be given safe passage to that not-so-abandoned town where they were keeping Rox, however. Getting me there seemed to be the goal. But that didn't stop me from searching for the deadliest branch I could find, looking underneath the hardwoods until I found a broken limb that could crater a skull. I found a solid, yet smaller branch with broken spikes sticking out from the business end, and handed it to Cassie.

She looked dubious. "You honestly think these two sticks are going to defend us against a horde of beast-men?"

"Better than nothing," I said.

"Actually," she said, dropping the branch and brushing bark from her hands, "I think we'd be better off not antagonising anybody."

"Suit yourself," I said, but knew she was right and now felt silly holding a branch like I was some prehistoric warrior.

"You didn't need to cut through the woods, you know," I said.

"No, I didn't know that."

"There's a road," I said. "In fact, you must have crossed it."

"I could have passed Dorothy on the road to Oz and wouldn't have noticed. I was in a blind panic just following those guys."

I can't imagine how terrifying that must have been for her. And here she is, doing it again, with only me to defend her. Given my status with this freak organisation, she was probably better off alone.

I led her to the dirt road I had driven up with Al. "Follow this down and it'll take us straight there."

It was ten degrees hotter in the open road, under the direct gaze of the sun. A wet heat that cooked you from the inside out.

Sweat trickled down my face and body and my shirt was already damp and clinging to my chest. Insects chirped from the trees, saying who knows what. Feed me! Fuck me!

I was hungry and dehydrated. Cassie pulled the hair off her neck, revealing the black stubble of her armpits.

"Jungle woman," I said.

"Shut the fuck up," she said through a smile.

The road wound downhill, which made the walk easier. We let gravity pull our feet forward. I scoured the tree line for skulking figures or camouflaged faces, but saw neither. Didn't mean they weren't there. Sweat dripped into my eyes and burned. The air felt like it was being filtered through an oven.

"This is really dumb," I said.

"You think?"

"I mean, we should devise a plan."

"I feel like we're part of some bigger plan and whatever we devise will just delay it or make things harder for us."

I had gone off script, at least I think I had, back at that place with Malia. And that hadn't seemed to help much. In fact, it had made things worse, placing me in the path of that echolocating clone that I may or may not have killed.

"So, what? Just walk in and announce ourselves and put ourselves at their mercy?"

"Pretty much. I mean, what's the alternative? You show off your big stick and demand Rox back or you'll start bashing heads?"

"I don't know," I said. "I'm just thinking we should try and scout the place out or something before we announce our arrival."

"Look," she said. "From what you've told me, and what I've seen, this isn't some upstart satanic cult that stumbled across an abandoned town in the woods to use as a hideaway. That town was constructed to conceal something. With rooms built underground and all that. I wouldn't be surprised if this whole mountain isn't somehow owned and operated by whoever is behind this."

"That's impossible," I said, naïve considering all I'd seen and been through. "Actually, you're probably right."

She nodded. We stumbled down the road, kicking up dust. I had turned my club into a walking stick at that point, not that it helped much. It took us about half an hour to get down to the section of road where I'd seen the abandoned town. We slowed, and I pointed to the decrepit cabins about fifty yards through the screen of trees.

"This the place?" I said.

She wiped sweat from her eyes and shaded them, looking for about a minute with her back hunched over. Then she pointed. "Yeah, that's the depot where they took me," she said. "It's got rooms underground. The cabin where we stayed is just past it. We're here."

We stood and stared for a long while, searching for some activity. From this place on the road it looked like nothing more than some old mountain town that had been deserted and left to rot decades ago. Clever, Mister O.

Sweat dripped from my chin and my shirt was drenched. Our combined stench could have offended a skunk. I used the branch to clear a pathway through a vine of thorns and it was the first and only thing it was good for. Regardless, I still got sliced a number of times hiking through the thorny undergrowth.

"Isn't there a show where people do this shit naked?" I said.

"Hush," Cassie said from behind me.

"We've all lost our minds," I said.

We stopped about twenty feet from the first cabin, sat on our haunches and conducted our final survey. When I was growing up, there used to be woods in every neighbourhood. My friends and I would take our bikes out into these woods and pretend we were secret commandos in some wide-scale war. Pre-teen Rambos. Using nothing more than our imagination, we would create these elaborate missions where we'd have to infiltrate a base and release hostages or assassinate an army commander. And it would feel so authentic, out in the quiet woods, that we'd manufacture real fear and adrenaline. The celebration after successful missions was genuine. But the stakes were not. Here, I had the same feeling I did as a kid preparing an assault on some imaginary fortress, but now my courage, or lack thereof, would truly be tested, and the outcome mattered. Fail, and I couldn't just return home to my mother's meatloaf and a warm bath and an hour of sitcoms before bedtime. Fail, and I might lose my son, the family I've fought to keep, and my sanity, if not my life. My bravado wanted to say, 'Failure is not an option.' But the voice in my head, the one that says, 'Just one drink won't kill you', told me it not only was an option, it was the most likely one.

We'll see about that. My bravado and insecurity are always at war.

"It looks empty," I said.

"Sure does."

"So, where did everybody go?"

"I'm guessing underground."

"Great." I stood and led us through the brush and out onto the rutted dirt road. I hesitated at the tree line, then turned and tossed my weapon-slash-walking stick back into the woods. "You're right. That's just likely to get us hurt."

The road was narrow, barely wide enough to accommodate a car, with crevices carved by water, and gnarled roots sticking out. Trees lined each side, merging overhead to create a canopy that shaded the sun. Shafts of light shot through like ethereal columns, landing as gold coins on the ground. My instinct was to avoid these columns of light, which worried me. Superstition would make me susceptible to manufactured fears. I forced myself to walk through a shaft of light and half expected it to trigger some booby trap like in *Raiders of the Lost Ark*, but I survived.

I went to the nearest cabin and peered in through the dusty window. The wood floor was caving, the mildewed walls warped and peeling, exposing the studs behind. There was a mouldering Raggedy Andy doll sitting in a small rocking chair in the corner with its stuffing spewing out. A spider of some kind skittered across its face as I watched. Then another. I felt something crawling up my leg and leapt away, resisting the urge to scream. I looked down expecting to see a spider, but saw black ants instead, streaming from a mound where I'd been standing.

I brushed them off and shivered. "Jesus, this place is creepy."

"It's not inviting." Cassie shivered, too. "Not at all."

My skin still felt like it was crawling with ants even after I'd wiped them all off. Phantom ants, like an amputated limb. We continued up the road, peering in windows as we went along. Baby toys in each of them, long abandoned. A Big Wheel covered in spiderwebs. A toy drum set folded in on itself like moulted skin. Deflated soccer balls holding stagnant water for mosquitos to breed. I wondered what these houses had held for Malia. For Priscilla, if she'd even come this way. None of this was in the book I'd read.

All of this for me.

I looked ahead and saw what appeared to be someone sitting on one of the two benches on either side of the depot entrance. A rigid man wearing a wide-brim hat with his legs crossed. I nudged Cassie and pointed.

"It's a statue," she said. "Of the original owner, I think."

I still approached cautiously until we got close enough for me to see that it was indeed a statue cast in copper or corroded steel. A man wearing a suit from the Fifties with thin-rimmed spectacles, looking stern, if not proud. Smooth skin splotched with grime. Folds in his clothes frozen in place. There was an iron plaque on the backside of the bench that was too dirty to read, but appeared to display the man's name and offer a tribute of some kind. The importance of this man and his make-believe mountain depot was beyond me, and didn't matter. We passed him and walked inside.

The place had been gutted. Aisles of empty shelves in various stages of disarray. Tilted price tags for absent products. Dust and spiderwebs everywhere. The old checkout counter was to the right, more empty shelves along the left and back walls. Cassie led me towards the door to the storage room and we paused for just a moment to listen before pushing through.

There was a narrow hallway that branched off into an employees' restroom with a shattered mirror and open plumbing where the sink and toilet would go. Someone had written 'I CAN TASTE THE BLOOD' in red ink on the sheetrock wall. Beside that was a smear that looked like shit. The hallway opened into an empty storage room with a stained concrete floor. Metal shelves were pushed together to create a dilapidated tower near the back corner. I followed her there and she pointed to the grey rug underneath the shelves.

"That's the hatch to the rooms underground," she said.

"Was it covered before?" I said.

"No."

I squatted and grabbed one end of the rug and pulled. It slid fairly easily on the concrete floor, the shelves rattling but holding in place. Cassie bent and grabbed a flap and together we moved the rug with its leaning tower until the hatch was exposed. It had a ring pull that was encased in the hatch door. I gripped it and lifted, revealing a black pit. Just a couple of rungs on a metal ladder leading down into pitch dark. I held my breath and so did Cassie and we listened to silence.

Cassie squatted and her knees cracked, loud as a starter gun. We both winced and waited to see if we'd been heard. I was about to whisper something when she called down into the underground shaft, "Hello! Anyone down there?"

I grabbed the hatch and prepared to throw it back in place. Expecting to hear the stampeding of footsteps or the flutter of wings or the buzz of locusts or the trilling sound of echolocations that would overwhelm my mind and drive me to murder. Instead, more silence.

Cassie shrugged. "Should we go down?"

I shook my head so hard I nearly sprained my neck. "Down into the dark? Fuck no." I closed the hatch.

We walked back through the depot and out through the front. Looked up and down the quiet and empty street.

"So much for the welcome party," I said.

"Must be a surprise party."

"I have no doubt we're in for a surprise," I said. "So, where's this cabin you slept in?"

"Couple of blocks that way." She pointed up the road, and we set off in that direction, arriving a couple of minutes later at a cabin on a corner lot that looked as dilapidated as all the rest.

"They clear this one out, too?" I said.

"No, this is just how it looks."

I followed her to the front door and we peered inside. I saw warped floorboards and mouldering walls. "Bedroom's in the back," she said. "It's comfortable, actually."

She turned the knob and opened the door, releasing a neutral smell less musty than the depot, or even the furnished cabin we had just left. Cassie stepped inside and I took one last look behind us, noticing that the benches in front of the depot were now both empty. The statue of the proprietor was gone. No, not gone. He was standing in the middle of the road, watching us. Not a statue, then. Just some guy dressed like one of those street performers you see in touristy cities. I waited to see if he would start walking, or running, this way, but he remained in place. I backed in through the doorway, keeping my eyes on him. He raised one hand as I closed the door, and waved.

"Well, they know we're here," I said, looking for a lock on the door and finding none. At least not one that I could latch. Cassie was heading towards a hallway that led to the back of the cabin. I scanned the room for a chair or something that I could use to barricade the door, but the room was bare.

She stopped and turned. "How do you know they know?"

"Come here," I said, and she did. I opened the door and the road was empty. So was the bench. "That statue?" I said. "That was a man in costume, surveilling us. He followed us partway up the road. Who knows where the hell he is now. Probably sounding the alarm."

Cassie put a hand to her mouth, letting the information sink in. "This is really happening."

"Something is," I said, and shut the door.

The cabin was stifling. Hotter than outside. I doubted any of the units out here had A/C. At least not in the rooms above ground. It wouldn't really fit the abandoned town façade Mister O had created should someone come stumbling along. Something told me unwelcome guests would be intercepted long before they made it this far, however.

Cassie was still staring at the door, maybe listening for footsteps, more likely paralysed by fear. I placed my hand on the back of her neck, and her shoulders jumped up by her ears. I waited until she relaxed. "It's all to scare us. I don't know why or what for, but I don't think we're in real danger. At least, not yet. Whatever is going on will soon be revealed. We'll get Rox back, we'll go home. Okay?"

She looked me in the eyes. "It won't be that easy."

"You're right," I said. "It won't."

A fly buzzed my ear and I swatted it away.

"Have you ever heard of anything like this?" she asked.

I nodded. "Yes, the book," I said. The one you're reading now.

"And what happened?"

I wasn't ready to go there, yet. "She survived."

But reading it had brought us here.

Cassie leaned in and I pulled her close. I could feel her heart beating against my chest. "Goddamn the shit we've been through," she said. Several retorts came to mind and I left them there, not knowing if she was talking about today, the past few years, or our entire lives.

"Where's this bedroom?" I said. I followed her back through the hallway, careful to avoid the splintered floor planks. I saw a spider in a corner web that could ensnare a pigeon. Was surprised I hadn't seen any snakes, but knew they had to be around. Malia and her little pets that she had unleashed on me in the culvert. The hallway was canted to the side like at a Fun House. But there was nothing fun about this house. I felt the itch of a mosquito bite on the back of my knee and it brought to mind a line Cassie used to quote from the Dalai Lama, 'If you think you are too small to make a difference, try sleeping with a mosquito.' Meanwhile, the only Dalai Lama quote I know comes from *Caddyshack*.

The walls were wood panelled. Mouldy and warped. Cassie stopped three quarters of the way down the hallway and stood before a splotch of mould that resembled a spray of buckshot. She placed four fingers against a configuration of mould splatter and pushed. The dark notches sunk into the wall with a click and a door-sized panel opened along one of the seams.

"I watched the lady do this when she brought us here," she said.

"That's actually pretty cool," I said, because it was. Appreciate whatever momentary joys you can find in this hell. We entered into a cosy room like you'd expect at a rustic bed and breakfast. Four-post queen-size bed with mosquito netting and a frosted dome light overhead. An antique Persian rug on the polished oak floor. A framed mirror that I wanted to throw the fuck out, and twin bedside tables holding large bottles of Mountain Spring water and an assortment of homemade granola bars wrapped in cellophane. I didn't give two shits if the water was poisoned. It would almost be a relief if it were. I uncapped one of the bottles and guzzled down a quarter-litre of cool, clean water. The room back here was windowless and more temperate, somehow. I moaned a bit as the water splashed in my stomach, not realising how dehydrated I had become. I ripped open the cellophane on one of the granola bars and took a bite. I tasted honey, roasted almond, chocolate, and fresh cherry. I moaned some more.

Cassie uncapped the water on her side, unwrapped a bar, and met me at the foot of the bed. We sat and ate our snacks and stared at the framed Japanese dragon on the wall. This was so much better than the Krispy Kremes and coffee in the break room inside that warehouse of horrors with Malia. I wondered if I'd see her again, and hoped not.

"I'm exhausted," Cassie mumbled with her mouth full of goo.

I sighed, feeling like a sail with no wind. A guitarist with no pick. A father with no son. The only movement in the room was our chewing. The only sound our swallows.

"We're going to have to fight," she said.

I had known that from the beginning. "I thought you said aggression would only antagonise them."

"Fighting and antagonising are two different things." She had not stopped staring at the dragon.

"What are you now, Bruce Lee?" I said.

She smiled without turning. "Steven Seagal."

"We're fucked, then. That guy is an overweight cop in Louisiana."

Cassie took a sip of water and so did I. I shivered as the damp T-shirt turned my body cold. Too bad I'd left my damn duffel bag with a spare change of clothes behind.

"I wish I knew who we were fighting," I said.

"Anyone who tries to keep us from Rox."

"Yeah, well. Height and reach may help. Weight class, preference of weapon. That sort of thing."

I wondered where the camera was positioned in this room. Not that it mattered. Best to assume you're always being watched.

"Life is war," Cassie said.

"I thought you said life was love."

"Life is love. And love is fighting."

"I thought love was letting go."

I opened another granola bar and split it in two.

Cassie scooted closer to me, our bodies now touching. "In the Bhagavad Gita," she said. It's a Hindu scripture. I'm telling you, this is what she does. "Krishna, who is like the embodiment of God, is preparing His disciple Arjuna for battle. Arjuna looks out at the army he is being commanded to fight and sees within it his brothers and sisters and friends, men, women, and children. 'How can I fight them?' he asks, thinking it would be better to surrender or run away than kill everyone he loves. Krishna answers by showing Arjuna His true form. And it's the most ferocious image you can imagine. His eyes are like angry suns, his mouth is a blazing furnace. Arjuna sees warriors gnashed to small bits inside Krishna's teeth. He's terrified. He thought Krishna was the source of all love, and wonders why he's presenting such a frightening image of Himself. And then Krishna says, 'I am the destroyer of worlds. These people you love will die whether or not you fight. I have killed them already. You fight to free them and find the greatness in yourself.'"

The granola lost some of its sweetness following that description. "Why are the gods such fucking assholes?" I said.

"Because," Cassie said, "love would be worthless if it wasn't so hard to attain."

I contemplated that as I chewed. "Maybe," I said. "Or maybe God just got bored after being alone in space for a few billion years and it made Him grumpy."

There was no way to tell time in the windowless room with its overhead light. After a while we lay back in the bed with its lace sheets, holding damp hands, our legs intertwined. The cotton pillows were cool and smelled like fresh air. Fear is exhausting. So is hiking in the heat. We slept for who knows how long. And woke to the sound of someone knocking on the front door.

The overhead light was still on so the room looked exactly as it did when we lay down. I've woken many times to rooms having no idea where I was or how I got there, and this was like that, but worse. Those rooms I could up and leave. In this one I felt trapped, and wasn't sure why until the full weight of memory slammed into my brain like a cannonball. Somewhere nearby our terrified son was being held hostage, and here we had slept comfortably in this dainty bed with its frilly duvet. Drinking our bottled water.

I heard another series of staccato knocks from the front door of the cabin and sat up, my head pounding, my vision swaying. I didn't feel rested at all. Cassie was still breathing evenly on the bed beside me, and I wanted to let her sleep. *Go away*, I thought, like it was just some Jehovah's Witness out there who would soon take his religion somewhere else. But whoever it was may be here to lead us to our son, or even have Rox with him. Or her. Maybe it was Malia.

I nudged Cassie as gently as I could. She woke during the next series of knocks and gasped to a sitting position. She jumped out of bed before I could say a word and stopped at the opening to the hidden panel when I shouted her name. From the corner of my eye I saw the word OBSIDEO scrawled on the framed mirror.

"Wait," I said. "I go first."

I could tell I had about two seconds to take the lead or she would go on without me. "Don't rush into this," I said. Silly, as I didn't have a plan or anything to protect us with. So, what? My strategy was procrastination?

Cassie was pushing up against my back as I manoeuvered through the canted hallway, eager to answer the door. The door was solid wood so I couldn't see who was on the other side, but a glowing amber light was shining through the windows. It was night outside.

I stopped a few steps before the door and held Cassie behind me. This whole situation was preposterous knowing there wasn't even a lock on the door. Come on in, already.

"Who's out there?" I said, my voice deep and gruff like some gate commander of the night's watch. Wishing this was fantasy.

There was a different quality to the quiet now. An expectation in the air. You can tell whether you're alone or not. Feel the energy of others even if you can't see or hear them. There were people outside, milling around. More than one. The shafts of amber light shifted in the windows.

"It's me, Malia," a woman said, but her voice sounded older than the Malia I knew, tinny and weakened with age. "Please open, no one will hurt you."

"Door's unlocked," I said.

"Yes, that's true. Though I'd rather be invited inside."

I felt Cassie begin to push past me, and held her back. "I've got it," I said, stepping forward and opening the door. To my surprise, it was Malia who stood outside. But not the one I had met. The lady on the doorstep was fifty years her senior, yet unmistakably the same person. Same height, albeit a bit hunched over. Black hair pulled up in a bun with a lock of white curling down the side of her face. She had aged well. Her skin was smooth and shiny, most of the wrinkles by her eyes and under the jowls. The dress was Victorian, but of a steampunk variety. Crimson with black lining. A form-fitting buttoned top with a billowing skirt, frilled at the bottom. High-heeled boots with black ribbons running up the open sides. Her eyes were unchanged. That sparkling jade.

This was not an old lady who merely looked like Malia.

"Hi, Jesse. Miss me?"

This was the same chick who had flashed her tits to me on stage. Had blown me in the bathroom back at the imaginary Mule. Had let me bend her over the countertop and take her from behind. And had photographed it all somehow and sent the pictures to my wife. Disgraced me in the eyes of Al.

"No," I said, my vocabulary reduced to this lonely word.

Torches lit the street behind her, held by statues of stone men that must have been men in costume. Fog from the Smoky Mountains hung in the air, creating a corona of haze around each amber flame.

"Don't lie," she said, her red lips twisting into a wry smile.

"I'm not," I said. "I've given that up."

"You give up everything and you'll have nothing left to give."

"I've got plenty left," I said, and stepped aside. "Come on in." She tugged her skirt in the briefest curtsy and came through, carrying with her the scent of autumn spices. I closed the door, and a large roach scuttled up the wall.

"Where's Rox?" Cassie said. "I did what you said, now I want to see him."

Imagine having versions of yourself in varying ages. I had my own questions, but none more pressing than Cassie's, so I held my tongue.

"I am happy to take you to him. As you'll soon see, he's doing extremely well. I think you'll be delighted."

"Bullshit." I grabbed her bare forearm, loose skin and bone. "This isn't a game anymore. Give us our son and let us go." I could feel her blood pumping against my hand.

"When has this ever been a game?" she said. Had this person also been abused by camp counsellors at Love Week? Watched the light fade from her daddy's dying eyes? Danced in a basement full of boys while high on ecstasy? Did they all have to endure the same torments, or was each version subjected to a different section of hell? I released her. Pitied her. Goddamn it, Malia's a clone.

So many thoughts and questions swirled through my muddled brain but only one mattered. "Where's Rox?"

"I told you, safe. Safer than he's ever been with you." These cutting words contrasted against her wry smile.

"Where is he?" I said.

The older lady stood in between Cassie and me. In this rundown room of a cabin fit to collapse. A town not listed on any map, crawling with monstrosities. She tugged at the front of her jacket, smoothed her ruffled skirt. "What if I told you," she said, "that Rox was better off without you? That we could restore the brain you wrecked. Allow him to enjoy the same quality of life as any able-minded boy and mature into a productive man. But that you would have to let him go."

No, this was not a game. "Where is he?" I said.

She skewered me once again with those preternatural eyes. "Would you do it?"

"We're not leaving without our son," Cassie said.

"And who does that benefit?" Malia said. "You or him? Would you not leave him in the care of a specialist who could restore his mental processes? Or would you take him home in his present condition where he cries from loud noises and can't tie his own shoes?"

"Stop it," I said. "This isn't the fucking Mayo Clinic. Cut the bullshit."

"No, it's not," Malia said. "They can't offer him the same opportunities in life that we can."

Her dress looked black in the dim lighting. Cassie's face was a half-moon.

"Where is he?" I said. It was the only question that mattered.

Malia smiled. Age had darkened her teeth. "Let's go see."

She led us through the front door. Cassie gasped when she stepped outside. The dirt road was obscured by a scrim of fog that refracted the amber torch flames. I didn't know if it was closer to midnight or morning. The moon was hidden and the forest was quiet except for the occasional chirp. There was a faint static buzzing in the air that seemed to be silence itself. Malia lifted her skirt as she stepped down to the road and her boots sank into the mist.

"You guys piping this shit in or what? Steam machine, dry ice?"

"It's the Smoky Mountains, smarty-pants," Malia said, and I could see the humour in her eyes. We followed her off the porch, turning right and travelling up the road away from the depot. I took a close look at one of the torch-bearing statues as we passed by and would have sworn it was chiselled stone.

But it wasn't. One wrong move and these cloned men would leave their posts and swarm Cassie and me and burn us alive. I wondered if they were separate individuals or if they shared a hive mind. If one eye opened, would they all open at once?

I sped up to walk next to Malia. "Where's the other you?" I said.

"There is no other me."

"The younger one. The one I met. Come on, you're going to tell me the resemblance is coincidental?"

"Different body, same person." She gave me a knowing look, one of a secret lover.

More connective threads.

I stopped talking, fearing what my questions might reveal. I took Cassie's hand and our fingers intertwined. Walking together down a street that had a ceremonial feel. More so than our wedding, which had felt more like a house party. The two of us and our closest friends, who were really cling-ons in retrospect. Our matrimony just another excuse to get wasted. It had been out on a little farmland at a place in Chattahoochee Hills owned by a friend of Caspian's, under a sprawling oak tree. Cassie had just started to show, but you couldn't tell in her dress. Her folks were the only family there, and they split right after the ceremony, which we had both laughed through so hard we barely heard anything the officiant said. Tripping on the absurdity of the situation. The embarrassment of having everyone's eyes on us as we went through some farce ritual. Both of us mutually unorthodox yet wanting to perpetuate systemic order for our offspring. Kids in adult costume.

It's the laughter that bonds us, I think. I've never been able to make anyone else laugh like I can her. It's like a frequency we both tap into. I can sense the laugh coming before I've formulated the joke. The darker the better. Bang our heads against the wall or bounce off the bottom of a drug binge and we look at each other dazed and laugh. Tuck us in our graves, cover us in dirt, and you'll hear a chuckle. I squeezed her hand and she squeezed back. I don't know who took more comfort, me or her. Probably me.

Speaking of graves, that's where we were headed. At first glance, it was a quaint little church. Methodist or Baptist, maybe Lutheran. Brick siding with a thin spire that would more accurately be called an obelisk. A cross at the top, but not a Christian one. More like a sun cross with a gaping eye in its centre. The wrought-iron fence behind the building contained the graveyard, which looked like something straight out of a George Romero film with the ground mist and canting headstones. Cue Michael Jackson's 'Thriller' and watch the undead claw their way out of the dirt.

Six steps led up out of the fog to a double-sided doorway. No nameplate or other building designation. Malia stopped at the top and turned.

"You need to prepare yourself for what you're going to see inside," she said.

"Which is what?" I said.

Her gaze shifted back and forth between us. "Your failings," she said. "And how to make them right."

"And we're to get this lesson in morality from who? You?"

"From Rox," Malia said.

Cassie's hand had begun to tremble. She released her grip and I wanted to grab hold of her hand again but she crossed her arms. "We know our son. We love our son. Take us to him," Cassie said. "Now."

I knew better than to cross that tone of voice, but wasn't sure how Malia would respond. She grabbed one of the doors by the handle and pulled it open, revealing a dark sanctuary lit by candle sconces. Smart lady. Much smarter than the chick I'd shot Jameson with, who had stuffed dollar bills down my pants while I danced on the bar.

The inside of the church was ransacked. Dusty floor with loose boards. A splintered pew shoved against the wall. Move it and watch the rats scatter. The collapsing rafters were draped in spiderwebs so large they flowed in the draft created by the open door. Were I to come across this church on my own I'd consider it a hazard. No way I'd trust the rotting floorboards to hold my weight. But they felt deceptively sturdy as we walked down the centre of the room. All part of the design.

I surveyed the rubble scattered across the floor. Saw bits of wood from broken crosses. A ceramic eye, a whiskered jaw, thorns embedded in brown hair. Jesus shattered into a thousand pieces. This house of blasphemy.

"Who are you people?" I said, my voice reverberating in the quiet room, and received no answer. Cassie was hugging herself. I felt watched.

The steps leading to the pulpit were broken with jagged edges. "Follow me," Malia said, and we watched as she carefully placed her feet on the few footholds that wouldn't cave. We followed her up onto the open landing. There was a stain on the floor where an organ once stood. A square patch where the podium used to be. Malia bent over as she walked and examined the boards, stopping by one on the left-hand side and lifting it up.

"Hold this, please," she said, and I did. She bent down and wiped dirt and sawdust off a crooked nail and pulled it. I heard a faint click. We moved to the backside of the pulpit and repeated the exercise. Then again on the right-hand side. This time when she pulled the bent nail a wooden board popped up ever so slightly in the centre of the floor. Underneath this board was a small hidden panel that slid open to reveal a series of buttons that blended into the appearance of packed dirt. It was a keypad. Malia entered the code and we heard the pop of locks disengaging as the outline of a hatch door emerged along the seams of the floorboards.

"It's heavy," Malia said, by which she meant, 'You lift it.'

I did, and it weighed every bit of fifty pounds. I had a flash vision of dropping the heavy lid on Malia's head when she moved underneath it, but resisted. She's a victim in this, too.

There was a steep stairway leading down. A faint light coming from the bottom. Malia went first, Cassie second, me last. I lowered the lid down after us, igniting the pain in my strained back. Heard the locks reengage when I let it go, and thought, *Here we are, served up on a silver platter.*

The stairway led to a long concrete corridor. Caged bulbs were spaced out along the wall, providing a sterile light. We followed Malia down a ways, could hear her Victorian dress sashaying in the tomb-like silence. Passed a couple of unmarked doors made from what looked like reinforced steel. Under other circumstances this would be the realisation of a childhood dream. Hidden bunkers, elaborate conspiracies, top-secret experiments. I didn't feel elated, though. I felt dread. Every step led me closer towards the realisation that this was something we'd never recover from. There was no way to return to a life of normalcy after this. No matter what, we would be forever altered, and it was all my fault.

I'm not sure how far the hallway stretched, because we stopped before we reached the end. A nondescript door, same as the others. Reinforced steel. Malia was nearly eye level with me in her high-heeled boots. Taller than Cassie by a few inches, looking very matronly standing there with her hands clasped before her. "Who wants to go first?" she said.

Cassie and I looked at each other. "First, where? For what?" I asked.

"To see Rox."

"Me," Cassie said.

"Wait, hold on," I said. "We're going together."

Malia shook her head. "I'm afraid not. It's one at a time or not at all."

Physically harming her would get us nowhere, but it's all I could think to do. Wrench her frail arm behind her back and threaten to break it. "I want to meet Mr. O, or whoever the fuck is behind this," I said, my voice trembling.

"Watch what you wish for," Malia said, and it caused the hairs on the back of my neck to prickle. The fear and sadness in her engineered eyes.

"Look, I don't care," Cassie said. "I just want to see my son. Please, take me to him."

I could see the pain this was causing her, and didn't want to prolong it with my puny negotiations. "Do it," I said, and Malia nodded.

"Follow me," she said, opening the door and ushering Cassie through, leaving me alone in the silent tunnel with my worries and toxic thoughts. Certain I was being abandoned again.

ⳋ

You're never really alone, even when physically isolated. Rocket up to the moon and you're still stuck with your mind. That chattering blob of negativity. Conjuror of doomed futures. Reminder of past mistakes. You think you control it until it turns on you and you realise how powerless you truly are. Where do those voices come from? Why can't we shut them up?

Dark thoughts chiselled at my resolve as I sat in that cold, empty tunnel. Alliances were being made without me. My fate was being decided by a jury of enemies. I had lost my agency, my testimony. Sitting in this hallway like a kid scolded for acting up in class.

Sometime later, maybe an hour, though it felt longer, the door reopened and Malia stuck her head through. "Okay. Your turn," she said, and my legs began to shake.

"Where's Cassie?"

Malia considered the question. "Recovering," she said.

Am I ready to see this? Are you?

I followed Malia into a windowless sitting room, everything grey, the carpet, the cloth chairs. Doors in three of the walls, nothing on the fourth. Malia pointed to the door on my right. "That's where you go to see Rox. I'll wait here."

I wanted more than anything to walk into a room filled with smiling faces and the combined shout of, 'Surprise!' Would have kissed everyone on the lips, even Caspian, and thanked them for the experience. The great gift of feeling alive.

But the room was dark and empty. An armchair sat in front of a glass wall. It was like the surveillance room back at the warehouse. I was on the viewing side of a two-way mirror that I couldn't see through. There was a door on the opposite wall that was locked. Only thing to do was sit, so I sat.

After just a few seconds the frosted glass began to clear like a car windshield in winter, offering a view into a room much like the one I was in. Rox was sitting in a chair directly across from mine. He was upright and attentive, hands in his lap, eyes alert. Typically, he'd be slouched down with his arms crossed trying to cram himself into the cushions or find a shell in which to hide his head. He looked like he'd aged a year. Been sent to boot camp or confidence school or given a brain transplant. What had they done to my son?

"Rox!" I leapt to my feet, placed my hands on the glass window. "Can you hear me?"

Rox calmly nodded his head.

"He cannot see you, however." A soothing male voice came from a speaker I hadn't seen in the corner. *"There is a mirror on his side."*

Doctor O and his goddamn mirrors.

I knocked softly on the window, this barrier between my son and me. "Hey, buddy," I said. "Daddy's here. I was just with Mommy. It's so good to see you, buddy. Are you okay?"

He nodded his head again. "I'm okay," he said. "A little tired. I was sleeping before."

This was the first time I'd seen him talk without squirming like he had to fight with the words to force them out. There was no stutter, no stammering. No squashed face of dire concentration.

"You were sleeping, buddy?" I said. "Yeah, it's pretty late, huh?"

"I don't know what time it is, actually," he said. "Nighttime is all. It's always nighttime here. I'm always sleeping. Even when I'm awake. Like everything's a dream."

"This is his first experience with the linear narrative of lucid reality," the voice said through the speaker. *"He is still adapting to his abilities to absorb, process, and comprehend the information his mind takes in."*

It was like having someone read over my shoulder. I just wanted that voice to go away. "You look great, buddy. I can't believe how well you're talking. I'm going to be with you soon and we're going to go home, okay?"

Now he looked uncomfortable for the first time. "But...." he said, the beginning of a stammer, the familiar look of pained confusion on his face. "I don't know myself there. I'm all alone. I have a friend here. He helps me think and see things and say what I feel and I'm not as scared when I'm with him."

Please do not take my son from me. "A friend? That's great. Can I meet your friend? Tell me about him."

Rox shifted in his chair; he looked down, concentrating. "I met him in the mirror. Only I can see him, I think. Like he's inside of me, kind of. Kind of like an imaginary friend? But I know he's real, because he tells me what to say and I can hear him. Or sometimes he'll use my mouth to say it himself. Which sounds weird, but I don't mind. And I know it's not just me knowing what to say, or saying the things he says. He lives in the mirror, I think. Because he goes away when I'm not near one. And then the bad dreams come and I can't think anymore or say the things I want to say. And then it's like being at home. And I don't want to go back to being that way if I can be this way, even if it's like being in a dream."

How can I make my son go back to the way he was if he doesn't want to?

"Does your friend have a name?"

Rox looks up and offers a sheepish grin, like he's embarrassed. "Yes. But it's not like a normal name. It sounds kind of weird."

"Yeah?" I said. I'd never had a real conversation like this with my son before. "He's got a funny name?"

Rox nodded, sitting upright and alert in his chair.

"Can you tell me what it is? Can I meet him?"

Rox nodded again. His eyes shifted back and forth as though searching his memory banks, or trying to put all the letters in the right order. Then he faced me, staring, I suppose, at himself, and prepared to speak. His mouth opened, and out came the sound of my damnation. That reverberating chirp from a sonar machine at full volume, tunnelling into my ears and drilling straight into my brain.

A flash of light, then I'm looking through a set of eyes that aren't mine. Typed words on a sheet of white, separated by symbols. A book, this one.

Please don't read this. Please don't read this.

★   ★   ★

Astaroth ⊕ Adoor ⊕ Cameso ⊕ Valluerituf ⊕ Marreso ⊕ Lodir ⊕ Cadomiir ⊕ Aluiel ⊕ CalnNeisso ⊕ Tealy ⊕ Pelorim ⊕ Viordy ⊕ Meusa ⊕ Calmiron ⊕ Noard ⊕ Nisa ⊕ Chenibaranbo ⊕ Calevodium ⊕ Brazo ⊕ Tabarasol ⊕ Come ⊕ Arastoth ⊕ Amen

★   ★   ★

I hear your inner voice, reading the future words I must write. That damned incantation that I read before and just read again, knowing now what it does. The soil it turns and the seed it plants.

I see my story rewind, and start over. I'm in the corner of my old apartment looking down at myself as I stagger and scream. I'm wasted on stage creating distortion. A spark and I'm staring into Caspian's severed head. The doctor with those walrus teeth. A voice now speaking inside my brain in a language I shouldn't understand. It's my son's secret friend and he's bigger than anything, than everything, and he's ancient and wise and he says he'll take care of us all. And he's my son's father, and he's mine, and we are all his sons and daughters, and his laughter is like breaking glass, and now that we've created the space for him to enter he comes.

"Stop!" I'm shouting. Maybe I've just begun or have been the whole time Rox began making that blasphemous noise. "Stop! Stop! Stop!" Screaming like a strobe light, crying because I can never compete with the father he has now. His secret friend.

And then I'm looking through my own eyes again, and my ears are ringing, and my face is wet, and my throat is sore, and my son is staring calmly in my general direction, but it's not my son anymore. I stop screaming. Let silence reclaim the room.

Strive for words that will reverse all this – the anti-incantation – and realise I have nothing left to say.

I flattened my hands to the window, pressing my forehead against glass so hot it nearly burns. "I love you, son."

Rox calmly nodded his head. "I know you do," he said.

Frost expanded out from the edges of the window until the view of my son was obscured. I staggered back and collapsed in the chair. Then my side of the glass took on the reflected surface of a mirror and I was staring at myself, pale with grey stubble, gaunt with hollowed eyes.

Then I heard Rox calling from the other side of the window, "Dadda! Dadda!" The addled voice of my true son. His hands pounding on the glass. "Me, Dadda. Here! Dadda, here!"

The door opened and I looked to see grandma-Malia step through. I turned back to the mirror and saw a different face reflected on its surface. A woman of frightening beauty. Long, thick hair. Swan neck. Smooth, ivory skin and ruby lips. Furious eyes.

"Dadda, no!" Rox was shouting. "No, Dadda!"

"That's enough for now," she said. Rox began screeching when he heard her voice.

The rage I felt at that moment was beyond anything I had ever experienced. A lingering residue from whatever had invaded my mind. The face of destruction from Cassie's spiritual story of war, but worse. An insatiable appetite for pain. And I was its vessel. I leapt from the chair and charged Malia, grunting, slathering. Rox screeching in my ears. I clawed her to the ground like a bear, falling on top of her and clubbing her with my fists. A mindless frenzy of flailing arms, spittle flying, a gurgling sound from my mouth and hers as my hands find her neck and squeeze. A pall of red films my vision, calling for all of earth's strength to enter my hands. I look down to watch her die and instead I see her smile. Find glee in her haemorrhaging eyes. This is what she wants. Or, if not her, the thing that compels her. Because if she dies so does my soul, creating a vacancy. A blank space for something to fill.

I let her go. My breath coming in ragged gasps along with hers.

There is still mercy in me. I have yet to succumb.

I stood and stepped away. Listening to her delirious laugh.

I won't kill out of anger. Out of fear.

But I will kill to protect my son, or to save him, if I can. Killing her would achieve neither.

Blood ran from her nose and split lower lip. Her left eye was already swollen. "You won't have another chance like this," she said, blood gurgling in the back of her throat. Rox had stopped shouting from the other room and I listened for the sound of people rushing to help, but heard nothing. They were going to let me kill her if that's what I decided to do.

"Chance like what?" I said, willing the red pall to recede from my mind. Uncurling my fists.

"To take control," she said.

"No," I said. "Killing you is losing control. Is that what you want?"

She laid her head back so she was staring straight up at the ceiling. "Wanting is a waste of time. I gave that up long ago."

I went and placed my hands against the wall and tried to collect myself. To calm my racing heart and quell my murderous rage. Cassie was right: we would have to fight to reclaim our son, but on our terms not theirs.

"Who are you?" I asked, still facing the wall. The question could have been for me as much as her. "What are you?"

"That's complicated," she said. "Might as well ask the river. You'll get a different answer each time."

My anger rose and I had to remember that she was baiting me. Suicide by nonsense. Cassie once tried to teach me a breathing technique to achieve a calm state of mind. All it ever did was make me light-headed. I turned from the wall, walked over and bent down by Malia. "What have you done to Rox?"

Her poor face was battered good, blood pooling under her thin skin like liver spots. Great, I'd beaten up an old lady. If there is such thing as a life review upon death, mine is going to be one sordid mess.

"That's not for me to say," Malia said.

"Well, I've got no one else to ask."

"You don't want to meet the one with the answers."

"You're wrong about that."

Malia tried to wipe blood from her face with her sleeve, but only smeared it across her cheek. "He doesn't make things better. He only makes them worse."

"What can be worse than this?" I'd take this question back if I could. It must have been accepted as a challenge.

Malia's bloodshot eyes softened for a moment, expressing sadness, pity. Then her lips peeled back to reveal crooked teeth coated in blood and she started laughing. The laugh of a lunatic staring into the great abyss. Eyes bulging, neck swelling, chest heaving. Malia was going to die from dark hilarity, choking on her own blood.

I grabbed her arms and lifted her to a sitting position, patting her on the back to clear her throat. A mist of blood sprayed from her nose and mouth as she continued to choke on my question. Intent, it seemed, on having me kill her one way or another. Her laughter went on for a long while. Several minutes, at least. Every time it seemed to be winding down in hitching gasps something would start her up again. I let it run its course, resisting the urge to silence her with my hands.

"Oh, my," she said. "Sorry, what was the question again?"

"Forget it," I said. "Where do we go from here?"

She smeared more blood across her face and looked at the wet sleeve. "You're free to leave whenever you'd like," she said.

"Great, let me go grab Cassie and Rox and we'll be on our way."

Malia stretched out a hand so I could help her up. I stood and pulled her with me. She swayed backwards and placed a hand on my shoulder for balance. Leaning on me for strength.

"Okay," she said. "I'll take you to them."

The far door clicked open as she approached it. We exited into another concrete tunnel. Took a right and passed several unmarked doors before Malia stopped beside one on the left. She opened it and we entered a spacious hospital room with a couple of sitting chairs, a wall of cabinets, a monitoring station on wheels with an IV stand, and a reclining bed where Cassie was currently sleeping, bathed in soft light from a bedside lamp.

Her head was wrapped in a dressing that ended just above her bruised eyes. Right forearm enclosed in a soft cast. Her dress had been removed and she was now wearing a paisley gown. Spots of rust-coloured blood dotted the fabric under her left ear.

I stopped by the bed and listened to her breathing. Slow and shallow. Likely sedated. I turned to Malia. "What the hell happened?"

"She...." Malia was still dazed. She struggled to recall some elusive word. "Resisted."

"Resisted? It looks like she got her ass kicked."

Malia touched the tender swelling on her own face with her fingertips. "She tried breaking through the glass barrier. That's how she fractured her arm. The injury to her head occurred when we were trying to subdue her. For her own protection, as much as our own. It took several men to restrain her. She bit two of them, gouged out an eye, and ripped off half an ear. Your wife got the better of the exchange, I can assure you."

I looked at her sleeping peacefully. Wondered what nightmares were running through her mind. Looks like we'd had our fight after all. And this is where it got us.

"She'll never leave without Rox," I said.

"No," Malia said. "She won't."

"So where does that leave us? What the fuck do you all want?"

The beep of the monitoring machine was like a metronome. A bag of saline, sedative, or poison dripped from a clear bag into a vein in Cassie's arm.

"Sacrifice," Malia said.

I felt like crying. I was physically and emotionally spent. What more could they want from me? My life? Fine, take it. I may still be drawing breath, but I quit living years ago. Eternal sleep sounded like a vacation.

"Just say it, and I'll do it. Whatever it is. Just tell me what I need to do to get them out of here."

"You go this route, there's no going back," Malia said.

I turned. "What option do I have? What the hell do I have to bargain with? I'm fighting shadows. I've fallen behind every move. I just want it to end, okay? I just want it to be over."

Malia approached me, leaned, and whispered into my ear. "Please don't give up," she said. "Never quit fighting."

I'm a rope being pulled on both ends. I started to dispute her plea and she hushed me. "Save it," she said. "Your words are wasted on me. I'll take you to who you need to meet."

My body began to vibrate. My stomach dropped several floors. "Mr. O?"

"If you're ready."

'Ready' is a misleading word. It's a mantra, nothing more. Tell yourself you're ready all you want. Tell anyone who will hear, and it doesn't mean shit. Because you don't know whether or not you're truly ready until you step into whatever experience you were getting ready for. Then your words are worthless.

"Yes," I said. Lying is a hard habit to break.

She smiled, a spark of compassion in her one open eye. This woman with her many twins. To think I had met two generations of the same genetic sequence in the span of a few days. The look she gave me now suggested affection. Maybe she had a shared memory of our time at The Mule Kick. Maybe I'd endeared myself somehow. Passed some kind of test that would garner mercy. Solved the great riddle in the game by accident.

Her open eye closed, her mouth opened, blood between the teeth, and out poured that unclean sonic reverberation, putting me to sleep.

ካ

I hear a guitar playing in my head. Acoustic strings strummed hard. I'm inside the hollow chasm that amplifies the sound. A temple of potential. Energy and vibration enough to move young and old. End or start a war.

I'm conscious now and can open my eyes but I'm not ready. The song in my head has never been played before. I'm its sole audience. Its lone witness. Without me, it doesn't exist. Without it, my life is empty. When it stops my soul will wither and die. Let me stay here a little longer, then. Me and this simple tune that makes my heart shine and my body shake and my worries small. Let me dance one more time before I die.

There was a first person to strum a guitar and there will be a last. A first eye to open and a final one to close. Melody in between.

At least I'm comfortable. Or was. Reclined in a cushioned chair. My face against the corduroy fabric that smells like a teddy bear I once had as a little boy. The familiar odour unlocking a memory of my childhood bedroom from some closed chamber in my brain. Light streaming through the window blinds on a Saturday morning. Teddy on one side, a Nerf football on the other. The day stretched out ahead of me like an endless road. No need to rush. No need to worry. Nothing to do but lie in the comfortable bed with my cushioned friends and wait for the smell of bacon grease to worm its way into my room. A day I'll never experience again.

There's a crackling fire. An amber glow on the other side of my eyelids. I'll stay like this until my body starves and the music fades and the soft light goes dark. I'm already under a graveyard.

Then I remember what Malia said. *Please don't give up.* I saw Cassie lying battered in the bed having fought several men. The army's on the battlefield and there's not a friend in sight. Given the chance, I'd kill them all. And that chance has come.

★   ★   ★

I opened my eyes to a room full of shadows. A study or sitting room, much like the one I'd looked in on from my prison above the mantel. Two chairs angled towards the fire. Me in one, reclined so that I'm lying flat. A figure in the other, sitting deep in the plush cushions, a vague shape within a shadow. I glanced above the fireplace and was grateful to find an oil painting, not some decapitated head with gaping eyes.

The chair squeaked when I returned it to a sitting position. My head was like the hollow of a guitar, waiting to be strummed. The music had stopped and all I heard was the flutter of flames. *I will not be the first to speak. I will not be the first to speak.*

"You the sick fuck behind all this?" I said.

A warm chuckle. "For all intents and purposes, yes. Though I am but one link in a chain."

That chuckle, like I'm cute. "Some chain."

"Indeed."

All I could see were twin reflections of firelight on his eyeglasses. "So many questions," he said. "And yet, no one ever has much to say."

"I've got something to say." I leaned forward for a closer look, but might as well have been talking to an oil stain. Silence. It's an invitation to speak, it seems. So I opened my mouth to spew out my most venomous insults, incriminations, and demanding questions, but all I could manage was a quiet gasp. My mind a ball of tangled yarn.

"Yes, it's a curious thing," he said, his calm, soothing voice coming through twin reflections of firelight.

I looked around the room. Bookshelves lined the walls. Some ancient-looking text was propped up on a round table in the centre of the room. Men stood in the shadows of the far corners, watching me. Same height, same age, same face. The same man I may have murdered.

I turned back to the figure sitting beside me. "Who are you?"

That warm chuckle. This smug fuck. "You ask that often," he said.

"You been watching me this whole time? Is this your entertainment?"

"No, this is my work."

I snorted. Having a regular old chuckle fest here. Us chums.

"You're a fucking sick, sadistic, evil psychopath," I said.

He said nothing. Those twisting flames.

"Let's cut the bullshit," I said. "What will it take for you to let us go?"

"Go where?" he said.

"Home."

"Why are you so eager to return? What awaits you there?"

"Give me a break," I said. "How'd you like to go through the shit you've put me through?"

"What makes you think I haven't?"

I hadn't thought of that. "I want my life back. My family."

"Is this not your life? Has your life ended?"

I sighed. "What will it take? What do you want?"

"I don't want anything."

"You're going to stop messing with me, you understand? I'm done."

I was having a staring contest with firelight, though I couldn't feel its heat.

"What did you do to Rox?" I said.

"Rox is capable of becoming more than he currently is."

"You're not taking my son."

"Please, tell me how he's better off with you."

I stood, took a step towards this man and had an arm around my neck cutting off my air before I even realised what I was doing. I was pulled back into the chair and released. I tried that calming technique that never works, sounding like a bull.

"He's our son. We love him."

"Love him so much you won't let him get well?"

"He has doctors."

"He has irreparable brain damage."

"Okay, so. How can you fix that?"

"I can't. But I can give him purpose."

"What, a job in your torture factory?"

"Is that what this is?" he said.

"I don't know what this is. Why don't you tell me?"

"This is my purpose. My calling."

"You're fucking nuts."

"Show me sanity."

"Sanity? Go take a look at Cassie."

"The woman who broke her arm hitting a wall and gouged out a man's eye?"

"Yes, trying to save her son, you idiot."

"And did she?"

"She wouldn't have had to do any of that if you weren't a crazy asshole kidnapper."

A period of silence follows every insult. "Remove all the struggle from your life, what's left?"

Please, put me back in the wall, I'd prefer it to this. Ten years from now and I'll still be sitting here talking in circles. "Bliss," I said.

"Bliss in the absence of suffering? How would you know bliss without a counterpoint against which to reference it?"

"Because bliss is bliss. You don't need pain to feel pleasure."

"Yes," he said. "You do. There is no peace without war."

"So is that what you are, then? War?"

Those flickering flames were mesmerising.

"Without us," he said, "there can be no peace."

"Us? What, you and your clone buddies? Your wolf men?"

"Everyone involved in this story is part of the army, including you."

"Yeah, well. We're on opposite sides."

"God and the Devil, yes? If not for the Devil, would we have need for God?"

He'd be better off having this conversation with Cassie. "That has nothing to do with me."

"You are the story," he said. "You are the great attractor of the most valuable asset in this plane of existence."

"Spare me the Deepak Chopra bullshit." Though he'd made me curious. "What valuable asset?"

"Human awareness."

This is why I warned you not to read this book.

"What are you talking about?"

"We are at war. Fighting for peace. For happiness. For love. For the achievement of our greatest potential. A bird cannot fly without resistance. Neither can man."

"What side are you on?"

"The side of resistance," he said.

"So, what. I'm the bird?"

"You are a casualty, I'm afraid. Collateral damage, as it's called. I need this story to spread the resistance. This is not my doing. I have my own masters. I only follow orders."

"What story?"

"The one you will write."

"I'm not a fucking writer."

"No, but you have a story. The author will come."

This book is ghost written, you'll see.

"What author?"

The firewood popped, sparks exploded in his eyes. "The one inside your son."

I sank back into my chair, watched the fire. Its purpose is to burn. And we call it cosy. Need it for heat, to cook our food. Just don't get too close or it will kill you.

"What is inside my son?"

"The key to our happiness. The cause of your suffering."

"What is it?"

"You will find out."

"What is it?"

"It either lives in him or you."

"What?"

"The dark that supplies the light. Without light, all is dark."

"Without you all was fine, you sick fuck. Give me back my son."

My breath was trembling. This man I couldn't even see.

"You can have your son. If I can have your story."

"Story." It sounds so simple.

"That's all."

This book you hold in your hands. It wasn't written by me.

"I'll fucking write whatever you want me to."

"I don't want you to write a thing."

"Fine, who then?"

I'm so sorry.

"You'll see."

My greatest regret atop a mountain of others is that I never got to see his face. But those twin flames are burned into my brain like an afterimage. I was escorted out of the room by two of the clones. So strange seeing them up close. Tall, dark, and handsome. Strong hands gripping my arms. I wondered if they work out or if their strength is genetically engineered. Create a pin-up calendar of the whole brotherhood and make a million bucks.

I was feeling strangely elated after my talk with the brains behind the operation. Having negotiated the terms of our release. This experience was ending and I had developed a minor case of Stockholm syndrome. Felt a sense of camaraderie with these clone chaperones, one on each side.

"You guys talk?" I said.

The hallway was long and empty. Concrete slab floor with cinderblock walls. *Who built this place*, I wondered. Probably these guys.

"The silent type, I get it," I said. "Part of your mystique."

"You killed our brother," the man on my right said, and that chilled me. I had forgotten what elder-Malia had said, *This is not a game.*

"I what?" Their hands gripped my arms, leading me forward. Just the three of us in this underground bunker.

The one on my left spoke with the same voice as the one on my right. "You killed our brother."

They halted me in one synchronised movement, turned and pushed me up against the wall, standing shoulder to shoulder. A paper doll chain turned flesh and bone.

"Closed his eyes to this world," they said together, blinking at the same time.

I held up my hands. What, was I going to apologise? After the hell they'd put me through?

"I had no choice," I said. "I don't know what the fuck you guys know about this world, but this isn't how it works. Your brother attacked me. If I killed him, it was in self-defence." Even that wasn't really true given how my mind had been invaded. If anything, I had been directed to kill, manipulated like a puppet. If anything, their brother had killed himself.

I was staring into human eyes, black, both sets, and not finding one bit of humanity.

"We know of this world and more. Murder never goes unpunished. It is a basic law."

"I've paid enough," I said, heat rising to my face. If they wanted to punish me, let them try.

"You have paid a grain of sand when your debt is the ocean floor," they said.

Christ almighty, I didn't expect something so deep from these lab babies. They are vessels, though. Their consciousness, as I now know, comes from another place.

"You know what? You guys are assholes. I've got nothing more to say."

They tried to grab my arms and I shrugged them off. No more manhandling. I can walk my damn self. They fell in behind so we walked the hallway like a flock of birds. We came to a double door and the men stopped me. We stood there for a few seconds and then I heard the clank of heavy locks disengage. The men opened the doors and we entered the access room to an elevator. Both men took turns punching numbers on a keypad for a solid minute. A green light flashed and the doors opened. We entered and the cabin descended, how many floors I don't know. It stopped and opened onto a featureless antechamber with four plastic chairs and a single door on the far side. I was instructed to sit and wait. Life, I've come to realise, is mostly spent waiting for something else to happen.

Waiting is inherently boring. Combine it with existential terror, and it's torture. No iPhone to surf. Not even an outdated *Field & Stream* magazine to read. Just my panicked mind with its worries over the past and future. Know what I did? Pushups. Jumping jacks. I shadowboxed a badass and won. Played air guitar to a packed stadium. Then I sat and pondered my predicament. Wondered if I had been imprisoned here and left to die of thirst. Down payment on my insurmountable karmic debt.

Sacrifice, they said? Isn't that what I've done? Abandoned my life's passion for a steady paycheck. Stayed in place long enough to establish roots. Why, though? Sacrificed for who? Could I still be a father and a rock star? Replace my addiction to alcohol with something that ignites my soul? There's no happiness for me in the centre of the road, so why stay there? Fear of disappointing some spit-shined version of myself I don't even like. I'd been wasting my life. Mister O was right. What would I be returning home to but a dull fear more insidious than the extreme one experienced here? If I'm a vessel, it's because I've become empty.

The door opened, and there stood Malia. My Malia, the younger one. My crazy mistress. She was dressed in a white lab coat that looked more like a priest's robe. Her black hair washed clean of coloured dye. Her face as plain as God made it. Or as Doctor O had. She came through and sat in the chair beside mine.

"You sure do get around," I said.

Her mouth smiled, her eyes frowned. "More like I'm led."

"You need to stop playing the victim. You said you'd help me, and you lied. Did you know they'd be taking my wife and son?"

She stared into her hands. "I knew that one way or another you'd wind up here."

I leaned my head back against the stone wall. "What's the point of all this? Why do you do it? You're a clone, aren't you? Made in a lab?"

She shook her head. "Not a clone, a conduit. It's not like you think. All bad, like. It's more like a vaccine. How you use a disease to strengthen your immune system."

"A vaccine? How did sending pictures of us having sex to my wife inoculate me?"

She shook her head again. "It's not.... You won't figure it out all at once. It's not something I can explain."

"Can't or won't?"

She remained silent.

"What about those stories of you growing up. All lies?"

"No." She turned and looked me in the eyes. "That's our initiation. Our education. Our suffering. It helps us understand."

"Understand what?"

"The stakes," she said.

As Cassie would say, we are all just men and women crushed in Krishna's teeth. The world would be a better place if everyone played guitar.

"It's changing, though," she said. "Evolving. It's working. The darkness gets lighter. I am not like versions before me. One of the woodsmen went rogue, rescued an initiate. Don't give up no matter how dark it gets. Fight it until your dying day."

I scoffed. "Fight what?"

She looked towards the door like my enemy waited in the next room.

"The force of resistance," she said. "The scourge."

I laughed and shivered at the same time. "Those sound like names for songs my band would play."

"I've seen your band play, remember?"

What was that, a century ago? "Oh, yeah. You seemed to be enjoying yourself. Or was that all an act?"

"Honestly?"

I wondered if she even knew what that meant.

"It was the most fun I've ever had in my life," she said.

It was up there for me, too. Why had I given all that up?

That reminded me. "Hey, what happened to Caspian and those guys? What happened to Al?"

She shrugged. "They're all alive, if that's what you mean. Just have a blank space where the memory used to be."

"What, you have one of those memory erasers like they used in *Men in Black*?"

She shrugged again. I doubt she consumed much commercial art.

I looked at the unmarked door. Someone had decided to paint it grey. Why not yellow? Why not pink? "What's in there?" I said. "What's up next?"

"Why tell you when I can show you. Are you ready?"

"Hell no," I said.

"Okay," she said. "We can wait."

We sat for about a minute in silence, staring at the blank wall. Show wouldn't start until I stepped on stage and every minute I wasted delayed our return home. The crowd was growing anxious, or maybe that was just me.

I stood. "The scourge," I said. "The vaccine. I've never been more confused in my life."

"The more you learn," she said, "the less you know."

"Shut up, then," I said.

She opened the door and we walked through. So this was where he kept his lab. Impressive. Big and spacious with drawers along the walls like at a morgue. Steel workstations with vials and syringes and other mysterious utensils. Tubular pods meant to hold a person standing up. The floor was gleaming, the air purified. If there was a speck of dust in there I'd be shocked.

A young man in a lab coat came walking towards me. Early twenties with streaks of grey already highlighting his dark hair. We both wore the same style goatee.

"Mr. Wheeler," he said. Someone must have given him my dossier. "This is very courageous of you. You have my admiration."

"Thanks, but I wasn't given much choice." Humour is my form of self-defence, and I had left it behind. Something about those tubes.

"Have you changed your mind?" This kid, what is he, an intern?

"No. Whatever is in my son, I want it out."

"Great. It's decided, then."

My choice. "Fine."

There are questions you can ask here, but the answers don't help. It's not really about what happens to me, anyway. It's about what has already happened to you. As Malia would say in her roundabout way, "I," meaning me, "am but a stone tossed in the pond for the purpose of creating a wake."

I'll say it more plainly: I write jingles for ads that get played on the radio. My goal is to get them stuck in your mind. Doctor O has a ditty of his own, and this is how he spreads it: through stories, the most ancient virus known to mankind. My story brought you here despite the clear warnings. To this book that is coded with symbols you aren't meant to read. That's how he finds you. It's how he found me. Now you are part of his army, soon to be recruited and put through your own personal initiation. May be days, weeks, years. But there's no removing the mark.

The young man with the prematurely grey hair led me to a vertical pod.

"Will you please retrieve the transmitter?" he asked Malia.

She left us alone together. The term 'awkward silence' was coined for moments like this. I stood there, studying him. Wondering how he fit into the picture. And I've thought more about him since. If only I'd gotten a glimpse of Mister O during our fireside chat, I'd know. But here's my theory. This young lab technician was Mister O's eternity plan. Always keep a younger version of yourself handy in case something deadly happens.

Malia returned with the transmitter. A.K.A, my son. He looked so thin and fragile. Long, loose limbs, fresh skin on bone. A neck I could wrap my fingers around. Eyeglasses with inch-thick lenses. Greasy hair, hand combed and parted on the side. Cutest kid on earth, maybe the whole universe.

"Call my son a transmitter again, and I'll fucking kill you," I said. Me and my empty threats.

When Rox saw me he rushed forward. I squatted down and received him in open arms. Crushed him against my chest. Whenever I would hug him like this I heard all the things I wished I could say to him in my head and hoped he heard it in his. We couldn't talk in a meaningful way, so I prayed for telepathy. I think his heart heard. Otherwise, why the hug? Why squeeze me like I'm the only thing floating miles from shore?

"You okay, buddy?" I whispered, and he shook his head against my neck. He's not a liar like me.

"We're going to go home. Soon, okay?" I hoped I wasn't telling another lie, especially when he nodded his head and repeated that crucial word, "Home."

"I can't stop the talking," he said. "All the words, all the talking. And then when it stops talking I hear all the talking come out of my mouth."

I thought I knew what he was trying to say. "I'll make it quiet again," I said. I'd do anything in the world for the little dude, and that's no lie. I'm a good person, damnit. A better father than I would have thought. I'd given up my life for him, and was now risking my soul.

"Quiet," he said, and I pressed our heads together, sending 'I love you I love you I love you' to him through my brainwaves.

But I said it out loud for good measure, "I love you, Rox," and he squeezed harder. Here's a little-known secret: rock and rollers have big hearts. Just don't tell anyone.

I could have stayed like that for the rest of eternity, but nothing ever lasts. I broke the hug and stood up. "Okay," I said.

The young lab tech led us back to a pair of vertical pods stationed side by side and connected with wires. He opened one hatch door and Malia opened the other. The insides of both concave tubes were coated in gleaming mirrors. Mirrors, once again. I had been told enough to tease out what was happening here. I knew Professor O's early experiments dealt with importing consciousness into compatible vessels. Clearly some form of intelligence had been implanted into my son, and was now going to be transmitted to me. What I didn't know was the nature of this intelligence or where it had come from. Questions would lead to more nebulous answers. Physical violence would end with me in a hospital bed like my wife, if not worse. Neither action would do anything to relieve my son of the unwanted passenger in his mind. Some chatty son-of-a-bitch, apparently. Sometimes inaction is the best option. Sometimes you just have to hold to your word and hope for the best. I don't believe I made the right decision stepping into that pod, but I can't take it back.

"It'll all be over soon," I said to Rox. "Be strong, buddy."

Tears were in his eyes. "You too," he said, then stepped into the pod and turned to look at me. I watched as the door was shut, and right at the final moment, saw him smile. But it wasn't Rox's smile. It wasn't the smile he gave me when we hung the mobile of fighter jets from the ceiling in his room. Or the one he'd sometimes give when Cassie smeared whipped cream on my face for fun. This was something under the surface, like a shark in shallow water, smiling through him. Cold and mean and eager to enter me. To enter you.

I felt Malia's hand on my back urging me forward. I walked robotically into the mirrored chamber. The door shut before I had the chance to turn around. No final words. No last requests. Just the reflection of myself from every angle, so bright and clear I could trace every wrinkle in my skin, view into every pore. Trapped with the last person I'd want to be stuck with.

The space was tight. Cold, too. I was surprised my breath wasn't fogging the mirrored interior. The three-hundred-and-sixty-degree mirror reflecting my image to infinity in all directions, making me sick. "Hey, what do we do in here?" I asked, nearly shouting. But my voice was contained to this soundproofed chamber. My words dying the instant they exited my mouth. Muffled like there's no air. A candle snuffed in space. Which made it hard to breathe. The thought of that. It felt like I'd been in for minutes and it'd only been a second or two and I didn't know how long this would continue. The final moments of me as the man I knew then. On the precipice of some unfathomable change. My eyes grew wide and I banged on glass that didn't rattle or crack or make a sound of any kind. Screaming in the silent vibration of my chest and throat.

And I couldn't stand to look at myself in that way. The impotent maniac in the mirror. The soundless rage that won't help me escape. I lowered my arms, tried to relax, and failed, but at least presented a believable image. He was watching, I was sure of it, and I wanted to maintain some dignity. Or at least fake dignity through composure.

I would have preferred blindness to the sight of my own reflection, but my eyes had nowhere else to go. They scanned my pot belly. My pale, flaky skin. The receding hairline that had revealed asymmetrical moles. Sagging flesh, craggy wrinkles, grey hairs. There was once a time I'd spend hours staring at my reflection, flexing like some amateur bodybuilder. Did I take a wrong turn somewhere? If so, how far back?

At last, my eyes found themselves. The only feature that doesn't change. Not physically, at least. But I saw a change in them nonetheless. Fear where I used to see confidence. Cowardice where I used to see 'fuck you'. The man who was going to storm the world got sucked down a sewer drain and wound up here. And now the echolocations are beginning – dear God, help me – widening the void.

The companion comes as a series of images. An unfolding rose, black. A spinning six-pointed star. The horned head of a goat.

I am ejected from my body, viewing it from above. This skin suit that can only inhabit one entity at a time. And my expression changes in an instant. The rage has returned. The anger. My snarling lips are trembling. The violence in my eyes is no empty threat. A furious laugh of silent malice that I now hear in the mind I've re-entered. The cackle of my companion, entangled with me inside my skull.

My eyes are blank. I feel complete indifference, the total absence of hope. Bracing against a frigid wind blown across eons of ice.

Finally, I've found you.

The scourge is the size of all existence and twice as old. An empty void without boundaries or shape. A shudder like a groan of such wretchedness my body vacates trying to purge this deadly infestation. Surging like a seismic wave.

The empty space I created.

Its colour is no colour and always changing. Shifting an instant before solidifying into view. An idea that all ideas are wasted. That life is futile. The creator of death.

I come for it.

It makes my mind laugh like an allergic reaction as it tries out every word. All the languages ever known spoken at once. My glazed eyes are a dead man's, my mouth a gaping idiot's, shapes and calculations churning my brain matter to mush.

OBSIDEO

And I see all the stories, a dizzying spectrum of fractal constructs branching off at an exponential rate, multiplying faster than anyone could track. And in it is mine, the one you read now. The one this bitter wind will make me write. So that it can invade your skin and steal whatever creative impulse you may have. Leave you blank-eyed like a fish on a trawl line. Remove from you the love that is not old but new and expressed in spite of our random creation. Rob your ability to fight the force meant to cease existence. To seize the wheel. To stop the clock.

The scourge is in me – not all these words are mine. Don't let it enter you.

I'm soft flesh on a hanger of bone. Dull eyes that reject light. Head full of mindless memories that flash from a broken recorder. I am plain. I am pointless. The fever dream of a sick God gasping on Its dying breath. Forgotten if It wakes, obliterated when It dies.

You are a dream, too. The ghost of imagination. Feel the stirring? The long slumber is ending as the universe wakes to the infinite dark and the potential shown in this flash vision shall be forgotten. The emptiness must return.

I spill from the pod like a passed-out drunk, covered in piss, shit, and puke. My son was right; this fucker doesn't shut up. A constant babble of archaic languages like a beacon from hell. My mind's eye watches a rapid-fire loop of complex geometric patterns and the pillar memories of my life. Some kind of encoding process. I don't remember being dragged away and cleaned up. My only bit of retribution is against whoever had to scrub me down, but it doesn't bring me joy.

Even when I see Cassie again, nothing. Not even when we're reunited with Rox, the three of us creating an awkward triangle. Like I'm watching from the far side of another two-way mirror where everything is muted. Observing Cassie's hysterical joy over Rox's newfound linguistic abilities but not feeling it myself. Some residual after-effect from our companion that will either last or won't.

Cassie is too overwhelmed and maybe concussed to make decisions, and I'm too disturbed. Rox clings to her legs, not mine. Part of me is still me, but I'm on the periphery. Like I'm on the outside of my life looking in. My own Peeping Tom. I can feel my companion settling in, unpacking its stuff, testing out the utilities, moving furniture around. There is no dialogue between us, although I try to get one started. Talking tough and offering a peace treaty at the same time. I hope I'm just going mad, although that may be even worse. Or maybe it's the same thing.

The town has been evacuated, although I doubt the residents have strayed far. Some underground bunker where they all live and eat and spread the resistance. There's probably someone new at the Purge Palace now, reading Priscilla's journal and realising they've been abandoned by someone they thought they could trust, preparing for their trip here. A heroine with her invisible following. Her own ripple effect.

They're out there now, I know they are. You will join them soon.

My mind blanks like during a blackout. I suffer the worst parts of binge drinking without any of the benefits. The looks Cassie gives me during my brief periods of lucidity, I can't tell if it's concern over my well-being or hers.

"Are you okay? Are you okay? Are you okay?" is the repeating chorus line on a scratched record. I'm not sure I've answered her yet. My limbs are rigid – movements stiff – eyes open so wide they hurt. Fucker doesn't know how to blink.

Yes, in my strobe-light memory I see, that's no look of concern. Cassie's scared. She's keeping Rox away from me, and he's not resisting. He's scared, too.

Elder-Malia is gone, hopefully to the infirmary, if not hell. So is the younger one, and I think I know why. She's either afraid of my companion, or the one in her is hopelessly attracted to it. I wonder if I'll ever see her again. I hope not, but will never stop looking. When does this end? How? With an exorcist, or a return visit to Doctor O?

I vaguely remember being in Cassie's hospital room following the procedure. Then Cassie, Rox, and I are being escorted by a group of six or more identical men, always travelling in sets of two. They keep their distance from me now. Like I'm some abomination to them. Up the elevator, back to the surface. Back to planet earth. It's dusk again, or dawn.

The street lamp statues are all gone so the road is dark and the stars are blinking softly overhead. The view you can't get from the city. Dead lights that we fill with false meaning. Ransacked stars snuffed by the scourge heading our way.

I want to go home so bad it's beyond anything I've wanted before. Rewind the tape to where? I wonder. To just before I read the book or further back, I don't know.

They take Cassie and Rox away in a police car with darkened windows. She doesn't protest, and neither do I. We huddle together, but again, I'm the wobbly third wheel, only wanting distance between us.

"Be safe," she says, like I have any control over that. No hug; no kiss goodbye. "We'll be waiting for you." I plan to stay far away.

I hover over Rox, but he shies away from me. My eyes open so wide he's blurred. I'm wrestling with the rage inside me to get my words through, shouting from the far side of a boundless chasm. "Be good, son." Because that's all I want from him. That's all we need. For people to keep pumping goodness into the world, regardless of their plot in life. For people to fight against this resisting force.

I don't recall them being driven away. Whether I waved, offered a final farewell. I don't even know how long ago it was. Don't know where I am. Thankfully there are no mirrors in here. Just a place to eat, to shit, to sleep, and most importantly to write.

A stack of papers. An old-timey quill pen. How many times has this story been told? Since the beginning of time?

I'm no writer, but Doctor O told me not to worry. I realise, as I pick up the pen, he's right. The story's inside of me, and wants to come out. Being pushed forth by the compelling force within. Encoded with hazardous symbols. Malignant seeds planted in your subconscious, soon to sprout and unfurl their deadly bloom.

I told you not to read this book, but it's too late for you now. He's planted the beacon, and there's no getting it out. No way to purge it from your mind. Whatever you do, don't look in the mirror. Ransack your home for surveillance devices, or better yet, move. Now that the story has ended, your time has come. Maybe a week or so from now. Maybe tonight.

I'm so sorry to have subjected you to this. I had to, for my son.

But I'm not done fighting. In fact, the war has just begun.

I'm going back to making music now, although this new guitar feels ungainly in my arms. And my companion howls in fury when I play. Music is my weapon. Every note I strum is a shot fired across the bow. And with every shot I grow stronger. But then my mind goes blank and I wake up with fuzzy memories of time wasted and wonder how much progress I've lost, or if I've made any at all.

Here I am, in my hidden corner of the world. Alone with my malevolent mind. Tuned into the one bit of distraction I've been granted aside from this guitar. A video monitor, like the one from back in the surveillance room behind the two-way mirror. My voyeuristic view into a world I'll never rejoin.

I'm watching Cassie and Rox on a seventeen-inch screen. Grainy, black-and-white feed. She doesn't leave his side, and that makes me both sad and relieved. I'm unsure who needs who more. But they're not alone, and that's what worries me. Malia was right – I would be told many lies, and they saved the worst for last. Not that this has ended, or will anytime soon.

I haven't seen them eat in over a week. They don't sleep. Sometimes they cry, and they hold each other and rock back and forth for hours, even days, inducing a kind of hypnotic trance.

Other times, like now, they sit facing each other, staring intently. Completely still. There's no volume, so I can't hear what sound is coming through their gaping mouths. Throats convulsing like homunculi chambering venomous spit. It looks like they're singing, but that's no song. That's no song.

Cassie's eyes have rolled back into her head, the lids fluttering over balls of white. Gorgeous on this ghostly screen. Rox turns and faces me like he knows I'm watching. Just like John B at that goddamn orphanage after he ruined all his friends. And he bares that dark smile again. The one underneath, like a shark in shallow water, his mouth opening wide.

I feel myself fade away as I drop the guitar, abandoning it once more, maybe forever this time. Another blackout in a lifetime of many. My mouth opens against my will. So wide I feel the skin split at each side. Type-O blood wets my wavering tongue.

This tune that will destroy us. I begin to sing along.

A B C D E F G H I J K L

M N O P Q R S T U V W X

Y Z TH EE NG EA ST

FLAME TREE PRESS
FICTION WITHOUT FRONTIERS
Award-Winning Authors & Original Voices

Flame Tree Press is the trade fiction imprint of Flame Tree Publishing, focusing on excellent writing in horror and the supernatural, crime and mystery, science fiction and fantasy. Our aim is to explore beyond the boundaries of the everyday, with tales from both award-winning authors and original voices.

•

Look out for Brian Kirk's next book *We Are Monsters* coming November 2019

Other titles available include:
Junction by Daniel M. Bensen
Thirteen Days by Sunset Beach by Ramsey Campbell
Think Yourself Lucky by Ramsey Campbell
The Haunting of Henderson Close by Catherine Cavendish
The House by the Cemetery by John Everson
The Toy Thief by D.W. Gillespie
Black Wings by Megan Hart
The Playing Card Killer by Russell James
The Siren and the Spectre by Jonathan Janz
Wolf Land by Jonathan Janz
The Sorrows by Jonathan Janz
Savage Species by Jonathan Janz
The Nightmare Girl by Jonathan Janz
The Widening Gyre by Michael R. Johnston
Kosmos by Adrian Laing
The Sky Woman by J.D. Moyer
Creature by Hunter Shea
The Bad Neighbour by David Tallerman
Ten Thousand Thunders by Brian Trent
Night Shift by Robin Triggs
The Mouth of the Dark by Tim Waggoner

•

Join our mailing list for free short stories, new release details, news about our authors and special promotions:

flametreepress.com